"Rebel Communists key their return to power on a secret document hidden accidentally in the effects of a brilliant young concert pianist who has no idea why threats surround every move she makes. Sue Duffy has mixed the mayhem of political intrigue with the melody of romance."

—DICK BOHRER, author, editor, and former
journalism professor

"I have just spent a wonderful evening reading Sue Duffy's *The Sound of Red Returning*. Wow! Intrigue and suspense come together in an incredible story of love and betrayal, commitment and courage, power and danger . . . and a God who controls it all. Sue Duffy is a wonderfully gifted writer and this book is a must-read. You'll 'rise up and call me blessed' for having recommended it to you. Oh, one other thing, this book is fun."

—STEVE BROWN, founder and president of
Key Life and host of Steve Brown Etc.

The Sound *of* Red Returning

A NOVEL

SUE DUFFY

Kregel
Publications

Library of Congress Cataloging-in-Publication Data

ISBN: 978-0-8254-2574-5

Printed in the United States of America
12 13 14 15 16 / 5 4 3 2 1

To my children:
Kimberly, Laura, and Brian

Acknowledgments

You can't write what you know if you don't know it. So you have to learn it. That's what the following people helped me do:

Marc T. Canner, director of the Institute of Strategic Languages & Cultures. He's also an adjunct professor of Russian language, culture, and history at Columbia International University. Marc's vast knowledge of all things Russian was invaluable help in authenticating this book.

My husband, Mike Duffy, my son, Brian Duffy, and my brother, Scott Railey—all experienced men of the sea—coached me in fishing, diving equipment, tides, navigation, and boat piloting.

Florance Anderson, audio-visual technician at St. Philip's Church in Charleston, South Carolina, filled in my information gaps on that historic church's bell tower.

I'd also like to thank my daughters, Kim Beasenburg and Laura Player, and my friend and fellow author Sandi Hendrickson Esch for their literary counsel and reviews of the finished manuscript.

To my dad, J.D. Railey: thank you for piano lessons, my first boat, and your gentle humor.

To my husband, again: thank you for your love, support, and enduring patience.

Prologue

It was just three small paragraphs in the *Boston Globe* that morning in October 2011:

Slain Professor's Widow Dies

Eugenia C. Devoe, wife of the late Schell M. Devoe—a prominent Harvard music professor who was murdered in his Boston home in 1996—died of natural causes Friday in Canada. She was 78.

An accomplished musician, Eugenia Devoe had been a popular band director at Boston Central High School for many years. Shortly before her husband's death, Devoe resigned her position and left the couple's home near the Harvard campus. Until now, her whereabouts had been unknown.

From Boston, Devoe had moved to the small farming community of Curien, west of Montreal, where she assumed her mother's maiden name, Holbrook. Neighbors say she

rarely ventured from her small rural home,
where she taught piano lessons. The couple
had no children. Mrs. Devoe had no surviving
family.

By dawn the next day, the isolated cottage that had been Eugenia Devoe's
hiding place lay in ruins. Even the boards had been stripped from the
ceilings and floors. Yet when the intruders left, they took only one thing
from the house—a letter Schell Devoe mailed to his wife just hours before
he died.

Chapter 1

ONE WEEK LATER

*W*hen the lights dimmed, a tall, trembling silhouette stood in a doorway to the East Room. The audience gathered there waited expectantly.

"Miss Bower, are you all right?" whispered the president's valet as he straightened a beaded clasp on the back of her gown.

Liesl nodded absently, but all was not right. From a time and place long buried, an alarm had just sounded, causing her gifted hands to tense and her mind to flash the unbidden image of a dark alley in Moscow.

A voice inside the historic room spoke, momentarily dispelling the fearful image, and the valet stepped aside. "The President and First Lady wish to continue this evening's festivities with a performance by one of the world's most acclaimed pianists. Please welcome the recent winner of the coveted Messenhoff Award for the Performing Arts, fresh from her victory recital at Carnegie Hall—Miss Liesl Bower."

A chilling inertia threatened to abort her entrance, but the stimulus of applause propelled her slowly forward. Her head held high, she passed beneath chandelier prisms that now, to her wary eye, cast a distorted light.

She had performed in royal courts around the world and in this very room before two sitting presidents. It was not the dignitaries and other guests of the president assembled before her, not the white-knuckle jitters that still plagued her no matter how often she performed, not the powerful scherzo she would soon unleash onto the keyboard. What had stricken her just moments earlier was a face in the second row, the same face she'd seen burn with rage that night in the alley. What was he doing in *this* place?

As she crossed the room, the clapping hands ringing in her ears, she risked the briefest glance at the man in the second row. But even in that instant, she felt his eyes breach the barricade she'd constructed around herself so long ago, that bulwark about her soul that isolated her from the hurtful world outside.

Though her mind was in turmoil, her slender body, now slick with perspiration inside her black velvet gown, moved with practiced poise toward the piano. When she reached the imposing Steinway concert grand with its three gilded-eagle supports, she placed a steadying hand on its fine, aged wood and turned to face her audience, knowing where she must *not* look again. She nodded to President Travis Noland before bowing grandly, then seated herself at the keyboard, the only thing in the room she was sure of.

As she always did, Liesl closed her eyes to summon the music, to place herself in the hands of the composer. Sometimes she would hope for the faintest breath of God. This was one of those times.

To settle the after-dinner audience, Liesl began a warm and rippling etude by Moszkowski. Later, like the times she had driven for miles in deep thought and couldn't remember anything about the route she'd taken, she realized she'd finished the etude without inhabiting it—a transgression for any concert pianist. *No more of this!* she scolded herself.

She rose from the piano to accept the applause. Careful to avoid the troubling face, she looked around the room and noticed one or two guests beginning to nod off. Even at this unsettling moment, the drooped faces amused her because she knew what was coming.

Moments later, her silken hands lifted like graceful swans from the even-tempered opening measure of Chopin's *Scherzo No. 2 in B-Flat*

Minor only to strike with a fury that caught her audience off guard and swept them into the stormy yet lyrical piece. It was President Noland's favorite and his special request for the evening.

Now, Liesl escaped her audience and plunged so deeply into the music, she no longer sensed if anyone else was there. Except once. After the pounding clash of the first passage, she was midway into a peaceful interlude when she surfaced long enough to dare look into the second row. *Gone! He's gone! But where?* No time to wonder; the music wouldn't wait. The storm was gathering again. It demanded she channel it down the length of the instrument and release it to the room. But in the finale, in the resolution of the strife, the victory of peace prevailed.

It was then she suspected why the president had selected this particular composition. She knew who else was in the room. The Russian ambassador and others from his diplomatic corps were seated so close to her, she could hear them breathe. She knew the strife of recent negotiations between the United States and Russia, knew that the delicate balance of power between them sizzled ominously. Of course, Ambassador Olnakoff would know the scherzo she'd just performed. A music scholar himself, a devotee of Chopin, he would surely translate the conflict-to-peace narrative of the music into the political message of reconciliation that Noland must have intended.

When it was over, Liesl rose from the piano to exuberant applause, her eyes falling on the empty second-row chair. Though she usually allowed the applause to roll over her in tingling, uplifting currents, at that moment, she was numb to it, feeling only the need to warn someone about the man she'd just seen.

She scanned the crowd for Ben Hafner, assistant to the president for domestic policy, perhaps her closest friend since their Harvard days together. *I've got to reach him!*

But the audience wouldn't let her go. They begged for an encore and Liesl knew she must oblige. But as she lowered herself to the tufted bench, she looked out once more and caught Ben's mop of brown hair and toothy smile beaming her way from a side door to the room. *Read my face, Ben,* she silently implored, then raised a summoning brow.

Once again, Liesl lapsed into the spell of the music, having chosen something she hoped would reinforce President Noland's mood for the evening: the disarming *Clair de Lune* by Debussy.

The piece had been a recital offering when she was just twelve. Under her grandmother's tutelage, she had refined her performance of it in the centuries-old house beneath the live oaks. Now, as she gently stroked the keys, she could almost smell the briny wind off Charleston Harbor; hear the creak of the kitchen floor as her mother and grandmother prepared the evening meal; and hear the bells of St. Philip's.

Was this selection for Noland? Or for her need in this hour?

As Liesl took her final bow, she was set upon by admirers, her path to Ben still blocked. The reluctant celebrity with the amber hair and eyes to match always drew more attention than she welcomed. She'd been photographed around the world, not just at the piano in one of her regal gowns but in baggy sweats leaving a produce market in Paris, even swimming in a remote grotto in Greece.

The White House photographer approached and asked her to pose next to the piano, between President Noland and Ambassador Olnakoff. When the president swooped in with the ambassador in tow, more than a few observers raised an eyebrow over the unnatural chumminess the two men displayed toward each other. Liesl overheard one tuxedoed gentleman comment to another, "A beautiful woman can bridge many a gap, eh?"

After the photos were taken, other admirers moved toward Liesl. Between the heads of those gathered about her, she finally made eye contact with Ben. She excused herself from some wanting to discuss the finer nuances of the scherzo, and quickly left the East Room.

"What's up?" Ben asked when Liesl reached him. "I still read you pretty well, don't I?"

"Right now, that's a good thing." She took his arm and pulled him down the hall.

"Whoa, take it easy. People will start talking again."

She stopped abruptly and turned into him. "Ben, you've got to listen to me!"

He stared down at her, then put both hands on her shoulders. "You're shaking. What's the matter with you?"

Before she could answer, he steered her across the hall and opened the door to a small, tidy office, then closed the door behind him. "Sit down and talk to me." He remained standing.

"Did you see the man in the second row wearing a red ascot? Black hair slicked straight back, hollow cheeks?"

Ben thought a moment, then nodded hesitantly. "Probably Evgeny Kozlov."

"Do you have a picture of him?"

"No, I don't have a . . . what's this about, Liesl?" he asked impatiently, his forehead bunching in creases.

"Who is this Kozlov?" she asked, her tone urgent. "Why was he here tonight?"

Ben took a seat opposite Liesl and looked intently at her, but didn't answer.

She knew there were many things Ben could never talk about with her. Perhaps this was one. She drew a hurried breath. "Ben, do you remember that last trip I took to Moscow with Dr. Devoe?"

He nodded solemnly.

"It was January 1996."

"I remember," he said softly.

"The last night we were there, Dr. Devoe came to my hotel room. He pulled me out into the hallway and asked me to take a walk with him. I was tired. I'd just played a concert that night at the conservatory. But he insisted. He said he had something to tell me. I asked why we couldn't talk in my room, and he said, 'Because they're listening.'"

Ben reached for one of her hands and held it.

She squeezed the hand of this burly, compassionate man she loved as a brother. The media had tried hard to make something more of their relationship, daring to suggest that Ben might stray from the wife he adored.

Liesl continued. "I had no idea what Dr. Devoe was talking about, and he refused to elaborate." She steadied herself. "When we walked out of the hotel that night, the snow was blowing hard, but we kept going. He was taking me to a small coffeehouse in the next block, he said. Before we got there, though, the flimsy hat I was wearing blew off and I ran after it. Just a silly thing. I had to chase it down the sidewalk.

"But when I turned back, Dr. Devoe was gone. I ran to where I'd left him and heard voices from an alley nearby. Angry voices. Dr. Devoe and another man were arguing in Russian."

There was a knock at the office door. Ben put up a hand to silence Liesl as he moved to answer it.

"Mr. Hafner," said Ben's chief aide, Ted Shadlaw, "sorry, but I happened to see you come in here."

"It's all right, Ted," Ben said calmly. "What is it?"

"Miss Bower's car is here."

"Tell the driver to wait, please." Ben closed the door. "Keep going," he told Liesl, returning to his seat.

She didn't know how exhausting this would be. She wanted to curl into a ball and draw the barricade closer. "I didn't know what to do," she said. "I was afraid to approach the alley until I heard a scuffle and went charging in. Dr. Devoe was on the ground. His mouth was bleeding, and a man stood over him. By the street lamp, I could see him clearly. Then the man came at me. He pointed his finger in my face and yelled, 'Don't ever come back to Russia!'"

Ben flinched.

"He ran off and I helped Dr. Devoe to his feet. I tried to press a tissue to his mouth, but he wouldn't let me. He held my wrist and looked hard at me. He told me to forget what I'd just seen, that it was just a common street thug trying to rob him. But I knew better. They knew each other, I was sure of it. And why would a random mugger tell me never to return to Russia?"

Liesl looked sharply at Ben. "I never saw that man again," she said. "Until tonight. In the second row."

Ben breathed a heavy sigh and stared at the floor. When he looked up, Liesl saw his frustration.

"Liesl, what happened to Dr. Devoe later, that ghastly thing you witnessed in Boston, is history. Fifteen years ago. It's over."

"But, it's—"

"It's like it happened yesterday for you, I know," he interrupted. "And now, after what you just told me, I understand even more why you disappeared after the murder. But why didn't you tell this to someone during the investigation?"

Her eyes clouded and she looked away. "You know the way they treated me. Like I'd done something to betray my country."

"The police?"

"No, the others."

Ben nodded. "Liesl, lots of people were questioned. Dr. Devoe had many associates, many students. None as close to him as you were, granted. And none of them had to watch him die. I'd do anything to erase that trauma from your life, but I can't. And you can't." He paused. "But you can break its grip on you. You have to let it go."

Liesl straightened her back as if a steel rod in it had just snapped into place. "Tell me who Kozlov is?" she persisted.

Ben stood up and raised both hands in surrender. "Someone Olnakoff recently brought over for counsel. He's a lawyer in Moscow."

"He's a punk!"

"Liesl, keep your voice down. And try to understand what's going on. Russia is back on a collision course with the United States, and President Noland is dealing every diplomatic card he can to keep our countries from a showdown. We can't go accusing one of their diplomats of brutish behavior nearly fifteen years ago. From your account, that's all it was. Scared the wits out of you. Probably had everything to do with Devoe's treason, though maybe not his murder. But that chapter's closed. What do you want from this man? An apology?"

Ben moved toward the door. "I know you think I'm insensitive. But you've suffered long enough. Make it stop. The man isn't here to terrorize 'one of America's classical darlings,' as that *Post* reporter called you." He smiled brightly as if trying to coax the same from her, but she fixed a stony eye on him.

"Liesl, come with me," he finally said with a hint of begging in his voice. "Your coach awaits."

Liesl let him pull her up from her chair and hug her gently, though she barely returned the gesture. When he let her go, she said, "Mrs. Devoe just died. Did you know that?"

Ben went still. "Yes, I know," he said, then tried again to lead her to the door, but she stood her ground.

"That warm, vivacious woman was living alone in the backwoods of Canada under a false name, Ben. Why did she have to do that?"

He looked down at the floor then back at her as though he'd had to compose the impassive face he now showed her.

She noticed this effort and understood. "You know something more about that, don't you?"

Ben straightened stiffly. "Liesl, please let this go. It doesn't concern you anymore." He waved an arm toward a draped window. "There's a whole world of beautiful music and adoring fans out there for you. You've worked hard for it. Now put this behind you once and for all and go live your life."

The limousine that had transported Liesl to the White House on that Tuesday evening pulled back onto Pennsylvania Avenue and headed toward her small, rented bungalow in Georgetown, where she'd lived for many years. She wrapped her velvet cape tightly about her and sank deep into the plush leather of the seat, resting her head against its high back. *Ben's right. It's over. Time to put it away.*

Soon, she gazed out the window at one of Georgetown's stately old houses, and her mind raced back to her childhood home in South Carolina. She wished she could climb the worn stairs to her room, to wander the neighborhood where she'd been just another kid on the block, not the prodigy others had labeled her. She wanted to go back in time and skip rope with her friends, canoe into the marsh, and catch fiddler crabs. It had all come too quickly to an end.

A few blocks from her house, the driver turned toward her and asked, "Miss Bower, are you expecting anyone at your home tonight?"

Liesl looked at him curiously, her mind still swirling in Charleston currents. "Why do you ask?"

The man hesitated before answering. "I just thought you might have arranged for someone to follow you there."

The impact of what he was saying suddenly hit, and Liesl turned quickly in her seat to look out the back window. A few car lengths behind was a set of headlights, nothing unusual. "I'm not sure I understand," she said, though something quickened inside her.

"So, you're not expecting anyone?"

"No, I'm not."

"In that case, ma'am, I'd like to call Mr. Hafner and tell him I'm returning you to the White House."

Chapter 2

Liesl stepped from the back of the limousine into Ben's sure grip. Flanked by two Secret Service agents, he escorted her into the West Wing.

"Ben, there was no one following me," she insisted as he steered her through the nerve center of the White House. It was largely deserted at this late hour except for security agents now questioning her limo driver in an open cubicle.

"Just precautions," Ben replied. He opened the door to his office, flipped a light switch and gestured for Liesl to take a seat on a worn, overstuffed sofa. He moved quickly to his desk and opened one of its file drawers. "Let me just gather a few things and then we'll go."

"Go where?" she demanded, still standing.

Ben removed several folders from the drawer and looked up. "I've already called Anna and the guest room is ready for you. Of course, the kids are asleep and you won't get to—"

"No, Ben. This has gone too far. I'm not going with you. So please ask the driver to take me home. There's no one out there waiting to . . . get me." Her irritation was unmasked. But inside, behind the barricade, her resolve had begun to crumble.

"Now, Liesl, until we're sure that—" Ben stopped, looked past her toward the door, and stood. "Sir."

Liesl glanced over her shoulder and pivoted quickly.

"I would be grateful if you did as Ben asks," said President Noland from the doorway. Still dressed in his tuxedo, he stepped into the office, filling it with his commanding yet gentle presence. His silver hair reflected the harsh overhead light, but his smile was easy.

"Mr. President?" The verbal salute spilled nervously from Liesl, but as a question. *What is he doing here?*

"You performed magnificently this evening, Miss Bower. Now let us repay you by tending to your security and exploring what happened tonight, if anything did happen."

"That's my point, uh, sir. Nothing happened."

"Probably not," the president replied, "but I'd feel better if you stayed with Ben and Anna tonight."

She turned an accusing eye on Ben.

"Yep, it's an ambush," Ben admitted as he dropped more papers into his briefcase. "I knew I'd need reinforcement to make you come peacefully."

The president laughed, but Liesl wasn't amused. *There's more to it than that.*

Then something occurred to her. "Sir," she said as the president turned to leave. "I was wondering about the music you requested for this evening."

"Yes?"

"It was a message to Olnakoff, wasn't it?"

She saw something flash in Noland's eyes. He glanced at Ben then back at her and the eyes softened. "From all of us."

On Wednesday night, Liesl flew to New York hunched against the tiny window. Only then did she realize how much the previous evening at the Hafner house had restored her. Anna and Ben had made her feel safe and wanted. As godmother to their two children, she was always welcome. Liesl knew that. But it was their home, not hers. Still, she'd slept peacefully in an antique four-poster bed. Secure for a while.

Liesl looked thousands of feet below at the densely populated corridor between Washington and New York. Flying had always made her feel so temporary, as if at any moment one of the thousands of critical parts that kept the plane aloft might malfunction. It made her wonder why so many sensible people flew. Still, she was drawn to the spectacle unfolding below. Against the black void, neon tentacles now crawled into view, and the aircraft tracked them all the way to the massive, pulsating body of New York.

The ride from the airport was uneventful, the Whitley Hotel near Grand Central Terminal welcoming as usual. It was small and elegant, catering especially to women who came to the city alone. As she entered the lobby, Liesl lifted a wave to the familiar concierge and followed the bellman to her room.

The next morning, a cab whisked her off to the venerable Juilliard School at Lincoln Center, where she was to teach a two-day piano workshop capped by a recital Saturday night. She was grateful for the diversion. But later, after the day's seamless itinerary of classes and private lessons, exhaustion crept in and she returned early to the hotel, declining an assortment of dinner invitations from students and faculty.

In the same top-floor corner room she always requested, she slipped out of her cashmere sweater and wool slacks and wrapped herself in a thick terry robe, compliments of the hotel. She pulled a chair close to the window and, nibbling on a room-service sandwich, gazed down into the canyon of Park Avenue, cut like a diamond, its neon facets brilliant against the night sky.

But this night, the city failed to dazzle her. Instead, it whispered too many questions through the glass. How many hotel rooms have there been? How many nights alone? Was someone really following her?

Liesl put down the sandwich and stood. She pressed her hands against the cold windowpane and watched strangers pass below her. The drenching loneliness rushed at her, and tonight, she couldn't fend it off.

Chapter 3

*I*n a vault room deep and sealed inside the Russian Embassy in Washington, D.C., Evgeny Kozlov drew a labored breath. Perhaps it was what lay before him that caused his distress. Even so, he'd returned to look at it again, his third time since it was recently recovered from a remote cabin in Canada.

Alone in the tiny room, the locking tumblers inside the steel door solidly in place, he sat at a table cleared of everything but the open metal box and what it held. They were just two small pages written in a bold, steady hand—not the hand of a man who feared imminent death, but one confident in what he was doing and those who protected him.

You fool! Kozlov raged silently. *Even if you had given your Americans what they wanted, they would gladly have dangled you before your executioner. You betrayed your country first, then mine. Did you think that warning in the alley meant nothing? Did you think I would not find you again?*

But too late. Kozlov knew that now. Schell Devoe's final communication had just been unearthed like a musty scroll bearing the key to an old mystery—and igniting a furor inside Russian intelligence. Now, KGB agent Evgeny Kozlov held the simple letter from Devoe to his wife and read it again:

Dearest,

Victory! I have uncovered the mole's identity, the name that will ensure our future. Just hours ago, I finished coding it in the usual way. It appears nowhere else. I will deliver it to my contact later this evening. But an unfortunate thing just happened. Liesl came to the house unexpectedly and while she was here, she accidently picked it up with other music on my desk. I didn't realize it was missing until she'd left. It worries me that something so toxic is in her hands, and she has no idea what it is. I was careful to raise no alarm when I called her. She is returning it to me tonight, just another sonata.

I will join you in three days, my love. The agency will take care of us, and we will begin our lives again. I am overjoyed.

Your devoted husband,
Schell

No matter how many times he read it, the damning irony remained. At the moment he killed Devoe for trying to expose one of Russia's most critical and highly placed informants, the girl stood before him with the mole's identity in her hands—and Kozlov let her go.

The locks clanged loudly in the door. Only three other people in the building had clearance to this room. He suspected which one it was now pushing the heavy door open.

"I knew I would find you here," said Pavel Andreyev, his smooth, square face set like granite. He approached the table and looked down at the letter, shaking his head. "I do not need to remind you of the urgency in finding this . . . sonata. The Americans cannot possibly know what we found at the cabin, but they are tracking us this moment, I am afraid. Without the letter, they stumble in darkness. But not for long." He bent toward Kozlov, who tensed even more. "You must be quick," Andreyev ordered. "And this time, Evgeny, you cannot fail."

Kozlov returned the letter to the box and slammed the lid shut. "My people are in place," he responded tersely. He barely looked at Andreyev as he pulled a file from his briefcase and spread its contents on the table—maps, field reports, dossiers, and photos. One photo, in particular, drew Andreyev's eye.

"Miss Bower?" he asked with a trace of admiration.

"Taken outside the White House two nights ago." Andreyev studied the young woman wrapped in velvet, her golden hair swept over one shoulder. "A pity." He tossed the photo back on the table. "You know what to do."

Chapter 4

*L*iesl arrived early at Juilliard Friday morning, determined to break free of her brooding. Before going in, she sat on a bench in the school's plaza and sipped the last of her coffee. It was an unusually clear autumn day, and the city seemed to cheer the Atlantic's temporary triumph over pollution. The sea had swept the air with its pure, sweet breath, reminding Manhattan that it was, indeed, an island. Liesl tilted her head to drink in the airy elixir. Now invigorated by the rush of oxygen, the caffeine, and the growing swell of students scurrying across the plaza, she fairly bounded into the school and up the steps to her first class.

Later that day, she joined a few other teachers leaving the school for a nearby coffeehouse. As they crossed the plaza, she tugged on a lightweight jacket, pulling her long, honey-gold hair free of the collar with one hand while gesturing animatedly with the other. She was telling a funny story about a nearsighted tuba player in a marching band when she noticed a woman standing directly in her path. Liesl paused in her story long enough to sidestep the woman, only glancing at her face as she passed. But a glance was all it took.

Liesl stopped and turned around slowly. Her eyes locked on Ava Mullins, and the last fifteen years—that slippery cushion between her and Devoe's murder—slid away.

As the woman moved toward her, Liesl turned to the others and fretfully excused herself. "I . . . I'm sorry," she told them, trying to calm her voice. "I'll have to catch up with you."

As they walked away, Liesl turned back and glared at the woman, now only a few feet from her. "What do you want?" Liesl demanded, unable to conceal her alarm.

"Don't be afraid of me," Ava said.

Liesl felt as though she were frozen in place, though her pulse hammered wildly.

Ava waved an arm toward the whole of Lincoln Center. "You're thirty-seven and look where you are," she said with unveiled delight. "At the top of your world, and I couldn't be more proud of you."

She seemed to wait for Liesl to respond. When no response came, Ava said, "I've come here to help you."

Liesl studied the woman, guessing she must be late fifties by now. Her body was trimmer, fitter than Liesl remembered it. But the woman's face was hard and lined, her short and shapeless hair streaked with dingy gray. "How did you know where I was?" Liesl asked bitterly.

The woman moved a little closer and in a near-whisper said, "It's what we do. You know that."

Liesl squeezed her eyes shut. *Why won't they leave me alone?*

"Will you walk with me, Liesl? Somewhere that's, uh—"

"Safe?" Liesl blurted.

"I think *private* is a better word."

Liesl swallowed hard. "Aren't you afraid to be seen with the traitor's accomplice?"

"You know I don't think that. I never did."

Liesl felt her lips begin to tremble.

"Come with me, Liesl. I just want to know how you are."

As they left the school, Liesl caught Ava scanning their surroundings. "Look hard, Ava. Make sure there's no boogeyman in the shadows." Liesl shoved her hands in the pockets of her jeans and walked faster, forcing Ava to try to match Liesl's longer stride.

A block off Broadway, Ava steered Liesl into a small café with few patrons at this midafternoon hour. They settled at a table in a back corner. Ava ordered coffee for them, even though Liesl asked for none. She remembered the last time she had seen Ava Mullins. It had been in the back of a paneled van near the Harvard music school, with two other CIA agents recording the conversation. No, Liesl recalled more vividly, not a conversation, a grueling interrogation.

Liesl dropped her shoulder bag on the table and looked sharply at Ava. "You didn't bring me in here to talk about my career. Someone at the White House told you about the man I saw there, and that maybe I was followed. That's why you're here, isn't it?"

The waiter brought coffee. Ava stirred milk into hers and took a sip. Liesl didn't touch hers. "I'm waiting," she said flatly.

Ava put down the cup. "The call came from Langley." She paused, picked up the cup, and took another sip.

That's right, Ava. Stall. Think of the right thing to say.

"The driver wasn't certain your limo was followed," Ava reported. "But Ben Hafner thought it suspect enough to report it immediately—even before taking you to his home."

"Oh, you know that, too. So what color nightgown did I wear to bed that night?" Liesl ripped open a package of sweetener and dumped it into her coffee, stirred it loudly, then plopped the spoon onto the table. The coffee sat untouched.

"We don't have time for your contempt, Liesl, even though you probably have good reason to unload it on me. We were hard on you, I admit. But I'm hoping to put that behind us to deal with more important things." She paused. "Now, I must repeat a question I asked you long ago. Did Dr. Devoe ever entrust any special sheet music to you?"

Liesl's eyes flared. "Reams of it!" A smirk curled about her mouth. "It's what *we* do, remember? You were once one of us." Liesl felt like she was spinning out of control, ashamed of her behavior but unable to stop it.

Ava shifted in her seat, her eyes darting quickly about the restaurant. "I'd like to explain something to you," she said, turning to face Liesl, who noted the woman's usual no-nonsense demeanor was still intact. "Please try to understand. And keep your voice down." Ava looked once again about the café, then at Liesl. "I spent twelve years teaching music at Harvard. For ten of those years, that was all I did, that and raise my son in peace after a disastrous marriage. But one day, I was asked to give more. To do things that were extremely uncomfortable for me." Ava looked down at her coffee, placed her hand over the top of the cup and let it warm her.

Liesl listened quietly.

"I was asked to pry into the life of a fellow teacher. To betray a friend whom I discovered was an enemy. I had been too immersed in my own world to understand that there were some in this country who, for some warped ideology or more money in their bank account, would sacrifice the rest of us. And then I understood that sometimes even someone like me can stop someone like that."

Liesl raised an eyebrow. "Are you suggesting I become a spy like you?"

"Of course not. I'm suggesting that you try to understand what people like me sometimes have to do to protect people like you."

Finished with the conversation, Liesl grabbed her bag and stood up to leave, when Ava said, "Who do you think asked for you to play at the White House on Tuesday?"

Liesl looked down at her. "My agent booked it," she snapped.

"What your agent doesn't know is that the Russian ambassador *insisted* that you appear."

Liesl didn't take another step.

"Didn't you think it odd that you were asked to play for the Russians? And with such short notice?"

"I studied in Moscow. I play the Russian masters. Everyone knows that."

"What everyone doesn't know is that just one week ago, after it was reported where Eugenia Devoe had been living all these years, her little cabin in the woods was torn apart by someone looking for something. Someone who got there before we did."

Liesl blanched, the news hitting hard. She hated to think how tormented Mrs. Devoe must have been the last years of her life. But Liesl failed to see the connection Ava was trying to make. "What does that have to do with me?"

"Maybe nothing at all. But we can't be sure. That's why I'm here."

"To do what?"

"To stand by and make sure you're all right."

"Or to see what kind of information you might get out of me . . . again. Well, too bad. I don't know anything more than I did fifteen years ago. But I would like to know what *you* were looking for in Mrs. Devoe's house."

"Please, sit down, Liesl."

In almost painful submission, Liesl lowered herself to the edge of the chair.

"All you know of Schell Devoe's link to Russian intelligence is what we told you after his death," Ava began. "I don't think you ever realized that this man you trusted, whom all of us on the faculty admired, could have been executed by our government for all his years of smuggling State Department documents to Russia. Of course, that was never reported in the media. His death is still filed as an armed robbery.

"Why did he do it?" Ava asked rhetorically, moving quickly to the answer. "It began innocently enough. His love for everything Russian became such a blind obsession, he eventually disconnected from the rest of us on the faculty, favoring long sabbaticals in Moscow and his friends at the conservatory there. Then came a simple request from a Russian colleague he admired and trusted: On his next trip to Russia, would he bring a file of documents supplied him by a contact in Washington? Would he just slip it into his music files? He told us later that he didn't know the contents of the file and that he'd refused payment for the courier service. He didn't know the Washington contact was a Russian spy planted in the State Department—until later."

Liesl hardly breathed.

"Everything changed, though, when the compensation grew irresistible and the threat unmistakable. The Devoes were given a dacha in the Russian countryside, cars, furs, and jewels—things I'm certain didn't charm Schell enough to betray his country. It was the KGB's threat to expose him as a traitor that secured his continued services to Mother Russia. We're fairly certain Mrs. Devoe knew nothing of his double life until the end when he insisted she escape to Canada."

"How did you know all that?"

"When I . . . when *we* caught him, he talked a lot. I think he was ready to. And then he told us something so incredible, we turned him and made him work for us, to go after something critical for us to know."

"What?"

Ava smiled and shook her head. "You know I can't tell you that. But we knew he'd just uncovered the information when he was killed." She looked intently at Liesl. "If it's true you were followed and there is any connection to Evgeny Kozlov's presence in the U.S., then it's possible the Russians think you have knowledge of that information."

Ava slid a few bills from her wallet and left them on the table. Then she reached back into her purse and handed several business-type cards to Liesl. They were all alike. "Put one by your bed, one in your purse, and one in your car. Call me at that number any time day or night."

Liesl held up a hand and refused the cards. "I don't need them. I don't have any secret information for anybody. I'm not a spy!"

Watching intently as more patrons entered the café, Ava said, "Let's go. I'll walk you back to the school."

But outside the restaurant, Liesl balked. "I don't want you to go with me. I want you to leave me alone."

The cards still in her hand, Ava reached over and dropped them into Liesl's bag. "If anything strikes you as odd, call me. It might be an encounter with someone you don't know, a message, maybe something out of place. It might be nothing at all, but let me make that judgment."

As Liesl started down the sidewalk, Ava called to her. "And Liesl . . . he loved you like a daughter."

Chapter 5

*L*iesl hurried blindly away from Ava Mullins and her parting words, but she couldn't distance herself quickly enough. The words found their mark and she swatted them from her mind as if they were stinging insects. A curse. *I am no one's daughter.*

As the faces streamed past her on Broadway, no eyes met hers. Just as well. She didn't welcome or trust any of them. That's the way it should be, she'd told herself since she was ten years old, hiding in the bell tower of St. Philip's Church and wondering why God called himself a father when the world was so full of bad ones.

Don't trust Ava Mullins, either, she warned herself.

As she neared Juilliard, Liesl glanced at her watch. She was to teach a private lesson at the school at 5:30. There was plenty of time. She looked east toward Central Park and took off like a homing pigeon. She could almost smell the hay-like warmth of the Sheep Meadow as it lazed beneath a generous sun. Even a half hour of rest there would be worth the walk. The broad, grassy patch of urban "country" had always cheered her during her frequent stays in New York. It demanded nothing of her but her company, inviting her to unfurl her long limbs and stretch like a contented cat on a sunny sill.

As she cleared the tree line bordering the meadow, a sudden wind hurled a blast of cold into her face, making her catch her breath and drawing her to a halt. Something about it made her think of her friend Max Morozov and that prankish trek across Moscow. She longed for the carefree innocence of even that short time, just a couple of music students on fellowship at the Moscow Conservatory, cutting class for a winter's romp through town. She so yearned to relive it that when she stepped into the light of the meadow, her mind saw it blanketed in Russian snow. In cinematic recall, she saw Max scrambling up the fire escape to the snowy rooftop of a small shop, snatching his violin from its case when he'd reached the top. She watched him treacherously assume the theatrical stance of the lone musician from *Fiddler on the Roof*, then gleefully stroke the opening notes of that iconic musical.

Now, as she lowered herself to the brown, withered grass of the meadow, Liesl remembered more of that long-ago day. At first, Max's impetuous act had been just a giddy, boyish stunt, something to make Liesl laugh and show off his athletic prowess. But the more Max played from his high perch and the more people gathered to stare, the more intense his playing became. There he was, an Israeli, a transplanted Russian Jew commanding a rooftop in the heart of Moscow, his violin wailing and moaning not from a Broadway score but from somewhere deep inside him.

Liesl smiled at the memory as she half reclined against the gentle slope, tilting her face to a sun slipping toward the skyline. She hoped Max was happy. When he wasn't trying to make her laugh, he tended toward the melancholy. Though he was fully immersed in the Israel Philharmonic and his teaching studio, he always made time for her—calls, texts, and e-mails. They would catch each other's concerts at least once a year. Her close friendship with him, as with Ben, had drawn media gossip that Liesl and Anna Hefner had finally learned to ignore.

There had been many overtures from male admirers through the years, but no one had ever stirred Liesl's soul as Max had. Why couldn't she love him as he wanted her to? She knew his feelings, though he'd never expressed them. They'd never even kissed more than lightly on the cheek. She'd never invited more. It just wasn't to be, and finally, he'd accepted that. In the past couple of years, they'd communicated less often. Liesl understood why.

She stretched in the sun's waning warmth, glad for the others who shared in it. Some tossed Frisbees to each other, couples huddled closely against the chill, a dog ran barking after its owner jogging the periphery of the field. Nearby, a man in a gray parka, its hood drawn snugly against his head, stretched out on his stomach with a book and a tall coffee. Children ran in orbits around their mothers, and a pair of old men played chess on a park bench, snatches of their conversation reaching Liesl in a foreign tone. A Baltic tongue, she guessed.

Max would know, she thought. Then she wondered why he and that particular memory had sprung so vividly to mind. But of course, she knew. She'd just snagged a trip line that ran from Moscow to Boston, where a masked killer had locked eyes on her just seconds before he pumped three bullets into the man who, reportedly, loved her like a daughter.

Chapter 6

*M*ax! Come down! You'll kill yourself!" But Liesl's urgent entreaty was lost on the young man on the roof of a tobacco shop just blocks from Red Square. With one foot lodged against a vent pipe and the other planted precariously on the roof's peak, Max Morozov clung only to his violin as if it alone would hold him aloft. In some ways, Liesl knew that was true.

"I *am* the fiddler, Liesl!" he shouted down to her, his unruly red hair tossed about by an icy wind.

"You *are* the fool!" Liesl scolded, shaking her head, but smiling. Her friend's bursts of disarming exuberance always chipped away at her natural poise. "Get down here right now!" she snapped, as though ordering a three-year-old to obey. But it served only to prod Max into another fiery stanza. She looked nervously about her as more amused pedestrians paused to watch the spectacle. *Always remember what and where you are.* Dr. Devoe's warning returned to her. *An American citizen in Russia. Watch yourself and those around you.*

Someone in the growing crowd poked her in the back. She turned to see an old woman dressed head to toe in black, shaking an arthritic crook of a finger in Liesl's face and proclaiming hotly in Russian. Knowing too little of the language, Liesl could only stare at the woman and hope her tirade would end soon.

"She says your young friend will die of vodka," interpreted an older man nearby. "Pay no attention to her. It is the mantra of all old crones. Maybe someday we drunkards will listen." He laughed, then suddenly gasped. The crowd sucked in a collective breath as Liesl turned just in time to see Max toss his violin free of his spectacular fall. Sliding upright on both feet down the full length of the Alpine-style roof, as an Olympic jumper heading for the "agony of defeat," Max sailed off the low-slung roof, tucked his slight, wiry frame into a ball and rolled into a snowbank, almost disappearing from sight. Liesl flew after him, clawing her way toward the only part of him she could see, one shoeless foot. But it was a moving foot, and Max soon emerged, spitting snow and mustering an "all's well" nod toward the spectators.

With the show over, the crowd dispersed, some laughing aloud at the silly stunt, some looking disappointed that Max hadn't done more harm to himself. The old woman shook her crooked finger at them one more time before scuffing slowly down the pavement.

"Where are you hurt?" Liesl demanded, looking for broken bones.

Max smiled at her with mischievous eyes. "Why do you assume I am? I told you, I am the fiddler, the resilient Jew."

"Yeah, yeah." Liesl rolled her eyes, slid an arm around his back and helped him to his feet. They stood at eye level to each other, both just over five eight. He gazed hard at her. "Why are you so pretty and I'm not?" he drawled in the fake Southern accent he often affected around her.

"You're not supposed to be pretty," she snapped. "But you are supposed to be smarter than this. Now grab your shoe and let's get out of here."

"First, my violin. Did you see it land?"

As the two looked back toward the tobacco shop, it wasn't the violin wedged upright in a small bush that they first noticed but the two uniformed officers standing beside it. As one reached to retrieve the violin and the other picked up the bow from the ground, Liesl felt a dark dread seep into her. She groaned aloud.

"Let me handle this," Max advised. "Since you don't know anything but magnolia-speak." Ignoring her glare, he approached the officers, speaking his perfect Russian and smiling graciously. In spite of her irritation with him at that point, she had to admire his zeal. She believed it had carried him through times untold, and suspected it might be his survival instinct. In the two years they'd known each other, he'd told her very little of his life in Tel Aviv. His family had defected from Russia when he was an infant. Liesl could only imagine what hoops he'd passed through to secure the coveted fellowships at the Moscow Conservatory. These fellowships were the only times they'd had together, just a couple of weeks each year. But it was long enough to know that something undefined smoldered deep in the heart of Max Morozov.

Theirs had been a fast and platonic friendship, bound by their love of the Russian masters and Schell Devoe. The preeminent Harvard music professor had taken both students under his wing, convinced of their greatness and devoted to their welfare. He'd been the father Liesl had lost. She'd spent many evenings with Devoe and his wife, Eugenia, in their comfortable Tudor home near the Harvard campus. It was through Liesl that Max now counted Dr. Devoe as his own trusted teacher and advocate.

Dr. Devoe! Liesl suddenly saw this unfortunate situation through the eyes of their teacher, the one who saw greatness in them. And here was one of the great ones now, in torn pants, wet hair stuck to his head, grabbing at a violin now tucked to the side of a Moscow policeman, and loudly proclaiming the injustice of—of being arrested!

No! Liesl hurried to his side and, in English that meant nothing to the two officers, pleaded for them to understand the impetuous prank of a "very immature, but innocent friend. And, by the way, a very fine musician who'd like to play a song for you." The ploy came to mind as she coaxed Max to offer his music in exchange for his freedom and their hasty return to the conservatory.

But that didn't work. Before they knew it, a car had been summoned for them. When it arrived, the violin and its case were fairly tossed into Liesl's hands as she and Max were ushered into the backseat like common criminals, Max in handcuffs. That was his undoing. The moment the metal clamped in place around his wrists, something turned inside him. Now, Liesl saw fear in his eyes.

As the driver skirted Red Square, the center of all things Russian, Max turned to gaze out the windows, now filled with a ponderous building. "And here I am," he said, "the pesky Jew versus the Kremlin." He sniffed derisively.

"Max, don't overreact. It's just disorderly conduct. They probably think you need a night in the drunk tank." She tried to laugh but couldn't. There was nothing funny about a drunk. She knew that too well. She also knew Max didn't indulge at all. "No pogrom for you, if that's what you're thinking."

He looked incredulously at her. "Why would you say such a thing?"

"Isn't that what's on your mind? The persecutions heaped on your people by this nation?"

"This nation *is* my people, Liesl. I am Russian. And a Jew. In Israel, I know myself and who they say my God is. But here, where I was born, where my ancestors lived and died, I don't know who I am." He looked toward the bright onion domes of Saint Basil's Cathedral. "And I don't know this God."

Liesl felt uncomfortable, knowing so little about the "religion" of God. That's all it was to her—empty rituals and obligations she didn't understand. But there was one thing she felt certain of. "Max, there's only one God. I don't know him either, not really. I've blamed him too long, for too much that went wrong in my life. But Max, something would happen every time I would run to St. Philip's. I could sense him there, waiting for me in my hiding place."

Max brightened. "I have a hiding place too."

Liesl cocked her head. "Inside that mysterious mind of yours?"

He pushed damp and dangling hair off his forehead and smiled. "Ever been to Corsica?"

"Charleston, Boston, Moscow. That's it."

"There's a tiny village on top of a mountain overlooking the bluest waters you've ever seen." He grew wistful. "It's ancient and isolated. No cars allowed. A few goats, cats, a little colony of artists. But few people live there full-time. A few tourists wander that way, but mostly, it's an end-of-the-line kind of place."

"What's it called?" Liesl was enchanted.

"Sant'Antonino." He said nothing more.

The car came to a halt with what Liesl considered an unnecessary lurch. She wondered if the two officers who'd accompanied them understood anything coming from the backseat. None of it would have mattered to them if they had, she decided. As she and Max were escorted inside a nondescript building swarming with people, she clutched the violin more tightly, then leaned toward him and whispered, "We've got to reach Dr. Devoe." She winced at her own words. What would he think of their careless behavior?

Deposited at the end of a long line of chairs, all filled with angry and anxious people, Liesl and Max waited almost two hours before anyone called them forward. A stern woman with bulging eyes motioned Liesl to a desk and shoved a phone her way. When Liesl reached Schell Devoe at the conservatory and explained what had happened, his reaction surprised her. Rather than the fatherly rebuke she expected, his manner was cold and oddly restrained. But he promised he would come immediately. Liesl and Max returned to their seats.

Barely twenty minutes later, the courtly figure of Schell Devoe entered the police station, and Liesl and Max began to squirm. He spotted them right away, but gave them only a nod as he headed straight to the main desk directly in front of them. In fluent Russian, he addressed a short, pudgy man with a shirt too tight and patience too thin, it seemed to Liesl. After a lengthy conversation, the officer motioned for Liesl and Max to approach the desk. Dr. Devoe and Max alternately spoke to the man in charge, leaving Liesl to guess what was being said. After a long and rancorous exchange among the three men, Max finally pulled her aside and explained.

"This guy's not budging. Dr. Devoe is pulling all the diplomacy he can muster to get the charges dropped. And yes, you were right. It's disorderly conduct, but they've concluded that demon drink wasn't the cause."

"Then why won't they just dismiss it and let you go?"

"The guy's evidently enjoying his authority too much, and I've never seen Dr. Devoe so rattled."

Liesl looked back at the officer in charge. "Uh-oh. Something's happening."

Max whirled to see the officer motion for two other uniforms to escort an outraged Devoe from the building. That's when Devoe slammed his fist against the desktop and demanded to place a phone call. Max and Liesl moved close enough to hear, Max interpreting.

Fury clouding his face, the officer grabbed the desk phone, "I will call. Give me the number," he barked rudely.

"You will call the Kremlin," Devoe instructed. "Federal Security Service. Pavel Andreyev."

The officer blanched.

"And you will do it now!" Devoe demanded.

Once that party was reached, the officer hesitantly explained the purpose of the call, listened gravely for a few moments, then slowly replaced the receiver. The angry set of his face contorted into something resembling a smile. "My apologies, please, sir. If you will, take this young man and his friend with you. And counsel him to stay off Russian roofs. Again, my apologies."

Before Max and Liesl could react, Devoe, without a word, moved quickly between them, took them both by the arm and led them outside to a waiting car. They climbed in the backseat as Devoe settled in the front beside the driver, a man Liesl and Max had never met, and no effort was made to introduce them.

The man didn't speak to them or even look their way but drove hurriedly to the conservatory. Just before they arrived, Devoe finally turned in his seat and said, "You have cost me a great deal today. You will repay me by never telling anyone what you just saw me do—or heard me say."

⁂

That night, Devoe insisted that Liesl and Max accompany him to dinner at a friend's home—"where I can keep an eye on you," he said in a disciplinary tone unfamiliar to his students.

"Are we on restriction?" Max teased.

"Exactly," Devoe replied stiffly. Liesl and Max waited for him to recover his good humor. When that didn't happen, they dreaded the evening to come. After Devoe, alone, picked them up for dinner, Liesl spoke only when necessary during their ride. Her beloved teacher's reproach had wounded her and she was indulging in a bit of a pout.

Later, they arrived at an apartment building quite a distance from their hotel and the conservatory. It was in a colorless neighborhood of unremarkable architecture, mostly residential. Small shops crouched beneath multistory apartment buildings lined up as though mass-produced from the same mold.

When they stepped from the car, a young child approached begging for money. "The street urchins are more common in this part of town," Devoe noted, handing the boy a few coins. "Better watch your pockets." Liesl watched Devoe tuck the wrapped bottle of vodka, a gift for the host, securely beneath his arm.

Except for some inspired stonework around the doorway, the building they entered offered little distinction. The elevator they took to the fourth floor made Liesl wrinkle her nose. "Not exactly jasmine, is it?" Max noted with amusement. He looked from Liesl to Devoe and back at her, his smile fading. He shrugged his shoulders as if there were little reason to pursue a thawing of relations with his professor or draw a playful retort from his friend.

Devoe led them down a narrow hallway and paused before the last door. "I probably don't need to remind you of the cultural differences, but I will. Don't cross your legs and present the sole of your shoe. It's an affront to many Russians. Max, don't shake hands across the threshold or stand with your hands in your pockets. Liesl, once inside, no effort will be made to shake your hand unless you initiate, and then you may receive a kiss to the top of your hand instead. And lastly, Russian hosts take great interest in their guests, but I suggest you refrain from supplying too many details about your personal lives."

"Otherwise, relax and be ourselves, right?" Max ventured as he faced the door and affected a ramrod state of attention. Liesl finally broke. An involuntary giggle escaped, which seemed to do Max a world of good. He fairly beamed at her.

Devoe had never shared Liesl's fondness for Max, she'd observed. She had never understood the near-subliminal friction between the two, unless it was jealousy over her affections, a notion that made her uncomfortable.

Moments after Devoe knocked at the door, it flew open and a large, red-cheeked man with bushy gray hair filled the doorway. Vadim Fedorovsky was a professor of musical composition at the Moscow Conservatory. Behind him were eight or nine other guests seated together and all talking at once. "Come. Come, my friends," Fedorovsky bellowed, then stepped aside with ceremonial flair. Even before the introductions, Fedorovsky vigorously shook Max's hand, kissed Liesl's when she extended it, then turned to Devoe, whom he gathered into a robust embrace. "Now, Schell, who are these charming young people you delight us with?"

As the two men spoke, Liesl studied her host. She thought the man's smile radiated a practiced warmth, but after the chill of Devoe's recent company, even insincere gaiety was welcome.

The room grew hushed as Fedorovsky invited Devoe to introduce his guests. "This is the esteemed pianist Liesl Bower of Charleston, South Carolina," Devoe announced with a softness and congeniality that, to Liesl, signaled some kind of reconciliation. Fedorovsky eyed her with obvious admiration and made a show of taking her arm. He turned her proudly toward the others as if presenting royalty. "Perhaps you'll do us the honor of playing for us this evening," he encouraged. She nodded graciously at him as one of the women in the group rose and showed Liesl to a nearby chair.

She watched as the gregarious host then fastened Max with a friendly eye. "And this young fellow?"

Liesl was pleased to hear the same conciliatory tone in Devoe's introduction of her friend. "This is one of Israel's finest violinists, Maxum Morozov."

A fleeting shadow muted Fedorovsky's bright face, Liesl noticed. But an instant later, he shook Max's hand again. "It is my pleasure to meet you," Fedorovsky said simply, with a crusty formality unlike his earlier greetings. "I hope you're enjoying your stay in Russia."

"Perhaps more than Russia is enjoying my stay," Max quipped, darting a dry glance at Devoe.

Fedorovsky's gaze lingered on Max for a moment more, then he swept an arm toward the dining room and urged everyone to take a seat at the long banquet table. As conversation returned to the room and people began to move toward the dining room, Liesl surveyed the small apartment. A baby grand piano anchored the living room, haphazardly arranged with an ill-matched assortment of chairs and side tables. The dining room was consumed by a large double-pedestal table and as many straight-back chairs as could be crammed around it. Liesl had heard that Fedorovsky, a widower, was known for an excessive lifestyle. Though this apartment didn't reflect that, she had heard from other students that the man owned a handsome dacha outside Moscow.

Russian dinners could take hours to finish, with course after course, drink after drink. The dried fish, fresh vegetables, and caviar served during the first course had been sufficient for Liesl. Everyone but she and Max also had indulged in repeated servings of ice-cold vodka. By the third course, they were surprised to see Devoe holding his own with those obviously accustomed to alcohol.

After dinner, no one seemed ready to leave except Liesl and Max. The others had dispersed into conversational units of twos and threes, speaking Russian only. Liesl was glad Fedorovsky hadn't asked her to play. She was too tired and bored now. Noticing a window at the end of a hallway, she motioned for Max to join her there. "Maybe there's something interesting to look at," she whispered.

Just before they reached the window, they heard hushed voices coming from a room off the hall, its door closed. They paused and looked at each other. Then they heard, in English, "You'll find all the names you need in this." It was unmistakably Devoe's voice.

"Too bad about our friend in Washington," came Fedorovsky's thick voice.

Fearing they'd ventured where they shouldn't have been, Liesl and Max were about to retreat back down the hall when the door to the room opened. Devoe paled at the sight of them. From behind, Fedorovsky pushed him aside and glared first at Max, then Liesl. Suddenly, though, his face relaxed, a transformation that Liesl found frightening. An awkward smile creased his face as he placed a firm hand at the back of each young guest and guided them down the hall. "I think the party is this way, don't you?"

Chapter 7

Another cold burst from the north roused Liesl from her memory of that Moscow night. She looked about her and noticed a legion of shadows had advanced far across the Sheep Meadow, steadily devouring the light on the ground. The Frisbee players had left. The children had been swept along with their mothers' retreat into the dinner hour. The man in the gray parka rose from the ground, snapped his book shut, and wandered off to deposit his coffee cup in a trash bin. But the old chess players remained, intent on the game and, apparently, needing to be nowhere soon. But Liesl did.

She would have to move quickly through the rush-hour throngs to reach the school in time for her 5:30 lesson. One block from Juilliard, her cell phone rang. Without stopping, she grappled deep into her shoulder bag and withdrew the insistent instrument, smiling at the caller's identification on the screen. "Well, if it isn't my nanny with the hairy chest," she chided, "calling to see if I'm eating my vegetables."

Ben Hafner chuckled. "Someone's got to tend to you."

Liesl's mood changed. "Someone like Ava Mullins?" She hadn't intended to fall so quickly into a combative tone.

"She made contact?"

"Oh yes," she answered with irritation.

"Liesl, if someone was indeed following you, even a deranged fan, I had to put somebody on it."

"Why her?"

"We felt it best. You already know her and can trust her."

"Why should I? She lied to me. Pretended to be my friend, my confidante, when all she wanted was information on Dr. Devoe. And then she fed me to her CIA interrogators. No, I don't trust her."

"You've got to, Liesl, and that's all I'm going to say about it. Now, when are you coming home?"

Liesl didn't answer.

"Are you pouting, Liesl? Because I hate it when you pout." More gently, he added, "Now, tell me when you'll be home."

Liesl drew a long breath. "Home. Hmm. I don't think I have one of those."

"Something's up with you. What's wrong?"

She finally wrenched herself from the flow of sidewalk traffic and headed for the school's entrance. "I'm sorry, Ben," she said, stopping just inside the doorway. "I'm in a neither-here-nor-there kind of mood. Lots of self-pity going on, and I promise to bring it all back to Washington on Sunday."

"And you're sure you're okay?"

"Everything's fine here, but I've got a class in five minutes. I'll call you later."

"Tell me then when to pick you up at the airport."

"No, Ben," Liesl said as she turned to look out the glass doors. "You don't need . . . to . . ." Something caught her eye, a man just entering the plaza. A man in a gray parka with the hood drawn snuggly against his head. The man from the park, only this time, carrying no book, no coffee. Carrying nothing a student or professor should. Now he moved to a corner of the plaza. He sat on a low wall beneath a tree and watched the door.

After her student left, Liesl sat alone at one of two grand pianos in the studio, glancing over the note in her hand. It was a hastily scrawled address to a brownstone apartment somewhere in the Upper West Side. Liesl was often asked to appear at opulent, fund-raising galas and private dinners hosted by Juilliard's wealthy patrons. But that night, she'd been invited to the home of an oboe professor who just wanted "to cook for some of my friends," he'd said. It was a last-minute invitation because he'd just that morning acquired a sizable and very fresh rack of lamb, he'd told her.

Another time Liesl would have welcomed the chance to unwind with her peers, but at this moment, she was focused on just one thing: the man in the gray parka. From the studio window, she had watched him leave the plaza midway through her lesson. But now, he'd returned, backlit by security lights that seemed all too impotent. How could they stop him? From doing what? Was she imagining too much? Probably.

Still, she hurriedly packed her things and headed for a more obscure exit on the opposite side of the building. After hailing a cab, she settled into the backseat and welcomed the end of the week. It had pushed too hard against the barricade. The Russian in the White House, the limo incident, Ava, the man in the plaza. And none of it was real, she told herself. Nothing of substance. Only coincidences.

Through the taxi's window, she watched the deliberate stride of pedestrians forging their route along Broadway, sure of where they were going. Had she forgotten what that was like? She'd quit being the sad little girl. No more the fool who trusted yet another "father" only to be betrayed again. Not the terrified witness forced to run away. But what *was* she? And where was she headed?

Night had fully cloaked the city by the time she reached the hotel, but she decided to end the day with just one simple victory—dinner out. A nonthreatening evening with friends and a rack of lamb, on second thought, seemed made to order. She showered and changed into black jeans, a white fisherman's sweater, boots, and a black leather jacket. After calling the concierge to summon another taxi for her, she grabbed the scribbled address and her bag, and took the elevator to the lobby. She would be a little late, if there was such a thing in New York.

She didn't have to wait long for the taxi, but as she climbed in, she wished she could have brought her own car from Washington. That wasn't a viable option, though, not in parking-starved Manhattan. Liesl handed the address to the driver and made a mental note to get her old Volvo serviced when she returned to Washington. She had neglected it and her little Georgetown bungalow too long. The anticipation of normal household chores, of polishing the tidy brick bungalow to a shine, made her feel oddly buoyant. She smiled to herself as contentment regained a partial foothold inside her.

After a long, jostling ride through a city anxious to get on with the weekend, the cab finally turned onto a tree-lined avenue lit by street lamps. Tucked behind the trees on both sides of the street were three and four-story brownstones that Liesl guessed were built in the 1800s, like many similar buildings in the area.

The cab came to a stop in front of an Old World–looking apartment building. After checking the address again, the driver craned his neck to look sideways through the windshield. "Dis must be 204 but I no see numbers," he said. "You knock, yeah?" He rapped on the dashboard, thereby illustrating his broken English.

Without budging from the backseat, Liesl studied the building in question, seeing light behind curtains at several windows, but no sign of anyone familiar, going or coming. She asked the driver if he was sure this was the right street and block.

"Oh, sure, sure," he insisted.

Just then, someone pulled back a drape from one of the upstairs windows, and Liesl saw a number of people moving about inside. "That might be 204-B," she said mostly to herself, but with little conviction. She paid the driver and asked him to please wait until she was sure.

As she opened the door, her cell phone rang. Stepping into the street, she noted the caller ID. *Ben. I forgot to call him back.* "Sorry, old boy," she answered, pulling the strap of her bag over her shoulder. "I was supposed to—"

"Where are you?" he demanded gruffly.

Liesl frowned. "Getting out of a cab and greetings to you, too." She reached with the other hand and shut the car door.

"Get back in the cab right now!"

"What?" Liesl stepped onto the sidewalk and approached the building where she hoped the oboe professor lived.

"Get back in the cab and tell the driver to take you straight to FBI headquarters! The address is . . ."

But Liesl didn't hear the rest. She had just turned to see the cab driver smile pleasantly at her as he drove away. "Wait!" she hollered at him, removing the phone from her ear and waving both arms. She ran into the middle of the street. "Wait!" But the cab rounded the corner and disappeared. *Great. What if this is the wrong address?*

"The guy just left, Ben," she reported, heading back to the sidewalk. "Now, what's the matter?" She looked around her. No one else was on the street.

"Liesl, someone broke into your house last night. They really messed up the place searching for something."

Instantly, Ava's words returned to Liesl. *"Eugenia Devoe . . . her house was torn apart by someone looking for something."*

"Liesl, listen to me. You have to get somewhere safe right now!"

Safe. That word again.

"Where are you?" he repeated.

"I . . . I don't know." The same paralyzing inertia she'd felt in the East Room returned.

"What do you mean you don't know?" Ben's tone grew more urgent.

"I . . . I gave the address to the cab driver. I was going to a dinner . . . I think it's here." She felt like she was moving and talking underwater.

"Then get inside quickly and call the number Ava Mullins gave you. Do you still have her card? If not, can you write this down?" Ben waited. "Liesl!"

"Yes, I'm going to the door now." But before she reached the stoop, a car turned onto the street and pulled to the curb a few doors down, its headlights full on Liesl. She watched as three men got out and headed her way. Slowly. Quietly. Passing beneath a street lamp. Still coming. Something familiar. A face. Another street lamp, and Liesl was certain. It was *that* face.

Run! Make yourself run! But sluggish legs resisted. And then it happened. Adrenaline. Flight!

Arms and legs pumping now, picking up speed, Ben's voice a frenzied garble in her fist, Liesl raced for the next corner, never looking back. She didn't have to; she heard them coming. Not slowing into the turn, her boots slid on the pavement, but her long legs corrected and saved her from a fall.

Hide! She looked frantically about her. Just ahead, a door was slowly closing, a hand on its knob, light from inside now shrinking to a sliver. But it was enough. It was all she had. She lunged for the door, catching it seconds before it latched, jerking it from the grip of a startled man inside and throwing it open just enough for her to pass through—into what, she didn't know. It was just a plain door in a brick wall.

With no regard for anything but escape, she shoved the man aside, then slammed the door shut and threw a dead bolt. Her chest heaving, she pressed one ear against the door and listened. Footsteps falling hard, just taking the corner. Now stopping. Suddenly, someone jerked the handle on the door she leaned against, and she lurched backward. Then came the voice. Russian.

"Evgeny, prya-muh." And they were gone.

Evgeny! She struggled to breathe. Her body began to crumple toward the floor until arms caught her and pulled her back up. She turned weakly in those arms and confronted the man she'd nearly trampled.

"Sit down, young lady," came his words. "I think you've had a terrible scare."

She felt her feet move and a cushion rise up beneath her. But her eyes fastened on the man in the long black robe. They were in a small vestibule of some kind. She watched as he hurried to an open doorway and called for someone to bring water. As he turned back to her, she leaned sideways to look through that same doorway, only then seeing the sanctuary beyond.

As if to assure her, the man said, "I'm Rev. Scovall. Please tell me what just happened."

All her senses came flooding back. "I'm so sorry. I nearly knocked you down." Then she tensed. "Are the other doors locked?"

He frowned and without even asking why they should be, said, "I'd better make sure. Stay right here." He nearly bumped into an elderly woman carrying a paper cup of water. "Give that to her and come with me," he instructed.

Liesl took a sip of water then remembered her phone, now gone from her hand. She looked near the door and saw it on the floor. *Ben!* After punching in his speed-dial number, she stood up, felt wobbly and sat back down.

"Liesl!" Ben answered on the first ring.

"I'm okay."

"What happened?"

Between gulps of air, she told him.

"Again, Liesl, where are you?"

She hesitated.

"You *still* don't know?"

"Just a minute." She rose again, this time more steadily. She walked to the door of the sanctuary and called for the reverend.

She heard a door slam and footsteps growing louder. He approached from a nearby hallway and motioned for her to join him in one of the pews of the sanctuary. He was out of breath. "The church is all locked up," he reported, his thick fingers raking strands of gray hair off his damp forehead. "Now, tell me what's going on."

"First, would you please give my friend the address here." She held up the phone.

Rev. Francis Scovall introduced himself to Ben and gave him the address for West Park Christian Church. Liesl was close enough to hear Ben's deep baritone.

"Sir, thank you for your service to Miss Bower. You have no idea how critical it is. But I have one more request."

"Certainly."

"Would you please stay there with her until a woman named Ava Mullins arrives? It shouldn't take too long. She'll show you her credentials." Liesl heard the name and knew there was no point in arguing with Ben over who would come for her.

Rev. Scovall studied Liesl with grave concern. "Of course, I will. And what is your name, sir?"

"I'm Ben Hafner."

"Are you here in New York?"

"No, sir. Washington. May I speak to Miss Bower again?"

Liesl took the phone and stood up. Excusing herself, she walked off to finish the conversation privately. Soon, she returned to the pew. "It's about time I introduced myself, sir. I'm Liesl Bower. I'm so sorry to impose on you this way." She managed a thin smile as he took her trembling hand in his. It was warm and doughy, a surprising comfort.

"But I'm deeply grateful for your help," she added, releasing his hand and looking around the ornate little church. It felt otherworldly. "It's been a long time since . . . since I was in a church."

He appeared to wait for her to continue.

"Do you have a bell tower?" she asked abruptly, a memory beginning to throb.

"Why, yes, we do."

She looked up at the ceiling as if she could see the bells through it. "I used to hide in the tower of a church."

"Hide from who?"

The question caught her off guard. She clenched her hands and wouldn't look at him. Wouldn't answer.

"Surely not from God," Rev. Scovall offered gently. "That would be impossible."

She looked back at him, and his eyes were full of sincere concern. "I don't know what kind of trouble you're in," he said, "but God knows. He's your Father, Liesl. The only one you truly need."

His words startled her. *Why did he say that? How could he know?*

Then he stood and asked, "Would you like to see the tower?"

She found herself following the man toward the double front doors to the building, then turning down a short hall to a stairway. After a climb, they emerged on an upper landing in the belfry. It was smaller than St. Philip's but she could almost see herself tucked on the stairs—ten years old and wishing her flesh-and-blood father never to find her.

From the landing, they climbed up a narrow iron staircase. When Rev. Scovall opened the door at the top, Liesl stepped forward into the night. With the twin bells anchored above her, a rough wood floor below her, she looked out at the city with little thought to who might be looking back. It would have been difficult for anyone on the ground to see her in the un-lighted tower. Still, Rev. Scovall urged her back from the high, brick arches. "I don't know who you're running from, but let's not invite them here."

Liesl realized the danger she'd placed this man in. "I'm so sorry for all this," she said.

He waved away her apology. "If I can't serve those in trouble, what good am I?"

She watched him gaze out over the neighborhood. "This is where I come to listen," he told her.

For what?

He smiled as if hearing her voiceless question. "I'm afraid I get so busy being me, I tune out God. Imagine that—a pastor who can't hear God's voice inside him. So I come up here to be alone and listen."

Liesl was about to ask what that voice sounded like, when they heard a car pull up below, doors open and shut.

They eased to the edge of the tower and risked looking into the street. Liesl laid a hand on Rev. Scovall's arm. "It's okay. It's time for me to go."

By the time they returned to the front doors of the church, the knock-ing had reached a fevered pitch. "Are you sure about this?" Rev. Scovall asked Liesl before unlocking the door.

"I'm afraid so."

"Just the same, I made a promise to your friend. So, if you don't mind, please wait out of sight while I check identifications."

Liesl smiled at this kindly man who'd harbored a stranger. She'd burst through his door and put him at risk. And that was okay with him. *What sort of things did God tell him?*

"Sir, we're here for Liesl Bower." Peeking through the crack of a nearby closet door, Liesl watched as Ava Mullins presented the picture ID that declared her a special agent of the Central Intelligence Agency. She even provided a small flashlight for clearly reading her credentials and badge.

"CIA?" Rev. Scovall asked, his voice rising. He peered at Ava as if it were a hoax.

"Yes, sir. And this is agent Reggie Diaz." The young man with Ava presented similar identification.

"Well, uh . . . my goodness, I had no idea . . ."

Liesl emerged from the closet and stepped into the front doorway, glancing awkwardly at Ava, then eyeing Reggie Diaz with caution. She looked toward their black Suburban parked at the curb and the man standing next to it. A man in a gray parka. This time, its hood was pulled away from his head. Liesl stepped back and gaped at the man, then at Ava.

Ava spun around to see what might have frightened Liesl.

The man had already turned his back to them and stood at full alert as he kept watch on the street. And suddenly, Liesl understood. Uncoiling, she fought the urge to laugh, fearing it would lapse into hysteria. "He's *yours?*" she asked Ava, her voice shrill.

Then it was Ava who grasped the situation. Her face colored and she sighed. "Yes, he's ours, and evidently in need of better surveillance skills."

Liesl shook her head slowly. *Could my life be more ludicrous?*

"Are you a CIA agent too?" Rev. Scovall asked Liesl, his brows arching high on his still-moist forehead.

She could see he was struggling to take it all in. "No, sir. Just a piano player with very strange friends."

"But friends, no less," Ava said pointedly. Eye to eye, something silent and conciliatory passed between the two women. Then Ava announced firmly, "We have to go."

It was then Liesl knew that a door had closed on the life she'd known, and that what lay ahead was out of her control. Impulsively, she wrapped her arms around Rev. Scovall and held on as if it were her last contact with the normal world, whatever that was.

"Thank you for keeping that door open just long enough," she said as she released him and turned to go.

But the reverend gently caught her hand and looked into her eyes. "I don't think it was me, child."

Chapter 8

*E*vgeny Kozlov rode the elevator to the fourth floor of the small, Rococo-style building near the East River. He emerged into a lobby dimly lit by gilded sconces on walls clad in ruby flocked wallpaper. Crossing quickly to one of the four doors fronting on the lobby, he knocked twice and waited. There was no sound from inside, but from the sidewalk below, he could hear the raucous laughter of late-night partiers spilling from the nearby South Street Seaport. *New York, the city that never sleeps*, he mused. *It better not.*

When Pavel Andreyev opened the door, he ushered Kozlov into the apartment without making eye contact. "Sit here," he ordered, gesturing to a crushed-velvet sofa hugging one wall. As Kozlov took his seat, his eyes swept the room, taking in its garish glamour, its pink-crystal chandeliers and gaily painted vases. The apartment's owner, Kozlov knew, was somewhere in the Middle East. An art and antiques dealer, the man owned homes throughout the world, each one a base of operations for his primary employer, the Kremlin.

Andreyev lowered his short, wiry frame into a green satin armchair that, strategically, sat higher than the sofa. Too quietly, too calmly he looked down at Kozlov, clearly waiting for the agent to explain himself.

"She turned the corner and vanished," Kozlov offered, his tone brittle.

"We checked every door. They were locked. We split up and searched the alleys. Nowhere. She was nowhere."

Repeatedly squeezing the cushioned arms of his chair, Andreyev asked, "And the music you took from her house?"

"My people continue to study it. We will find what we are after."

The composure finally snapped. "But not soon enough!" Andreyev roared. "There is too much of it to search. And too little time. The girl could have found it for you. It would be out of the Americans' reach, and this whole episode would be over. But now you have chased her away. What do you propose to do?"

"We tracked her here today, we will find her again. My men are in place at her hotel, at Juilliard, and in Washington. Even Boston, where she has friends."

"And Charleston?" Andreyev asked.

"It is most unlikely she will go there. There is no one but the grand-mother and she is"—Kozlov circled his finger about the side of his head—"of little use. Still, I have two men down there now, watching the house and the nursing home."

Andreyev stood and went to the window, gazing down into the street. "And if the code is not in the music you now have?"

Kozlov did not answer.

Andreyev looked back at him. "If they haven't already, the Americans will soon realize that their young pianist has had it all along. The question is, where? And where is Miss Bower at this moment?" He turned back to the window and tapped the pane. "Somewhere out there, she is scared and looking for a place to hide. She may have already gone to the authorities. You should hope to uncover the code before anyone uncovers your mission here." He cut dark, hooded eyes toward Kozlov. "Or have they already?"

"What do you mean?" Kozlov's voice grew to a nervous pitch.

"The man who surprised you at Miss Bower's home. Are you sure he was just a curious neighbor?"

Consciously lowering his voice, Kozlov answered with only shallow authority. "Our operation last night was meticulous. My men are loyal and well-trained. No one could have known our plans." With certainty, he added, "He was, indeed, just a curious neighbor being an American cowboy trying to, as they say, save the day." Kozlov smirked. "He will think twice before doing so again. One of my men left him with a souvenir of his ill-timed heroism, a knife slash to his shoulder."

"And he could never identify you?"

Kozlov grew more confident. "Ski masks. Otherwise, we would have killed him."

"And the license plate on your van, the one he must have seen?"

"Stolen." Kozlov cocked his head. "Do not worry."

"But you should, *comrade*. I call you that to remind you of the ranks you rose through—and our ways. You know what happens in just six weeks. You know the fate of our man in Israel, the fate of this entire operation if you fail your mission." Andreyev turned to look once more into the street below. Kozlov thought he detected the slightest gesture of the man's hand. His eyes still locked on the street, Andreyev added, "It would be your fate as well."

After a severe silence, with Andreyev never looking again at him, Kozlov rose slowly and let himself out of the apartment.

Chapter 9

A few miles east of Big Pine Key, the serrated teeth of a coral reef rose for a bite of the Atlantic. Into that feeding ground, Ian O'Brien dropped a hooked shrimp and waited for a dinner-sized yellowtail snapper to oblige him. They were plentiful in these clear, shallow waters over the Florida reef. There was only one thing that might interfere with his catch—the grandson hanging over the other side of the boat, emptying the contents of his stomach into water that was no longer clear.

"If you don't beat all," Ian grumbled, glancing over his shoulder at the bent-double figure. "You're a one-man chum line, you know that? The kind fish don't find real appealing." He shook his head slowly as he adjusted the rod, not budging from his spot.

Cade O'Brien slowly raised his head and wiped his face with a towel, trying to balance himself against the relentless swells rocking the boat. He looked back at his grandfather. "Don't overdo the sympathy, Pop. It's embarrassing."

"What's embarrassing is the charter captain with a first mate who keeps throwing up on the paying customers," Ian said with a throaty laugh. "At least we're alone today." He looked at Cade and smiled, deep fissures spreading across his ruddy, bearded face. "Okay, we'll go back," he moaned and began reeling in his line.

"Nothing doing," Cade said, straightening to his full six-three height and replacing the wide-brim hat on his head. "It's over and I'm good for the day. I wouldn't deprive you of your last sunset on *The Dolphin* for a while."

"Yeah, well, if you're sure you can handle the seas today," Ian said, already letting out more line.

Cade wasn't sure of any such thing. For nearly two years, he had tried valiantly to measure up to first-mate standards aboard the forty-foot Bertram. But most every time his grandfather had gunned the twin inboards and headed for open water, a thrill to most of their customers, Cade had grabbed a nearby bucket. If he made it through the churning acceleration and gas fumes, the rolling swells beyond got him, and nothing had helped, not patches, pressure bracelets, or pills. Nothing except the newspaperman from Charleston.

He was an editor from the *Post and Courier* who had boarded *The Dolphin* just a customer gunning for tuna, and eight hours later, disembarked as Cade's new employer and ticket off the boat. The man had been impressed by a few feature stories Cade had written for the Key West *Citizen*, and, as rarely happens, offered him a newsroom job on the spot—though on a trial basis given Cade's relative inexperience. Just a year later, the recessive economy had forced a downsizing of the newsroom and the last-hired-first-fired maxim held true. Cade had been laid off with five other reporters. As he'd done many times before, he had retreated to his grandfather's nurturing refuge in the Keys, long enough to regain his bearings. After a couple of weeks, he was ready to return to Charleston and find new employment.

"Pop, I hear the black fins are hitting pretty hard farther out. Want to give them a run?" He'd settled into one of the fighting chairs with a cold can of ginger ale, which he held as much to his forehead as his mouth.

Ian gaped at him. "You mean you want to go farther and stay longer?"

"Last day, Pop. Make it count."

"Son, I'm just going to Charleston with you, not the moon. I'll be back in time to—"

Ian's words were cut short by Cade's sudden and hasty departure from the chair back to the side of the boat, his hat sailing from his upside-down head.

"That's it!" Ian declared. "We're going home." This time he cranked the line all the way in.

Two days later, Cade awoke in his ground-floor apartment to the sound of a branch skittering lightly across his windowpane. Autumn winds off Charleston Harbor had lifted with the sun and come rattling down the narrow lanes, sweeping the warm covers off the slumbering city.

He turned toward the window in his bedroom and pulled the blanket up to his chin. He thought of the slaves and servants who'd done the same thing in this very room centuries earlier, wishing they could spend the day roaming the town instead of polishing the silver and ironing the linens of those who lived upstairs.

It was this town that Cade was eager to show his grandfather. The job hunt could wait a few more days, he decided. Proceeds from the recent sale of his sprawling Atlanta home would pay the bills until he decided how to market himself. His wasn't the usual skill set: corporate executive in his parents' real estate empire, charter-boat mate, news reporter—in that order. He watched the tree branch bend to trace its own wobbly path across the windowpane, then suddenly right itself in the buffering wind. And he smiled. *All is well*, he believed.

Cade inhaled the damp air that persistently clung to the apartment, even with the windows open. The place had been ripe with both charm and mildew when he moved in a year ago. "This close to the water and tucked under the belly of this old house, you can't escape mold and mildew," the rental agent had admitted. "And since the gardeners disappeared a couple of years ago, the old growth is closing in on this place, making it even damper. You might ask the owner if you can clear out some of it. Beat back Borneo, you know." He chuckled. "Anyway, she's in a nursing home. I'll get the contact info for you."

Lying in the tender light of approaching day, Cade decided to do just that, only he didn't think he needed permission to prune back the obtrusive shrubs that nearly blocked the path to his door. The owner would surely thank him for tending her untidy grounds. And it would give his grandfather a project.

This was the hour the old man usually rose to coffee and the Scriptures, but Cade hadn't heard him that Thursday morning. Probably still worn out from the trip. They had arrived late the previous night. In an impulsive moment during Cade's recent visit to the Keys, Ian had insisted on going home with him for a "look-see at the place where you think you belong."

He smiled to himself as he often did when thinking about his grandfather, the only one who'd thrown him a lifeline when his parents' careless lifestyle threatened to suck him into the abyss with them. The smile faded with memories of his parents' boozy, all-night parties at their lavish house in Atlanta, but deft with practice, he clambered to the other side of those visions and kept going.

Cade pulled on jeans and a sweatshirt and crossed the combination living room-kitchen to the spare bedroom on the other side, and quietly opened the door. The bed inside was empty and neatly made. He checked the bathroom and his nostrils flared from the freshly applied Old Spice aftershave. Slipping into loafers, he stepped outside to search for his grandfather, and locked the door behind him.

As he crossed the ribbon of grass to the sidewalk, he gazed back at the old white-painted house with the black shutters and high porches. Looking at it always gave him pleasure. He didn't know what a Charleston single house was until he moved into one. Like most of its kind, this one was three stories, counting his ground-level apartment. The house was one room wide with the length of it running perpendicular to the street and fronting on a side lawn and garden. An elaborately carved wooden door at ground level facing the street led to an open-air stairway that rose to the second-floor porch and the main entrance to the home. The place had captivated him at first sight.

Before Cade had arrived in Charleston to start his job at the newspaper, his editor had advised him to find an apartment in one of the "young professional" developments off the peninsula. "They're more plentiful and far cheaper than any place you'll find in town," the editor had said. "In town" was the peninsula where proud old Charleston preened between the Ashley and Cooper rivers.

Once Cade had driven onto the peninsula that first day, he could drive no longer. He had entered another land and had to absorb it slowly on foot. He parked the car and walked back in time, down the narrow cobblestone streets, through the meandering old Slave Market, beside homes built in the 1700s and 1800s, past imposing wrought-iron gates into gardens where trees planted by the early colonists still fluttered in the salt breeze. There was no going back to the redundant apartment complexes cemented along the byways. Cade was home, though he didn't know why he believed that.

After pondering which way his grandfather might have gone, he turned and walked briskly toward the harbor, knowing that's where the old fisherman would most likely head. A couple of blocks down the road, he spotted Ian seated on a bench facing the water, his floppy fishing hat sitting low on his head. He was watching the fishing boats head east toward Fort Sumter and the open sea.

"How long have you been out here, Pop?" Cade asked, coming up behind Ian.

"Long enough to get some air," Ian said, his eyes following the boats. "I don't know how you stand being jammed up so close on every side. Everywhere you look there's a brick wall or a gate in your face." He finally looked up to see Cade smiling down at him. "Well, what's so funny?"

You, you grumpy and wonderful old man. "Come on. I'll make breakfast for you."

"Already had mine."

"Now where did you find food between my place and this bench?"

"I found some beef jerky and one of those Little Debbie cakes in my jacket pocket. The cake was a little squashed, but it went down tolerably well."

Cade laughed out loud, breaking the stillness of the early morning.

"And which artery did you slice open to cram all that saturated fat into? Is that what a heart bypass teaches you?" Cade tugged on the back of Ian's jacket. "Come on, Pop. Let me fix you something healthy."

The two men ambled down Tidewater Lane, Cade's street, which was lined on both sides with other tall, stately dwellings, many of them on the National Register of Historic Places. Some were built of handmade brick or stone, or both. Others were clad in hand-planed boards thick with paint, their colors preapproved by the local historic preservation board.

As they approached the big white house with the black shutters and snug, though damp, basement apartment, Cade noticed a thick-bodied man in a plain white sweatshirt and loose-fitting gym shorts studying the house from across the street. Tourists often stopped to ogle the houses in the neighborhood, but this seemed a little early in the day for sightseeing. He gave the man a courteous nod as he and Ian crossed the grass toward the house.

As Cade turned the key in the door, he glanced discreetly over his shoulder and was glad to see the man had moved on down the street.

"Strange-looking fella, don't you think?" Ian commented, watching the man. "Bet he's not from around here."

"Neither are you, Pop," Cade teased. He pushed open the door and went straight to the kitchen. "Now, knowing your penchant for bacon and eggs, I'll get right on it."

"And that's healthy?"

"If you do it right."

A little later, Ian asked, "Where's your TV?"

"Don't have one yet."

"How am I supposed to watch *Jeopardy*?"

"That doesn't come on until tonight."

"Well, when it does, what am I supposed to do?"

Cade ran a hand through his dark hair and sighed. "Maybe we'll just have to find something even more exhilarating than watching *Jeopardy*." He put a plate of bacon in the microwave, then stirred the eggs.

"How about we let ourselves through that fancy door out there and take a sit on that big old porch upstairs," Ian said. "I'll bet you can see the harbor from up there."

"I don't think we should do that."

"Well, nobody lives up there, right?"

"That's true. The woman who owns the house moved to a nursing home a couple of years ago."

"So no one ever comes around?"

Cade spooned eggs onto a plate for Ian, then added the bacon and a stem of red grapes. Ian inspected the food and looked up with a big smile. "Well, son, that's a respectable breakfast right there." He nudged the grapes aside and dug in hungrily to the rest. After just a couple of bites, though, he put down his fork and eyed his grandson suspiciously. "Something funny about this." He looked past Cade to an assembly of containers on the counter beside the stove, then got up for closer inspection. He picked up a few and read: "Eggbeaters. Turkey bacon. Salt substitute." He turned back and fixed Cade with a smoldering eye. "If I'd wanted imitation food, I'd have eaten the package that jerky came in."

Cade walked over and wrapped an arm around Ian's bulky shoulders. "Nothing funny about the food. Nothing funny about a heart attack. So admit it's pretty good and finish your breakfast. We've got work to do today."

"And what's that?"

"I'd like you to help me trim back some of the shrubbery."

"Well, I think I can manage that. I hate to see a fine old place like this neglected. You never did say—does anyone ever come around to see about the house?"

"The agent said the owner's granddaughter pops in occasionally for just a few days, but not for over a year now." Cade handed Ian a cup of coffee. "She's a pianist. Lives in Washington."

Chapter 10

WHEN LIESL WAS SEVEN

"Hey Liesl, my dad says your dad's a drunk!"

"He is not!" Liesl yelled back at nine-year-old Buddy Prentiss, riding his bike up and down the sidewalk.

She turned to one of her friends jumping rope with her. "What does that mean, Angie?"

Buddy overheard. "Ah-ah, you don't even know, do you?" he taunted.

But Angie Ryall just shrugged her shoulders, then turned to glare at the boy. "Go home and leave us alone, Buddy."

"You can't make me!" he yelled.

"Oh yes I can." Angie ran to her backyard gate and opened it. The barking black Doberman that rushed out chased Buddy until the girls could no longer hear his screams.

Later, Liesl walked down the cobblestone street to her house. It was really her grandmother's home, but she and her parents had lived there for almost a year now. "It's ten times bigger than the apartment where we used to live," she'd told her new friend Angie soon after the family moved in. "It's like a house in a storybook, where the princess lives." Then she'd taken Angie to show her.

Liesl's grandmother, Lottie Bower, had let the girls ramble through all the rooms and play the big white piano where Liesl practiced her lessons each afternoon. Lottie brought homemade scones and sweet tea to the girls as they played dress-up in Liesl's third-floor corner room. It was smaller than the other bedrooms, but from its tall windows, Liesl could see all of the garden that rambled from the side yard to the back.

It was to the garden that Liesl now headed, hearing the loud buzz of her dad's electric saw. The old wrought-iron gate off the driveway squealed as she opened it and shut it behind her. She ran along the flagstone path to one corner of the backyard, carefully gauging her stride so that each foot landed squarely on a stone.

"Dad!" she called when the buzzing momentarily stopped.

Henry Bower looked up to see his daughter running toward him and a smile spread across his face. He removed the red baseball cap from his head, revealing the same sunburnt-gold hair he'd passed down to his daughter. He waved the cap at Liesl. "Hey, Punkin!" he called. His only child's earliest attempts to say "pumpkin" had coined the endearment he used frequently—so much so that Liesl had given him a small gold charm in the shape of a pumpkin for his birthday. He'd strung it onto a gold-chain necklace and sworn he'd always wear it.

He set down the saw, the wide gold wedding ring on his finger catching a ray of light. He placed his cap sideways on Liesl's head, then gently pulled her to him and kissed her cheek. "You're a sweaty one this afternoon," he teased, releasing her with an exaggerated frown. "What have you been doing?" He picked up a long tool Liesl had never seen before and continued working.

"Jumpin' rope at Angie's," Liesl said, scanning the progress of her dad's project. "What's that?" she asked, pointing to the level in his hand.

"This is what keeps all the boards of your new playhouse perfectly level so that when it's finished, you don't have to walk crooked when you step inside." Demonstrating, he bent sideways and shuffled awkwardly through the doorway, deliberately bumping his head in a clownish performance that drew a fit of giggles from his young daughter.

"Dad, you're so silly," she said, hugging him hard around his waist.

Then she looked up at him and asked, "When you were a little boy grow-ing up here, did you have a playhouse too?"

Her dad seemed not to hear, so Liesl repeated the question.

"I heard you," he said gently, resting the level on a board he'd just placed on top of another one. "And no, I never had one. That's why I'm building this for you." He looked proudly at the half-finished little house that would, he had promised, have window boxes and a real front porch. "This will be your special place," he told her as he picked up his hammer. He swung it soundly, driving several big nails into place before turning back to Liesl.

"Everyone needs a place that's just for them," he continued. "Where they can be alone and try to figure out who they are." He paused and looked away. "Before it's too late."

Liesl pushed the cap out of her eyes and frowned. "I don't know what you mean, Dad."

He stroked her lightly on the chin. "Of course you don't, darlin'. Not yet."

"Dad?"

"Yes?" He picked up another board.

"What's a drunk?"

That night, before Liesl climbed into bed, she went to a window and looked out. Through the loose canopy of trees, the moon had cast shad-ows like black lace over the lawn. But Liesl could clearly see the playhouse. It looked like a rough, wooden crate without a lid, its interior dark. But outside, where the porch would soon be built, gauzy beams of light fell on the figure of a man, rendering what would become an indelible image in his daughter's memory.

The baseball cap on his head, he sat alone in a plastic chair. Liesl caught the glint of glass and watched as he hoisted the bottle to his mouth and drank. She kept watching until finally he placed a cap on the bottle, crossed the lawn slowly, and shoved the bottle deep inside some bushes against the house. He never looked up.

Later, when the angry voices from her parents' bedroom grew silent and the house was still again, Liesl slipped out of her bedroom, down the wide staircase and through the back door. Barefoot, she ran to the shrubs and found the bottle. Uncapping it, she took a sniff and wrinkled her nose.

She couldn't read the label in the dark, perhaps not even in daylight, the words were so unfamiliar. But it didn't matter. If her dad was pouring such awful-smelling stuff inside him and making her mother cry, she would put an end to it, she decided. She poured the brown liquid into the dirt. Then she screwed the cap back on the bottle and put it back where she'd found it.

Chapter 11

Ian was the first to wade into the thicket of wax myrtles on one side of the house. "You can forget the clippers," he called to Cade, who was gathering the garden tools he'd borrowed from a friend. "We'll have to use a saw, maybe dynamite to cut through this stuff. Why anyone would let a place like this go to the dogs is beyond me."

"Here you go, Pop," Cade said, handing his grandfather a large handsaw.

"Here you go nothing. You get on in there and see what you can do, and give me those clippers. I'll start on these little bushes over here."

"Sure, Pop. Wouldn't want you to mess up your manicure with the hard stuff." Cade shot his grandfather a wily grin and plunged into the thicket. He cut back enough growth to open an airway between the myrtles and the side of the house. That's when he noticed the rot. Though the basement level of the house was brick, the wooden frames around the windows fairly crumbled to his touch. *This is a job for the old handyman*, he decided.

He turned the front corner of the house in time to see Ian closing in on an old camellia bush. "No, Pop! Not that one."

Ian's head jerked toward Cade, but the long shears remained just inches from the ornamental shrub now loaded with magenta blooms the size of saucers. "Why not? It's too big."

"It's a camellia, Pop. They're like sacred cows around here. You just leave them alone and let them do what they want."

Ian turned back to study the privileged plant, then back at Cade. "Like me, right?"

Cade laughed and motioned for Ian to follow him. "Come look at this."

Leaving Ian to determine the best way to repair the window, Cade went to inspect the others on ground level. He'd just pushed his way through more thick shrubs when his foot struck something hard in the dirt. He stooped to see an old, empty liquor bottle. Retrieving it, he noticed only a fragment of a label, the letters too faded to read. And the cap was screwed down tightly.

He passed Ian on the way to the garbage bin.

"What have you got there?" Ian asked, still probing the woodwork.

Cade held up the bottle. "Looks like the end of a party."

The next afternoon, Cade and Ian left the peninsula and headed for Hidden Pines nursing home in North Charleston. "You really don't want to go, do you?" Cade asked.

Ian grimaced. "Those places make me queasy. I don't know why you couldn't have just asked the woman's permission over the phone, or let the rental agent handle the repairs like he offered to."

Cade drummed his fingers against the steering wheel of his old Chevy Blazer. "I really want to meet this lady. I've been living under her lonely old house for a year now. I can almost hear it breathing up there, but we've never been introduced."

"You and the house?" Ian asked blankly.

"Yeah, it's this stranger I want to know. Just like her." Cade glanced over and caught the puzzled look on Ian's face, then sighed. "Okay, I can see I'm not getting through."

"Oh, I'm hearing you. But as soon as the owner tells you it's okay to be friends with her house and even patch up its lonely little windows, can we leave?"

Cade set his mouth in a tight line and stared straight ahead. "You got it, Pop."

Thirty minutes later, he pulled the Blazer into the parking lot at Hidden Pines. It was nice enough, he guessed, but there were no pines and nothing much was hidden. In fact, all around was a wide-open stretch of shopping centers, car dealerships, and a new elementary school plunked down on a treeless plain. The nursing home was also new, its flat grounds scattered with tiny, round bushes that, from the air, must have looked like a connect-the-dot game. Near the main door, a couple of newly planted river birch trees were crutched up with two-by-fours to keep them from falling over—sadly appropriate, Cade thought, for a place housing the disabled.

He watched Ian eye the propped-up trees in much the same way, and caught a trace of fear in his aging face. It wasn't anything Cade was used to seeing and it troubled him.

Cade opened the polished glass door for Ian, studying the solemn old face as it passed wide-eyed into the gleaming reception area. "Now behave," Cade admonished lightly, hoping to draw fire and break the gloom. But Ian failed to deliver his usual sharp retort.

"May I help you?" came the pleasing voice of a woman at a receiving desk near the door.

"Yes, ma'am. We're here to see Mrs. Lottie Bower. I called earlier. I'm Cade O'Brien."

"Oh yes. She's expecting you. Just sign in here and I'll direct you to her room."

Formalities over, Cade and Ian followed a broad linoleum hallway hung with cheery prints to reflect the region: sailboats bobbing on the ocean, a horse and buggy delivering hoop-skirted women to the entry of a white-columned plantation home. Lush silk greenery rose from pots stationed along the hall.

"Very pleasant, don't you think?" Cade asked Ian.

"It smells."

Cade smiled to himself. *There's hope.*

"Mrs. Bower is almost ninety," Cade informed his grandfather as they walked. "The rental agent says she's had a series of strokes. She's in a wheelchair. And she suffers from mild dementia."

Ian's expression grew more pained.

At the partially open door to room eighteen, Cade stopped and rapped lightly on the door frame. "Mrs. Bower? It's Cade O'Brien."

"Hello?" came the soft reply from inside.

"Is it okay to come in, Mrs. Bower?"

"Who?"

Ian turned to Cade. "Let's just leave."

Cade shook his head and slowly stepped into the room. He didn't see her at first, her thin body sunken into the wheelchair in front of the window. Light pouring in through the open blinds backlit the woman, leaving her face in darkness but the top of her head in shining silver. "Oh my, you're here," she said. "I've been waiting." Holding her left arm awkwardly against her body, she offered her right hand.

Motioning for Ian to come inside, Cade went to grasp the delicate hand, finding her grip surprisingly firm. "It's a pleasure to meet you, Mrs. Bower. I'm Cade O'Brien." He turned. "And this is my grandfather, Ian O'Brien."

She released Cade's hand and waved timidly at Ian.

"Ma'am," Ian said, approaching hesitantly. As he bent low and closed his rough hand over hers, his face relaxed. Cade watched Ian's bushy-browed eyes search the woman's clear blue ones before finally releasing her hand and straightening. "I hope we're not disturbing you."

"Of course not," she said sweetly. She looked at Ian intently. "You remind me of my husband," she said to him. "Except you're alive." She paused. "How old are you?"

"Seventy-two, ma'am."

Her gaze grew bright. "I'm just thirty-six. You're much too old for me."

Ian shot Cade the briefest glance then smiled warmly, genuinely, at the woman. "Yes, ma'am. You're much too young."

Her right hand fluttered to her face and she beamed with delight. "Now, tell me who you are."

Cade cleared his throat. "I live in the basement apartment of your house, Mrs. Bower. My grandfather is visiting me. We've come here to talk to you about your home."

"Home?" Her voice rose and her eyes danced. "I'm going home?"

Cade panicked a bit. "Well, I'm not sure that—"

"Is Henry there? He's been gone so long. He won't even recognize Liesl." Then her hand came swiftly to her forehead, rubbing it as if to coax something from inside. "Oh dear, I've forgotten. Henry's dead, just like Liesl's mother." She turned to a small table next to her bed and lifted a framed picture. Handing it to Cade, she said with renewed cheer, "Except for her hair, doesn't she look just like her mother?"

Cade evaded the question he couldn't possibly answer and took the picture. He gazed at the young woman he assumed was the granddaughter, the one who seldom visited. She was dressed in a fur-trimmed gown, her golden hair worn loosely about her wide, bare shoulders. He studied the set of her face, beautiful yet somehow severe. "This is the pianist?"

"I taught her first. Before that man took her to Russia and nearly got her killed." She turned to Ian. "Would you like some tea, dear?"

Ian sputtered a no-thank-you and, to Cade's surprise, pulled up a chair close to her, motioning for Cade to do the same.

"Mrs. Bower," Ian began slowly, "we've found some rotted wood at your home and would like to replace it if that's okay with you."

She looked toward the picture still in Cade's hands. "What does that have to do with Liesl?"

"Well, nothing really," Ian answered patiently. "But she might appreciate it if we fixed your house for you."

"Is she there?" the woman asked hopefully.

Compassion flooded Ian's face and he tenderly touched the woman's arm. "Liesl is not there now, but I'm sure she'll be—"

"Because if she is," Lottie interrupted, "that man wants to see her. He told me so."

Cade raised his brow as the woman continued.

"He's an old friend of hers who wants to surprise her. Have you talked to him too?"

Ian drew a deep breath and stood up, looking firmly at Cade. "Mrs. Bower, I think we should go now and let you rest."

Cade jumped in. "It was so nice to meet you and I hope you'll see your granddaughter very soon."

"And then I'll tell her about her friend," she said. "I don't think he'll mind. He was such a nice man. With such an unusual accent."

Chapter 12

*A*t FBI headquarters in Manhattan, Liesl slowly ran her finger around the rim of her coffee cup, willing the room and all those in it to disappear. It was almost midnight on Friday, and she was certain there would be no Saturday night concert for her.

She thought of Rev. Scovall and knew he was probably asleep, the strange episode at his church that night now over. But not for her.

"Miss Bower, I know you've answered many questions about your relationship with Schell Devoe, but I think you'll agree that the recent break-in at your home in Washington and the attempted attack on you tonight forces us to reopen this investigation." Liesl gazed at the man as if he were commuting sentence on her.

FBI Special Agent Mark Delaney continued. "We have learned that the man you told us you saw at the White House on Tuesday and who pursued you on the street tonight is a known operative in the Russian intelligence community. Now, can you think of any reason, besides your association with Devoe, why you would be of interest to such a person?"

Liesl glanced down at the man's tie, drawn by the white smudge against the royal blue. A powdered donut, she guessed, eyeing the green and white box sitting next to the coffeepots. Then she looked back at Delaney's face, the stubble of a beard growing darker with each passing minute. The agent had been reasonably kind to her, insisting she rest from her ordeal before the questioning began. But now, he was joined by a small contingent of FBI and CIA agents around a table in a windowless room. Ava sat next to her in what Liesl assumed was some show of support.

"Miss Bower?" Delaney prodded.

Liesl closed her eyes as she drew a long breath, feeling the walls close in around her. "No, I cannot."

Delaney studied her a moment, then asked, "How long did you know Devoe and just how close to him and his wife were you?"

Just give them all they want. Liesl looked away as she answered. "Dr. Devoe saw something in me he believed in, he told me." She paused, the memory of her old friend beginning to warm again. "He became my mentor. He would invite me to his home where Mrs. Devoe always cooked for us while we played duets together in the living room." Liesl could feel herself growing wistful as she recalled that nurturing but short-lived capsule of life she'd lived at Harvard, and the many pleasant hours spent in the Devoes' home.

One of the other agents cleared his throat and asked, "He took you to Moscow with him on two occasions. Did you at any time observe anything you thought was out of place or unusual?"

The alley. The fight with Evgeny Kozlov. Liesl remembered Ben's question after she told him of the incident: *"Why didn't you tell this to someone during the investigation?"* Now she knew why. It wasn't just because they'd treated her as if she were Devoe's coconspirator. It was also to protect him from more damning incriminations. Even though he was dead and a traitor to his country, she had cared deeply for him.

But suddenly the memory cooled. He'd deserted her and his country.

Liesl glanced at Ava and saw something she'd refused to see earlier—compassion. It was enough to move Liesl forward. "There is one thing," she offered. "Two, actually."

When she finished the story of that snowy night in a Moscow alley, she told them about the encounter with Professor Vadim Fedorovsky in his apartment. No one asked why she hadn't related those incidents before. They didn't seem to care. There was an urgency in the air that

Liesl sensed had less to do with what happened all those years ago than with something that lay ahead. She read it in the faces of those around her.

"Do you have in your possession anything that Devoe gave you just prior to his death?" Delaney asked. "Maybe for safekeeping?"

Liesl fought the urge to yawn in the man's face. Despite the coffee she'd swilled, she was fading quickly. "Such as?" she responded absently.

Liesl noticed an unspoken exchange between Delaney and Ava, the slightest nod, a go-ahead, it seemed, from Delaney. Then Ava turned toward Liesl.

"I know you're tired," she said. "Tired of this day, of us and our questions. But it's critical that you think hard about your answers." Ava looked again at Delaney, then back at Liesl.

"Yesterday, I told you that Devoe had been working for us as a double agent," Ava continued. "To save his own neck, he not only cooperated in a sting to catch Russia's informant in our State Department, but he agreed to uncover a piece of information that would more greatly impact security of the United States and one of our allies."

Liesl locked on Ava with growing interest.

Ava continued. "I also told you that we believe he made that discovery just before he was killed. "

"But you wouldn't tell me what it was," Liesl reminded her.

Ava looked steadily at Liesl. "You're the one they're hunting. You must have something they want. We think we know what it is. And now, you should know too."

Liesl straightened in her seat, the fog in her brain suddenly clearing.

"We believe Devoe had just identified an undercover Russian agent operating inside Israel's Ministry of Defense."

Liesl didn't move.

"We have reason to believe this agent, this mole, is still there. And now, it's more imperative than ever that we know who it is."

Delaney interjected, "Of course, you must see what's happening with Russia, Liesl. Its mounting aggression toward U.S. interests, its overtures to form alliances with those countries that could threaten U.S. security."

Ava jumped in. "Russia is attempting to build an oil and gas cartel to leverage power over Europe. And its arms sales to Iran and Syria leave the security of Israel hanging in the balance. The Russian mole is in place to detect when and how Israel will retaliate against those neighbors who are growing nuclear arsenals."

Sloughing off the fatigue, Liesl was now fully engaged. "How did Russia know that Dr. Devoe hadn't already reported the identity of their agent to you? Before they killed him?"

"We have to assume they didn't," Delaney answered. "But fifteen years of no reprisal against their mole proved he, or she, was safe in Israel. The Israelis also never detected a military intelligence leak. They thought Devoe must have been mistaken about a mole in Israel, and that the Russians killed him just because he'd turned against them. The Kremlin probably made the agent lie dormant—until now. Now, they'll do anything to protect their mole's identity." Delaney didn't explain why.

One of the other FBI agents asked, "Did Devoe tell you why his wife moved out of their home and where she was going?"

Liesl vividly remembered that conversation with Devoe. "He announced one day that he was going to retire soon, and that he'd already bought a place for himself and his wife. I was surprised at how sudden it was and that he wouldn't tell me where it was. He said she was going ahead of him to get it ready. She'd been gone less than a year when he was . . . when he died."

"Tell us about what you saw that night," Delaney said casually, as if he'd asked Liesl to describe her last trip to the dentist. He pulled a sheaf of papers from a file and spread them before him. He must have noticed her staring at them. "Yes, it's a transcript of your testimony in 1996. Go ahead."

She eyed him darkly. "You're asking me to go back there—to that night?"

"Yes, I am," he said flatly.

There was one hard pound of her heart before it began to race.

"It's important, Liesl," Ava urged.

Liesl heard but didn't look at the woman, only at the table before her.

It was a laminate of fake wood, no grain of its own, no life. An imposter. Was she? Had she concocted a life that no longer fooled anyone with its elegant illusions? *Just tell the story and get it over.*

So she began. "We were going to have dinner together after my last class. His house was an easy walk from the Harvard campus. When I got there, I was about to knock on the front door when I heard yelling inside. Then I saw the door was slightly open. I went inside and the house was in shambles." Liesl squeezed her eyes shut and saw the front rooms of the house clearly. "Everything was on the floor, pictures off the walls and drawers hanging open. A man in a black ski mask ran from a hallway, dragging Dr. Devoe beside him." A tremor rose in Liesl's voice, but she kept going.

"Dr. Devoe yelled for me to run. Just then, the man shoved a gun into Dr. Devoe's chest and . . . and fired." She didn't realize her voice had grown louder, that her whole body was shaking until Ava slipped her arm around Liesl's shoulders to steady her.

But it didn't help. Liesl felt like a runaway train as she surged further into the story. "Dr. Devoe fell to the floor and the man shot him two more times. Point blank. Blood sprayed against the walls. Then he turned and stared at me. I was paralyzed. I felt like my backpack would pull me backward onto the floor. Then he would shoot me too." Ava's grip grew tighter around Liesl. "But instead, he ran out the back of the house. And I . . . I . . ."

"We know the rest, Liesl," Ava said gently. "It's okay."

"It's not okay!" Liesl jumped up and walked to the water cooler. She drained a cup of cold water and paced back and forth in front of the door, wishing she could run back into the night. Alone.

Delaney watched her a moment, then said, "Tell me about the backpack you carried that night. I don't see any mention of it in your old testimony. What was in it?"

Liesl looked incredulously at him. "I just described a horrific murder to you and you want to know what was in my backpack?" Liesl wanted to defuse her anger but didn't know how. She waved a dismissive hand in the air as if nothing else she said mattered. "A sandwich I didn't eat at lunch," she answered robotically. "Class notes. Music. Stuff." Liesl refilled her cup with water and just held it, looking at no one.

"Music?" Ava asked.

"Of course music," Liesl snapped. "There was always music."

She watched as another silent signal passed between Delaney and Ava. "That's how Devoe passed his coded information to the Russians, mostly the names of American undercover agents," Ava confided. "Later, after we turned him and he started passing Russian secrets to us, he used the same technique."

"Through music?" she asked, dumbfounded.

"Devoe created a very simple but effective technique for coding secret information. He would carefully alter certain notes and rests on commonly published sheet music," Ava explained. "Using professional-grade equipment, he would then scan and reprint the altered music. These changes were undetectable to all but another trained musician."

Liesl went still. Something deep in her memory now hurtled to the surface.

Ava kept talking. "Knowing what to look for, Devoe's musician-counterpart in Russia would then find the erroneous markings in the composition, apply them to a letter code, and decipher the message."

Liesl's cup suddenly slipped from her hand onto the floor, splattering water over her boots. Her mouth went dry and she stared at Ava without really seeing her. "The sonata," she half whispered to herself.

All eyes were on her as she now stared at Ava. "The sonata . . . it was his. I took it home by mistake." She looked away, excavating more from her memory.

"Keep going," Delaney urged.

Liesl stared hard at the floor as that afternoon returned to her. "I had visited Dr. Devoe at his home earlier that day, and later he called to ask if I had accidently taken a Tchaikovsky sonata from his desk. It was the *Grand Sonata in G Major*, a new copy he'd just ordered." She looked up at Delaney. "I had it. Dr. Devoe had been helping me with some arrangements I was writing, and when I gathered up my music to leave, the sonata must have been underneath the pile. I didn't know."

"But why does that music stand out to you now?" Ava asked.

"Because . . . before I took it back to him, I played it. It was a favorite of mine."

"And . . ." Delaney broke in impatiently.

Liesl looked at him but saw the music instead. "There was something wrong with it. Some of the rests were all wrong. What should have been whole notes were quarter notes, and others were wrong too. I know the piece well, and the errors were obvious to me. I was going to tell Dr. Devoe to alert the music publisher when I got to his home that night."

"Why didn't you tell us about the music," Ava asked.

"I never thought of it again. Even if I had, I wouldn't have seen any connection to what happened." She looked earnestly at Ava. "You asked me if Dr. Devoe had ever given me music, and of course, he had. All the time." Her thoughts were gathering quickly. "Why didn't you tell me then what you were looking for? I would have known it had to be the sonata."

No one spoke.

Liesl knew why. "You didn't trust me, did you?" She looked accusingly at Ava. "Did you think I'd try to sell his music to the highest bidder?" Her words spewed like venom.

Ava stood. "Calm down, Liesl. It doesn't matter if we did or didn't trust you then. But it matters now, especially to you. You must trust us to protect you. You're the hunted one—and now we know why." She paused for only an instant, then, "Where is the sonata now?"

Liesl suddenly felt light-headed. She pulled a chair from the table and sat down, her mind tumbling through possibilities. Delaney motioned for one of the agents to get more water for her, but Liesl waved it away. She closed her eyes and saw herself running blindly from Devoe's house that night, straight to her little apartment where she locked the door and drew the shades. What did she do with the backpack and its contents? A blackness had spilled through those moments in her apartment as she reeled from the atrocity she'd just witnessed, and all the years had cast no more light on those hours.

"All of my music is at home in Washington." Though Liesl couldn't recall having seen that particular sonata since she'd moved from Boston.

"If they'd found what they were looking for at your house, they wouldn't have come after you tonight," Delaney said confidently.

"Why come after me at all?" she blurted. "How do they know what I have? If I have it."

Ava smiled uneasily. "We can only assume they discovered some clue at the Devoe cabin in Canada. Immediately after it was torn apart, Evgeny Kozlov arrived in the U.S. and you became a target."

Liesl thought of her bungalow that surely lay in ruins, just as Mrs. Devoe's own home had. Her library would be destroyed, every piece of music she'd collected throughout a long career gone. She hung her head trying not to imagine the carnage. But just then, somewhere in the fog surrounding the time of Devoe's murder, a pinpoint of light began to trace the days and weeks afterward, and Liesl now watched them unfold: The questioning by local police at the station downtown, the secret interrogation by CIA agents in the back of a van parked behind the music school. The shock of discovering that Devoe had been a spy. The shame of being linked to his traitorous double life. And then, her escape. Ben had called it her "disappearance," though he'd known where she was.

As if a lazer had just pierced a long-forgotten tomb, Liesl suddenly recalled those moments after her release from questioning: fleeing to her apartment, throwing a few belongings together, then racing from Boston in her old Volkswagen, heading south.

Now with clarity she remembered what else she'd tossed into the car before she left, a hurriedly packed box of music. Inside were the piano arrangements she'd been working on—and all the sheet music from her backpack.

She raised her head and met the anxious eyes fixed upon her. "I know where it is."

Chapter 13

The old Blazer rumbled over the James Island connector heading onto the peninsula. In the backseat was a used television crammed into a dilapidated cardboard box.

"See, I told you we'd get a better deal out there," Ian said, a smug curl at the corners of his mouth.

Cade changed lanes for the exit into town. He hadn't wanted to talk much about the television since leaving the flea market almost fifty miles from Charleston. But it was time to unload, just a bit. "You're right, Pop. It would have been foolish for us to buy a brand-new television from the store five miles from my house . . . when we could drive almost to Savannah to buy a used one from a guy in a Deadhead T-shirt. And here's the best part—to save forty dollars."

Ian eyed his grandson with scorn. "Well, I for one enjoyed the drive and you will be slobbering down your chin when you dig into these watermelons we picked up along the way."

Cade nodded in mock agreement. "You're right. Those watermelons will more than make up for no warranty on the television."

Ian sulked. "Not to mention that you didn't spend a dime on any of it."

Nodding concession, Cade offered, "I do owe you a bit of gratitude, don't I?"

Ian didn't answer.

"Okay, Pop. Truce." Cade made a sharp turn at the next corner and headed away from his neighborhood.

"Where are you going?"

"I'm taking you to lunch at a very special place."

"Do they have anything besides organic vegetables and bean sprouts? I don't think I can stomach much more of that stuff you feed me."

"That's why I'm taking you to Shem Creek, home to everything fried, just as much as you can shove inside those veins. Maybe one well-deserved gorging won't kill you."

As they crossed the Cooper River heading off the peninsula toward Mount Pleasant and the Atlantic, the wind through the open windows grew thick and pungent. Winding through a commercial grove of beachy, low-rise businesses, they crossed the bridge over Shem Creek and turned in at a row of wharf-like seafood restaurants, their timbers weathered to a shabby-chic gray. Tied up outside was an assortment of recreational boats, their passengers having stopped for a leisurely Saturday lunch along this narrow waterway.

But it was a sight farther down the docks that seemed to catch Ian's eye, and as soon as they parked the Blazer, he steered Cade that way. "I've just got to touch 'em and smell 'em," Ian said, his expression almost winsome.

Cade followed Ian's line of sight to a fleet of commercial shrimp trawlers tied up one behind the other farther down the waterway, and could do nothing but follow Ian's quick steps in that direction. They passed behind creekside dining porches where lunch patrons clinked silverware against plates, past a row of pastel-painted houses built high above the floodplain. Just beyond a dusty field of sand spurs and fish bones picked clean by circling gulls, Cade and Ian left one world for another. Gone were the shiny white pleasure craft tied up behind the trendy restaurants. Here where the creek opened into the harbor were the grimy troops just back from duty, their rust-streaked hulls now stilled, their crews weary from a night of hunting the white shrimp—the kind that ladies in crisp linen dresses feasted on just down the dock.

As they approached, a man with a beard that hung like Spanish moss eyed them dismissively from one trawler. He was hosing down the decks and anxious to get the job over, it seemed. "How was your catch?" Ian called cheerfully.

The man grunted a one-syllable response. "Fair."

Ian waited a moment then looked at Cade. "They're a lot more talkative in the Keys, don't you think?"

Before Cade could stop him, Ian attempted to board the boat. "Hey, buddy, you can't come up here," the man growled.

Ian stopped. "But I'm a fisherman like you. Got a charter boat in Big Pine Key."

"I don't care where you got a boat. You're not comin' up here." The man jabbed a finger toward the rigging, strung like a tangled web over the whole boat. "You could get hurt."

"Hurt? Why I grew up on a boat like this and I could—"

"Pop," Cade broke in, "let's not make trouble here. Come on." He tugged at Ian's sleeve.

"But I just want to see it."

"Why? You've been on boats like this a thousand times."

Ian suddenly looked stricken. "But how many more times will I?"

Then Cade remembered his grandfather's fearful reaction to the nursing home where Lottie Bower lived, to the trees propped up outside in the barren yard.

Ian looked down at the splintered boards beneath him. "How much longer do I have, son?" He stroked his beard, then squinted up at the trawler again. "I've got a body like that old rusted bucket there. How many more trips to sea has either one of us got?"

Cade thought a minute. "Which sea do you mean?"

Ian looked puzzled.

"There's this sea and there's the one you've been telling me about since I was a little boy. Have you forgotten?"

Ian still didn't answer.

"It was the John 14 passage about Jesus going to prepare a place for us in heaven and when the time was right, he would come for us and take us there. He said there were many rooms there. Only you told me that he really meant boats." Cade beamed at his grandfather. "You said there was a boat just for you and another one for me, and that we would sail on God's safe seas forever." Cade cocked his head slightly. "And I still believe that, Pop. So it doesn't matter what day either one of us stops riding this polluted ocean. There's a better one waiting."

Ian turned his craggy face to Cade and said, "Let's go eat."

Chapter 14

The attractive blond waitress showed Cade and Ian to an outside table overlooking Shem Creek. When they were seated, she cast a long and lingering gaze over Cade before handing him a menu. "Enjoy your lunch," she drawled sweetly, looking only at him, then started to walk away.

"Uh, miss," Ian called, his hand out. The girl turned to look at him and rolled her eyes. "Sorry," she demurred as she handed a menu to him. She smiled awkwardly at Cade and left.

As Cade studied the menu, Ian chided, "You're just going to pretend that didn't happen, aren't you?"

"What?" Cade asked, focused only on the fresh-catch specials of the day.

"That girl going all la-la over you."

"Pop, real men of the sea don't say 'la-la.'"

"And you're evading the issue."

"There is no issue."

"Well, what if I told you that before I go sailing off on that hereafter sea you've assigned me to, I'd like a few great-grandchildren."

"I'd say borrow someone else's for a while. Hey, how about a grilled tuna steak?"

"How about you going out on a date every once in a while? You haven't so much as looked at another woman since . . . well, for a long time. At thirty-nine, you're too young to be a confirmed bachelor."

"You are."

"That's different."

"You don't think Gran would have wanted you to marry again after she was gone?"

"She didn't know she was going. Heart attacks take you unawares. Why, even before I finish this sentence, I could—"

"Okay, Pop. Let's just focus on the menu." Cade drew a deep breath and let it out all at once. He took off his sunglasses and carefully wiped the lenses, feeling his grandfather's penetrating stare.

"You're afraid of women, aren't you?" Ian persisted.

Now Cade was amused. He smirked at Ian before replacing the sunglasses against his handsome, tanned face. "You think so?" he asked, stretching his mouth into a teasing smile.

"Look at you making light of what I'm saying. But you hear me out. The only two women in your life did their best to ruin it for you. My reckless, party-time son picked a woman just like him and the only good thing she ever did was bring you into this world. I'm sorry to talk about your mama that way, but she's as lost a soul as there ever was. And you let her handpick a wife for you. I just don't—"

"That's enough," Cade said more curtly than he intended. "I'm sorry, but I can't let this go on." He looked up into a cloudless sky and let the breeze sweep over his now perspiring face. When he turned back to Ian, he saw the hurt on the face he loved so well, in the eyes that had always harbored strength, but too often now sagged with despair.

Cade laid his hand over Ian's. "Pop, there's no one in this world I love more than you. Maybe one day I'll give you those kids. Maybe not. Right now, I'm just trying to start my life again, so be patient."

Ian didn't move his hand from Cade's grip, but his head bobbed in evident agreement as he looked back at the menu. "When you get around to it, I'd like to have at least one great-grandson to be my first mate, someone not prone to puking. But for now, I'll just have the fried shrimp."

Returning to the peninsula over the soaring Arthur Ravenel bridge, Cade looked into the shipping channel of the Cooper River below. "You know, Pop, you could run a charter out of Charleston as easily as Big Pine Key."

"Why would I want to do that? You'll be moving on from here one day."

"I don't think so. Something about this place intrigues me, even haunts me a little and I don't know why. I'd never seen this town until last year." Cade looked out over the Holy City, as the old town was called. Only steeples rose above the rooftops of buildings no higher than four stories. As a reporter, Cade had covered city hall and knew that historic preservationists had to continually fight the scourge of high-rise development. They were roundly supported by most Charlestonians and a tourism board that knew its bread and butter lay sandwiched in centuries-old mortar, not to be disturbed and certainly not dwarfed by a soaring Holiday Inn.

"I believe God led me here," Cade declared, "even if the job dried up. He'll help me find my way." He glanced at Ian. "Maybe you should be here too, Pop."

Ian was unusually quiet the rest of the way home. Once they arrived, he and Cade launched into the job of replacing rotted wood around the basement windows.

"Pop, do you mind if I leave you alone with this for a while? We need some groceries."

"Sure, go ahead. And get me some Tums, will you?"

"Uh, would that be for the fried shrimp, fried hush puppies, and fried onion rings you just downed?"

"Yeah, yeah. Just get me the Tums and hurry back."

Chapter 15

Saturday morning, three identical black Suburbans with dark tinted windows pulled away from FBI headquarters in Manhattan, each traveling in a different direction. The one carrying Liesl, Ava, FBI Special Agent Mark Delaney, and two of his agents drove straight to a private hangar at LaGuardia Airport. An hour later, a small jet lifted off with those passengers on board.

An hour into the flight—after more questioning, briefings, and Ava's calls for police support ahead—Liesl finally reclined her seat and turned her whole body toward the window. She willed an impenetrable membrane to cloak her against the others. Though she understood their intentions, she abhorred their tactics. She'd been invaded and laid bare, like a rape victim trotted into court—innocent yet shamed, angry yet overpowered. And now, they were mounting another offense into what was left of her life's sanctity.

She closed her eyes and saw the tall white house among the oaks, the hydrangeas that in springtime bobbed their giant blue mopheads next to the dainty, sachet faces of gardenia. She could hear the treble squeal of the front screen door as she flung it open for what seemed a hundred times a day. Her lids fluttering open now, she looked through the plane's tiny portal into the vaporous whiteout beyond. Against that gossamer screen, she watched the little girl she'd been, running up the steps to the porch, sweaty and winded from one of her escapades with the neighborhood kids. She remembered one summer afternoon in particular.

"Wipe your feet," her grandmother had called as Liesl threw open the screen door and rushed inside. "And come here, darlin'."

As it often was, the house was filled with the aroma of something fresh-baked. Today, it was unmistakably her mother's coconut praline cake, and Liesl wondered if she'd forgotten someone's birthday. When she reached the kitchen, the oscillating fan on top of the refrigerator stirred the airborne molecules of caramel frosting. "Want to ice it for me?" her mother asked.

"Who's it for, Mom?" Liesl glanced first at the cake, then at the tall windows over the sink. There was something odd about them. Normally, the plantation shutters were opened wide for an unobstructed view of the garden. But today, they were latched together, every wooden slat closed tightly. Before she could question that, her mom answered.

"Oh, no one in particular. We just had a hankering for something obnoxiously sweet." Liesl's mom glanced at her daughter's pants. "What in the world have you gotten into?"

"Pluff mud." Liesl looked down at the dark stains on her shorts with unconcern.

"You didn't get that in this neighborhood. Where have you been?"

"Angie's brother took us crabbing down the Ashley."

Norma Bower gasped, her mouth forming a perfect O. "On the river?" she asked her daughter with alarm. "And you went without my permission?"

"Did Angie's mother know about this?" Lottie Bower asked calmly.

Liesl shrugged. "No, ma'am. But we didn't think anybody would mind. And look what I found." She dug into one pocket and pulled out a half-dead fiddler crab, which she set down next to the bowl of icing.

Lottie looked at her daughter-in-law and both women burst into giggles.

"What's so funny?" Liesl asked, nudging the crab in hopes it would perform its sideways scurry.

Norma Bower wiped her eyes with the back of her hand and hugged her daughter. "One day you'll play Carnegie Hall. And when the *New York Times* wants to know about the upbringing of such an esteemed musician, be sure and tell them about pluff mud and fiddler crabs."

The back door suddenly opened and her dad bounded in with sweat on his brow and a gleam in his eye. He noted the fiddler crab on the counter and scrunched up his nose, but it seemed nothing was to keep him from some mission.

"And here you are, finally. Now we can begin."

Liesl didn't understand. She glanced from one grinning adult to the other and clamped a hand on each of her curveless hips. "Okay, what's going on?" she demanded with all the authority she could muster.

With arms stretched wide, Henry Bower gathered his daughter, wife, and mother and steered them through the back door and into the garden. All eyes were on Liesl.

Her dad had spent months building the playhouse. Liesl thought she knew exactly how it would look when he finished. He had promised a porch and window boxes, even the flowers to go in them. But she never imagined what loomed before her. It hadn't been there that morning. When had he done this?

Soaring from the roof of the playhouse was a replica of the steeple on top of St. Philip's Church, the building she loved most in all of Charleston. "It's your sanctuary, Punkin," he said. And something in his voice made young Liesl pause. *He sounds sad,* she thought. *Why?*

There was no time to ponder it. Her family quickly ushered her to the door of her new playhouse.

Later, the Bower women made a pageant of dinner. Lottie and Norma brought country ham and all the fixin's from the big kitchen to Liesl's miniature one. Proudly, Liesl served her family, seated in plastic chairs on and near her own front porch. Her mother even let her serve the cake on Lottie Bower's fine, bone-china plates, the ones rimmed in dove gray, each one centered by a creamy magnolia blossom. For the rest of the day, they basked in the light of each other, in the cool overhang of home, and all that meant to a girl of eight.

Lulled by the drone of jet engines, Liesl's vision slipped into a deep slumber where she remained until a woman's voice pierced the protective membrane and called her back. "Liesl, we're about to land." And again. "Liesl, wake up."

Liesl slowly surfaced to consciousness and the cabin of the aircraft. She blinked and ran her tongue over dry, parched lips, then turned to see Ava watching her.

"Can I get you something to drink?" Ava asked pleasantly.

"Cold water," Liesl mumbled. "Thank you."

Ava returned with the water and sat down. "Now Liesl," she began in her all-business tone, "there are a few things we must insist that you do once we arrive."

Though the cool water slid easily down her throat, Liesl was far from soothed. She closed her eyes again and wondered what cosmic order had aligned her with these people, in this time and place. And for what?

"You must stay close to us at all times." Ava pulled a cell phone from her briefcase. "And for the time being, you'll use this phone. It's untraceable, and all calls to your own phone will be forwarded to this one. You'll have to report all incoming messages. As for outgoing calls, texts, e-mails—clear them with us first." Ava frowned regretfully. "I'm sorry to lay this on you at the last minute, but I didn't want to disturb your sleep. You're going to need a clear head."

"Is there anything else?" Liesl asked, not with compliance but sarcasm. "Did you inject me with a tracking pellet while I was asleep?" Immediately, she regretted her hostility. She looked squarely at Ava. "Forgive me. I'm . . . I'm having a hard time with this."

"I'm certain of that. Hopefully, it will be over soon."

"What will be over, Ava? My career? Yours? Someone's life?" She seemed to have no control over her anger—apologizing for it one minute, indulging it the next.

Ava stood, seeming to ignore the taunt. "You'll probably want to freshen up before we land. And I'd suggest grabbing a sandwich from the galley. It's past lunchtime." She stepped aside for Liesl to slip from her window seat. But as she did, Ava stopped her and looked quickly about the cabin. Delaney and his men were in the back, cradling cell phones and huddling over files spread on a long table.

In a low voice, Ava said, "If there were any way to untangle you from this whole affair, I would gladly do it. I'd cut you loose and let you run back to your safe little world. But the truth is, Liesl, your world is not safe. No one's world is. Not anymore."

Something in Ava's eyes sparked. In a firm, measured voice, she said, "There are things you and the others on this plane don't know." She paused as if for Liesl to absorb that. "Things that make finding the coded sonata more critical than saving a life, even yours. Not finding it could mean the extinction of a whole nation. You must know which one I mean."

Liesl gaped at the woman.

"I'm not a very religious person, Liesl. But I know that there must be some holy edict from God himself that Israel must be preserved at all costs." Ava peered out the window, and Liesl heard her whisper, "God help us all."

Chapter 16

As the plane began its descent over the South Carolina coast, it dropped through sun-drenched skies. Liesl sat alone, peering expectantly through the window, eager for the first signs of home. When the cell phone Ava had just given her vibrated, she checked the small screen and was glad Ava had momentarily joined the others in the back of the plane, glad for a conversation the woman wouldn't overhear. "Ben," she answered expectantly. She hadn't heard from him since her escape into Rev. Scovall's church the night before.

"Are you all right?" he asked.

She didn't know if she was or not, but other things mattered more just then. "Tell me what happened at my house."

She heard a loud sigh on his end. "I'll be straight with you. It's a total wreck and not a sheet of music left anywhere."

Though the words stung, Liesl couldn't flinch anymore, as if a continuous-drip venom had finally paralyzed her. "What else?" she asked without feeling.

"Well, there's the desk. They probably didn't have time to read everything of interest to them, so they cleaned it out too. All your correspondence, bills, receipts. They must have had a van load when they left."

"How do you know it was a van?"

"The guy who called in the tip saw it."

"What guy?"

"A late-night jogger said he heard breaking glass and saw a van in the driveway. He called 911 on his cell but wouldn't give his name. Just a passerby who didn't want to get involved. By the time the cops got there, there was no one around." Another pause. "But there was one peculiar thing hanging from the light fixture over your dining table. I'm certain you didn't leave it there."

Liesl waited. She believed there was no more surprise reflex left in her. She was wrong.

"It was a ski mask. A black one dangling from a coat hanger."

Liesl pounded her fist into the back of the seat in front of her, stabbing into the vision of the gunman firing into Schell Devoe's chest—a gunman wearing a black ski mask. Now the killer had invaded her own home and she was certain who it was. She'd finally made the connection. "Evgeny Kozlov killed him!" Liesl cried. Ava and Delaney came running, but Liesl told them it was Ben and turned them away.

"It could be, Liesl, though we can't prove it," Ben said. "But that's past. What concerns me most is what they might have found in your papers, like your Charleston address."

Liesl felt suddenly chilled.

"You'll need to get in and out quickly," Ben instructed. "Find the music you're looking for and get out of there." After a few moments of silence, Ben said, "Liesl, do you hear me?"

Liesl nodded slowly to herself. "I hear a warning, Ben. Is that what you meant it to be?"

"That's exactly what that was. But you've got a good team with you. There's another one already on the ground in front of the house, waiting for you and watching. And one other thing, Liesl. Do what you're told."

Liesl smiled faintly, looking up into Ava's stern face. "Time to go, Ben. Watch for me on the evening news."

"That's not funny, Liesl. You've got to—"

But Liesl had already snapped her phone shut and turned to see Ava dropping into the seat next to her. She watched the woman buckle her seat belt and settle in for the landing.

"Why do you do this?" Liesl asked without preamble.

For a long, unguarded moment, Ava held Liesl's gaze, then looked back at the file folder in her hands. She thumbed the edges of pages stuffed inside. Finally, she said, "There is something more powerful than guns and missiles that will save our soldiers. Something that would have prevented the deaths of thousands on that morning of September eleventh." She gripped the folder and held it up. "Information. It's the most critical weapon we have against our enemies."

Liesl studied the hard-edged face before her, the dark shadows around the eyes. But beneath all that, she saw something else clearly—fiery determination. It popped and sparked like a severed power line.

"There's more, isn't there?" Liesl asked, though she wasn't sure how she knew that.

Ava looked down at the file on her lap then back at Liesl. "My son is a Marine serving in Iraq. Every day, his life depends on the accuracy of information his commanding officers receive from people like me. That's why I never returned to Harvard once the CIA recruited me. You might say the war drowned out the music."

Liesl waited for more.

"My son had just enlisted when the CIA asked me to track Devoe. They needed someone close to him, who knew his habits and could monitor him day to day without arousing his suspicion. Later, I begged the agency to take me on full-time. I had no choice but to protect my son in that way. But now that I know the things I know, I do it for all those who go to sleep at night *not* knowing those things."

It was the first time Liesl had looked beyond the woman's harsh veneer, and she warmed to what she discovered there. Before she could respond, though, Ava ordered her to fasten her seat belt. The command was quick and dry, inviting no further conversation.

On the ground, the plane was met by two black vans. Liesl, Ava, Mark Delaney, and his two agents were joined by two local agents, a man and woman dressed too casually, Liesl thought. Hasty introductions were made all around, but Liesl didn't log the newcomers' names. She didn't even know the men Delaney had brought from New York, and she was in no mood to socialize. Get in and get out, Ben had said. She would be gone from here before the need arose to call these people by name. Except maybe Ava. Something about the woman had suddenly intrigued her.

The vans sped from the airport onto the nearest highway into town. "I assume you know where you're going," she commented to Ava.

"We know the distance from the sidewalk to the front door and what your neighbor likes to feed her cat for breakfast. At this moment, we know how many cars are parked on the street and how long each has been there."

Liesl remembered Ben telling her of the team already at the house. Were they camped in the yard? Already inside the house? She didn't like the idea of strangers rummaging through her family home—turning up its secrets, defiling its sacred places.

"Of particular interest right now," Ava groaned, "is the old gentleman repairing windows on the ground floor of the house."

This surprised Liesl. "I haven't authorized any work on the house. Who is he?"

"Best we can tell, he's staying in the basement apartment with a young man we've just discovered is an unemployed news reporter. Just what we need during an op like this. But we'll work around him."

Liesl did know of the renter, but nothing about him personally. She'd always relied on her rental agent to keep the apartment occupied and maintained, and, after deducting his fee, to send the monthly rent proceeds to Hidden Pines nursing home.

The vans swept onto the peninsula heading for Tidewater Lane, the quiet street where the Bower home still held its ground. When they pulled onto the street, they slowed to a stop before approaching the house. Then the lead van, the one carrying the man and woman who'd met the plane, inched slowly ahead, leaving Liesl's entourage stopped a safe distance away. Moments later, Mark Delaney's cell phone rang and Liesl heard his end of the conversation.

"How long has he been gone?" Pause. "And the old man, where is he now?" Pause. "Well, try to get him to go inside." Pause. "I don't know. Tell him you're local police watching for a dope deal to go down next door. Tell him anything, but get him out of there. And if you see this O'Brien guy coming back, head him off before he reaches the house."

Chapter 17

The job had been harder than Ian expected, even with the right tools. He'd borrowed them from the widow next door whose husband had kept a fully stocked workshop at the back of their garage. Ian felt a pang remembering the woman's tears when she unlocked the workshop for the first time since her husband's death several years ago. Ian hadn't wanted to disturb the place, but Mrs. Fowler insisted. "You take anything you need, Mr. O'Brien," she'd drawled in a voice as sweet and slow as the sorghum syrup she'd sent home with him. "I've lived next door to Lottie Bower for over thirty years and I'm glad to do whatever I can for her and her home. It used to be a happy place before, well, before her son's difficulties. Before she threw almost everything of his away."

Her words came back to Ian as he pried the last piece of old wood from another window. He tried to imagine Mrs. Bower tending her family inside, who they all were and why they stopped being happy.

The wood around each window was so rotted, it had yielded easily to the pry bar once the caulking had been stripped. That had been the hard part for Ian. He had chiseled and chipped away at caulk the consistency of concrete, completing just two small side windows since Cade left for the grocery store. Now, he moved toward the front of the house where a double window faced the street. He'd just dug his putty knife into another long run of caulking when he heard movement in the grass behind him.

Before he could turn around, he heard a man's voice, "Afternoon, sir." With the blunt-edge putty knife still in his hand, Ian turned to see a young man and woman approaching, both in jeans and T-shirts with no markings.

"Hello," Ian said hesitantly. *Probably tourists*, he thought. He glanced past them and noticed a black van parked across the street. "Can I help you?" he offered.

When the man paused to scratch the back of his head, something inside Ian went on alert. To him, the gesture meant the young man didn't know what to say or maybe how to say it. Either possibility didn't rest well with Ian.

"Sir," the man began, "we have a bit of a ticklish situation, and I'm hoping you can help us with it."

Ian didn't move but his grip on the putty knife tightened. "What are you talking about?" As he spoke, he quickly swept eyes over the street, noting that no one else had emerged from the van.

Just then, the man and woman both reached into their pants pockets, and Ian wasted no time reaching for another weapon. He turned and grabbed the pry bar behind him, but when he whirled back to face the suspicious pair, holding the bar before him, he saw two badges thrust at him.

"Sir! Now calm down," the man blurted. "We're FBI and we really do need your help. I'm sorry we frightened you." The man looked at the heavy iron pry bar in Ian's hand. "But right now, you're scaring *me* a little."

"You just toss those badges over here," Ian ordered.

The pair did as he told them. Ian picked up the leather cases housing the badges and glanced them over. He'd seen fake badges before in the Keys. Some of the guys at the docks liked to brandish them to impress the girls.

"Sir, the only thing we'd like you to do is go inside and stay there for a while. We have a team of law enforcement officers needing to occupy the upstairs of this house for about an hour. Then we'll be gone."

Ian tossed the badges back, unsure if they were real or not. But now he was more irritated than frightened. "You know, for FBI agents, or whatever you are, you just did a real boneheaded thing. You just don't creep up on somebody in their own yard and tell them you've got a 'ticklish situation.' What's that supposed to mean?"

The young woman seemed to fight back a smile as Ian kept charging.

"I mean, you just about got yourselves hurt here." Ian held up the bent putty knife instead of the pry bar. "You don't want to mess with me. And what kind of business have you got here anyway?" His eyes burned into the agents and his body stretched to its full six feet.

"Surveillance, sir. I really can't discuss it."

"Then I really can't let you into this house."

"Sir, with all due respect, we don't need your permission. But for your own safety, we need you to go back into your apartment. And do you know where Mr. O'Brien is?"

"I'm Mr. O'Brien and how do you know my name?" Ian barked. He felt his heart beating too fast, but he couldn't stem the tide of his outrage.

Just then another van, identical to the one at the curb, pulled right into the driveway of the house and parked in front of the ornate iron gate to the garden. Ian's eyes bugged. "You people get out of here. I'm calling the police." Just as he moved toward the door to the apartment, the front passenger door of the other van opened and a man dressed in a business suit got out and hurried toward the trio in the yard.

"Way to handle the situation," he growled at the young man as he walked past him toward Ian. "Sir, I'm FBI Special Agent Mark Delaney." He, too, offered his badge, but Ian didn't even look at it. That something inside him that had gone on alert with the other two was now telling him that this man was legitimate. Maybe it was the suit. Maybe Ian just needed to believe he wasn't about to become a statistic. But there was something even more critical for him to know right now.

"What do you want with my grandson?" Ian demanded, realizing which O'Brien they must have wanted.

Delaney held up a surrendering hand. "Absolutely nothing, sir. I assure you. We are searching for something we believe might be in this house. That's all."

"Then why is it so important for me to get inside?" Ian refused to back off. Though he'd only been there a few days, he'd slept in the shelter of the house, visited its owner, and looked into her pleading eyes. There was the budding of an allegiance to this particular spot and he would not suspend it easily.

"We wouldn't want anything or anyone to compromise our efforts," Delaney answered tightly.

Ian frowned. "Is that the same thing as a ticklish situation?"

Delaney looked confused.

The young man in jeans cleared his throat. "Uh, those were my words, sir," he said to Delaney.

"Look," Delaney said, now with bristling authority, "we need to end this and get everyone inside. Mr. O'Brien, you have to—"

Cade's Blazer came screaming down the road and skidded to a stop at the curb. Barely turning off the engine, he jumped from the car and raced toward the knot of people in the front yard. "Pop!"

Ian raised a hand. "It's okay, son. Slow down now."

"Who are you?" Cade demanded of the three intruders to his property, rented or not.

Delaney stepped forward. "Mr. O'Brien?"

Cade was at Ian's side now. "I asked who *you* are. And who just tried to stop me down the street?"

"I'm Special Agent Mark Delaney of the FBI, Mr. O'Brien. We need to search this house. I'm asking you and your grandfather to remain inside your apartment while we're here."

In the flat rays of the afternoon sun, Cade squinted at Delaney. "Does Mrs. Bower know you're here?"

Delaney hesitated. "We have permission to be here."

"From who?" Cade asked.

But Delaney ignored him. The agent anxiously looked up and down the street, then back at Cade. "Time to go, Mr. O'Brien. We'll let you know when we're leaving."

"Come on, son," Ian urged. But as he and Cade turned toward the house, they heard a door open in the van parked in the driveway. They saw the head of golden hair from the photo on Lottie Bower's night table.

Chapter 18

At first sight of the house, Liesl choked back a guttural cry. The wail clawed at her throat as she strained to contain it. Nothing could have prepared her for this visceral response to home. She didn't see strangers on her lawn, didn't hear the voices around her. At that moment, there was nothing in her realm but the old house that looked back at her with a greeting only she could hear. What madness had kept her away for more than a year?

When the van had turned into the driveway, she felt it take one, then two familiar bumps in the cracked pavement where bulging tree roots still prevailed, the same two bumps Liesl had surmounted hundreds of times on her bike and roller skates. Now, she slid from the backseat of the van and looked at the carved front door, wishing it to open. How desperately she wanted to run inside and find her family intact. They would call to her as if she'd just come in from play. They would gather her into the kitchen and sit her down before a fresh coconut praline cake and a glass of cold milk. Liesl sniffed the air expectantly, still watching the door, knowing there was no one there anymore.

Finally, the tears burst through and she turned away, only to catch the eye of someone watching her intently from across the narrow lawn. She squeezed her eyes tight as if to wring out the last bit of moisture, then quickly swiped at her cheeks. She glanced back at the man whose gaze wouldn't let her go. *Who is he? Why does he look at me that way?* And then she knew. *The renter. The reporter! Of course. He thinks he's got the scoop on a big story. Let him think whatever he wants. He'll get nothing from me.*

"Let's go, Liesl," Ava prodded from behind. Liesl's efforts to mask her tears failed. "What's wrong?" Ava asked.

Liesl answered with the shake of her head as she fumbled in her purse for the house keys. The tender moments were over, dispelled by the unwanted presence of others, too many others for Liesl to willingly usher into her home. But she would do what she had to do, then one day soon, she would return alone. She made that promise to the house as she led the way to the door.

As she turned the key in the lock, she was tempted to steal the slightest glance back at the renter. She resented his wordless intrusion on her privacy. She resented them all. This was not going to be pleasant.

But once through the door, the planets shifted again and her world tilted on its axis. She slowly climbed the open-air stairs to the second-level porch and headed toward the main door to the house. It didn't matter that four people were in tow behind her. She had to stop, alter course, and take in the garden below. Drifting to the porch rail, its faded white paint peeling away in thin shards, she looked into the far corner of the yard. The playhouse beckoned to her from the deep indigo recesses. Weeds now cloaked the little windows and a careless vine had clambered over its pitched roof. But the steeple rose unencumbered, persistent in its effort to link something righteous to the man who'd built it. Liesl pressed her lips together hard, fighting back more tears. *Stop this!* she commanded herself.

When Mark Delaney reached the porch, he issued a low whistle. "This is some place, Liesl," he offered with as much of a grin as she'd seen on him. "Right out of a storybook. You must have been the little princess growing up here." The words triggered her memory of describing the house in those exact words to her childhood friend Angie. Only "storybook" and "princess" didn't fit any longer.

Ava shot him a cautionary glare, to which the agent shrugged his shoulders, clueless. Liesl caught the warning. "It's okay, Ava. Let him think what he wants." With that, Liesl hurried straight to the door.

She would allow them entry to her home, but not the life she'd lived inside it. They had no right to it. She glanced back at the steeple on the playhouse and saw him as clearly as if he were really there, hunched over his saw, his shirt damp against the strong back. She heard that silly name *Punkin*. She watched him take off his old red cap and place it on her young head, then embrace her in arms that had always been tender, even in those moments when she wished he would die.

"Liesl?" Ava said gently.

Turning obediently to her task, Liesl grabbed the handle on the screen door and braced for what she knew would come. Pulling it open, the worn door's familiar screech made her shiver with longing. It told her nothing had changed, but she knew better. Nothing would ever be the same. Ava held back the screen as Liesl turned the key in the solid, sun-bleached mahogany door and pushed it open. It was as though the house suddenly exhaled a breath held too long, and all the leftover molecules from another time escaped through that one open doorway. Liesl fairly leaned into the stale, bittersweet gust as she stepped inside the entrance hall, the others close behind her.

The hall ran front to back, bisecting the main floor into two equal halves, like the tubular body of a butterfly sprouting mosaic wings. Her grandmother's palette barely clung to the walls and floors, the upholstery and drapes. It had been pale greens and vivid corals punctuated by black, which lent its solid order and boundaries to the rambling colors. But the colors had faded beneath an overlay of dust and mildew, and Liesl ached at the sight. *I have allowed this to happen. This house was the one thing I could have controlled, and I didn't.*

"Okay, Liesl, where do we start?" Delaney asked briskly.

Liesl looked toward the wide stairway rising before them. "Up there."

The top of the stairs opened onto a hallway that ran the length of the house. Four bedrooms branched from there. "It should be in my closet," she offered as she led them down the hall to the corner bedroom, the one overlooking both yards. Once inside, she hurried to the small closet. Some of her clothes from high school still hung there. Dust-caked shoes and trinkets lined shelves at either end of the closet. Yearbooks, old textbooks, and shoe boxes of photographs were stacked on the top shelf. But there was no box of music on the floor where she'd left it. Fleeing home after the murder, she had shoved it to the back corner of the closet and covered it with a dark cloth, like a shroud over the body of a blood-soaked spy.

She had never again wanted to see anything Devoe had given her, including that last semester's assignments. Neither could she throw all that music away. And so she had never disturbed it, never moved it. But someone had. On all fours now, she removed everything from the floor of the closet, searching for any remnant of music. Then she unloaded all the shelves, heaping their contents onto her childhood bed, a fitting repository for the evidence of years past. But still no music.

"It's a big house," Ava said. "Lots of places to look. Let's get started."

Liesl shook her head. "There's no place else it could be. After I came home, no one else lived here but me and Lottie, and she never bothered anything in my room."

"Lottie?" Ava questioned.

Liesl felt herself smile. "She said *grandmother* or any derivative of it made her feel old. She insisted on Lottie." At that moment, Liesl was desperate to run to her grandmother and throw her arms around the frail shoulders, to beg her forgiveness for staying away so long. *And for what? So I could escape into a world of strangers. Because I loved the music more than anything or anyone else?*

Delaney cleared his throat. "We're going to search every inch of this house, Liesl. I'm sorry if that troubles you. But we're going to do it right now." He turned immediately to his agents and ordered them to work their way down from the attic, leaving no drawer, cabinet, box, or closet untouched.

"No!" Liesl cried. "You will not dismantle my home!"

Ava intervened swiftly. "Liesl, you must calm down. You and I will make certain nothing is harmed." Her voice was compassionate yet firm. "But you must understand one thing: we have no choice but to search this house. There is much more at stake here than sentiments."

Liesl rounded on Ava, barely catching her breath. "My mother is dead. My father is dead. My grandmother hardly knows who I am. There is nothing left but this house!"

"I'm sorry," Ava said, and Liesl read sincere regret in the woman's face. "I didn't mean to belittle your attachment to your home. But—"

"But we're not going to waste another minute pawing over each other's feelings, are we now?" Delaney said coarsely. "Liesl, please show these men to the attic."

Her mouth agape, Liesl held the man's eyes long enough to know she had lost, that once again she was helpless to stop the demise of everything she'd loved. This strip-search of her home would leave nothing as it had been before.

She glanced once at Ava then started for the door where she called mechanically over her shoulder, "This way."

An hour later, everyone but Liesl had moved onto the main floor, fanning out in their ongoing, methodical search for the sonata. Upstairs, Liesl lingered in her parents' bedroom, where, she had insisted, only she would handle the belongings still assembled in the deep drawers of the dresser and inside the towering, solid-cherry wardrobe her father had built as an anniversary gift for her mother. On the top shelf of the wardrobe was the plain wooden box that even now she refused to open, as if it were a coffin.

On the shelf below was a stack of men's sweaters. Ava had just entered the room when Liesl discovered the near-empty pint of vodka beneath them. Unaware that someone was watching, Liesl lifted the bottle and stared into its benign-appearing contents. Ava stirred behind her and Liesl quickly returned the bottle to the wardrobe. She knew Ava had seen it, but that made no difference now. The whole town had known the fall of Henry Bower and the torment it had visited upon his family.

Ironic, she thought, *that inside this great gift of craftsmanship lurked the very thing that would destroy the craftsman.*

As she slipped the bottle back to its hiding place, Liesl gently, almost imperceptibly, patted her father's worn Citadel sweater that lay on top of the pile. Then she closed the heavy doors on it all.

She and Ava had just left the room when they heard a loud crash below. Both women bolted down the steps.

In the dining room, they found three men squatted over the remains of Lottie Bower's antique punch bowl. When Liesl approached, all three faces turned up to her with such cringing dread, it disarmed her and she found her anger sliding quietly back into its holster. Despite the shattered crystal heirloom, the sorrowful hangdog eyes looking back at her made her ashamed of her earlier outbursts. "I'll help you clean it up," she said simply and left to get a broom and pan, four sets of bewildered eyes watching her every step—not knowing that each one was taking Liesl deeper into the spiraling vortex of one certain memory she couldn't hold back.

Chapter 19

WHEN LIESL WAS SEVENTEEN

It happened during Spoleto, the international performing arts festival that swept Charleston and its legions of visitors into a frenzy of artistic indulgence each summer. For seventeen days, the stars of theater, music, and dance would cast their brilliance onto the collective stage of this ethereal city, and audiences would pant for more.

An invitation to perform at Spoleto was coveted, an anointing. So when Liesl's mother and grandmother helped her and her long, full-skirted gown into the backseat of the family station wagon, the enormity of the approaching hour was almost too much for them to bear. As the women fumbled with car keys, sheet music, performance schedules, and breath mints, Liesl sat patiently awaiting her first appearance on a Spoleto stage. That she was to perform at the venerable Dock Street Theatre was like framing her debut in pure gold leaf.

Still, Liesl was too quiet. As Lottie Bower finally backed over the uneven bricks of the driveway, Norma Bower turned to look at her daughter. "Are you all right?"

Liesl smiled weakly. "Sure, I am, Mom." She absentmindedly dug her hands into the soft deep folds of her skirt, the silken hands that no longer captured fiddler crabs or twirled a jump rope.

"You have no idea what this means to me and your grandmother." Tears spilled down the woman's cheeks.

"Don't cry, Mom. We're supposed to be happy today." But there was something in the car that draped darkly over the three women. An absence. Norma Bower might have called it a blessed relief. Even Lottie Bower might have reluctantly agreed. But on this particular day, one Liesl had been groomed for since her fourth birthday, Liesl mourned her father's absence, and so they all did. It was more like an abscess, an old fissure that kept rupturing deeper, throbbing with each new pulse. She didn't know how to make it stop hurting her and those in the front seat. The child prodigy, the native daughter whom old patrician Charleston had taken to its heart despite her spotted lineage, felt helpless to lift her family's shame.

At three o'clock that Saturday afternoon, Liesl strode resolutely to the concert grand piano and turned to face her audience, nodding sweetly to her mother and grandmother in box seats near the stage. She'd played before many audiences on many occasions, but not in this legendary hall. The original structure, built in 1736, had been America's first theatrical performance hall. Rebuilt twice, the theater remained at the epicenter of Charleston culture.

Before turning back to the piano, Liesl inhaled and imagined that what filled her lungs was the breath of those who'd gone before her on this stage. A girl of seventeen, she felt like a waif in their shadows, unable to bear the weight of their legacy.

Liesl lowered herself to the bench and smoothed her skirt. As she did, one more thought pushed ahead of the Rachmaninoff prelude to come. *God, if you can hear me—if you're real—keep your eye on Dad and help me get through this.*

Striking the three-note salvo that launched the *Prelude in C Sharp Minor*, Liesl moved fluidly into the somber first part. Escalating into the urgency of the second section, she reached full stride, her long fingers galloping over the keyboard until they slowed into the final soulful stretch.

When she finally lifted her hands from the piano, the hall erupted. "There seemed to be an added flourish to their applause, perhaps in appreciation for the artist's youth as much as her performance," the *Post and Courier* would report the following morning.

Liesl was glad for the lilting *Claire de Lune* to follow. It was Debussy who would soothe her back to peace. Having stood to receive the adulation of her audience, she settled before the keyboard once more and began her grandmother's favorite piece, the one she'd taught Liesl before handing off her granddaughter's advanced musical training to the College of Charleston and, later, Harvard.

Liesl was sailing so contentedly through the undulating currents of the piece, she didn't notice the slight upset at the back of the auditorium. She was fairly swooning in Debussy's moonlit composition when a voice called out, "Show 'em what you can do, Punkin!"

The music lurched to a sudden halt as Liesl turned in horror toward the sound.

A tall figure moved from the shadows of the balcony overhang and started down the left aisle. "Show these self-righteous bluebloods what a Bower can do." Fending off a frantic female usher, Henry Bower shuffled toward the stage, unable to walk a straight line. He wore an ill-fitting sport coat over a T-shirt and baggy jeans, his faded red ball cap on his head. One might have thought so preposterous an entrance was, though ill conceived, part of the performance—until Liesl sprang from the piano and hurried off the stage, hearing one more entreaty from her drunken father before she fled the theater. "Aw, now come on, Punkin. Daddy didn't mean no harm."

Just then, two armed guards rushed toward Henry Bower, who, with surprising agility, outmaneuvered them and slipped out a side exit.

Liesl was already half a block ahead of him, running as best she could in her strappy high-heeled shoes, the sequined purse she'd carried to the concert and hastily retrieved from offstage now slung over her shoulder. The streets were full of tourists and Spoleto patrons, many now stopped to stare at the frantic teenager in the long, billowy gown racing past them.

Midway into the next block rose St. Philip's Church. Just as its imposing two hundred–foot steeple had once guided mariners into Charleston Harbor, the old church had always drawn Liesl to the safety of its inner sanctum. No one but her aunt Bess had ever attended church anywhere. St. Philip's wasn't a house of worship for Liesl, only her hiding place when the demons of her father's alcoholism chased her from home—and now, from the moment of her highest achievement.

The old cathedral called to her. So did her father. From a block away, she could hear his raspy howl pleading for her to stop. *Go away!* she answered silently.

Without looking behind her, she dashed across the street and headed for the open south doors rising high in the stucco wall. Built like a Roman temple in 1835, St. Philip's was home to an Episcopal congregation dating to 1680. But it had all been new to her when a fourth-grade field trip first ushered her inside the marble-cool sanctuary.

Heels pounding the steps, she finally slowed her pace as she entered the narthex and saw only a few tourists studying the stained-glass window behind the altar. She looked quickly toward the right balcony, at the rows of small pew boxes, each one contained by four low walls and a latched door. Centuries ago, each family bought the seating box where they worshipped. Liesl didn't know who owned the box she'd claimed long ago as her personal refuge. On any day but Sunday, she could crouch low to the carpeted floor, backed by the cushioned bench and white-painted walls, and no one could see her, at least from below. Not the father or mother who would run after her.

It was on the floor of the pew box where she had first sensed the thing that drew her again and again to the old church. A stirring inside her that made her close her eyes and hope. For what? Was it God who stirred inside? How mindful could he be of one wounded girl? Besides, if he was a father anything like her own, did she really need him?

Now, she looked toward her hiding place and saw a woman cleaning the woodwork there. *That's my place*, she pleaded silently with the woman. *Go somewhere else!* She peered back through the open doorway and saw the red cap bobbing behind a tour group massed along the sidewalk. *Hurry!* She whirled toward the north doors to exit on the other side of the church, but saw them closed. Probably locked, she guessed. Then she turned and glanced up the familiar staircase to the right balcony. On the landing, before the stairs turned again, she saw the strange little wooden door with the rounded top, too small for a full-sized man—even a tall teenager like Liesl—to enter without ducking. It was the access door to the bell tower. She'd always wondered at the disproportion of the mouse-hole entrance to such a colossal tower. Only twice through the years had she found it unlocked and hid inside, once during Sunday services. She'd remained there the whole hour listening to words from the pulpit that she didn't understand.

Now, she turned to look once more through the open south doors and saw her father emerge from the crowd of tourists. As he ambled toward the church, she rushed up the steps and gave the small door a mighty yank. The force of it flying open almost sent her backward down the steps. But in an instant, she reversed the energy and lunged forward through the opening, shutting the door firmly behind her and hoping no one had witnessed her escape.

Wishing more than the roughly planed wood of the door to separate her from the approaching calamity, she moved away and looked up. The inside of the tower was raw and unwelcoming, but the ascending steps offered her only avenue of deliverance. She kicked off her shoes, dropped her purse to the floor, lifted the skirt of her dress, and hurried up the steep masonry stairs. She tripped once over her skirt and fell hard against the rough steps, hearing an angry rip somewhere in her dress. But she couldn't stop to locate it. It didn't matter. She pushed higher and higher as if she would soon rise to another realm where there were no liquor bottles hidden in the shrubbery.

Beyond the first landing, the steps were built of rough-hewn wood and rose more steeply. As she approached the four free-swinging bells, she heard the voice. "Liesl!" She stopped and clung to the railing, heart lunging in her chest. She glanced up. *Not much farther.*

Then again. "Liesl, don't you dare hide from me!" His voice boomed from the narthex below.

This is your house, God. Make him leave! She didn't know if the prayer of a wayward soul would make it through the rafters, but surely in this place, God would hear her and have mercy.

Determined to outdistance the voice, she had just begun to climb higher when the three-quarter-hour chimes split the air. The slashing percussion so close made her collapse into a protective ball against the steps, her hands clamped tightly over her ears. When the last note sounded, Liesl remained curled against whatever else might hurl itself at her. *God, are you just a place? A noise? Can you not hear me?* Moments later, she resumed her climb.

By the time she reached what seemed to be an observation window, she heard other insistent voices below and imagined the efforts to subdue her disruptive father. Pulling back a wooden shutter, she peered through the window, then heard the frightful wail of a siren. With a clear view of the street below, she watched the police car stop in front of the church and two officers get out. She knew what would happen next, and it did. Only the head was bare now as the tall, shuffling man was led to the car and helped into the backseat as if he'd been merely sick. *He is sick.* Liesl slapped at tears stinging her face with humiliation and fury.

Without the siren, the car pulled slowly down the street. Liesl didn't blink until she could see it no more. *Don't ever come back!*

Like sinking to the bottom of a dark sea where the weight of water crushes human life, Liesl descended slowly to ground level. It seemed to take twice as long as the ascent, longer to gather her wits than relinquish them to fear. When she reached the little door, she paused to listen. Hearing no one on the other side, she slipped back into her shoes and grabbed her purse. When she cracked the door open to peek out, she saw a workman with tools dangling from his belt making his way toward the tower. *That's why the door was unlocked.* She was in no mood to explain herself. As she prepared to throw open the door and dash from the tower, risking interference from the workman, she heard someone call to the man and he reversed his steps. She was able to slip unseen from the tower and flee the church.

Just beyond the south doors, though, something on the ground stopped her—the faded red ball cap. She stared at it for a moment, then picked it up. She didn't know why. She rolled it up and tucked it tightly inside her purse and started across the street. As she did, the St. Philip's chimes erupted again, this time tolling the full hour as if it were marking a waypoint in her life. When the bells finished their tolling, no one in Charleston doubted that it was four o'clock.

All her senses were at full alert. The police had removed her tormentor, but she felt hunted still, the flight instinct continuing to fire inside her. She paused long enough to get her mental bearings and noticed the alarmed faces of others on the sidewalk. One couple drew to a sudden halt in front of her, then stepped quickly aside. That's when Liesl looked down to see that her skirt had ripped from the bodice on one side and a trickle of blood snaked down her right arm. She remembered her fall against the rough steps in the bell tower and was surprised by the damage it had done. When she looked up, a young woman came cautiously toward her, her arm outstretched in a gesture of help.

Liesl looked back at her torn dress and bloodied arm. She felt alien, misplaced. Waving off the approaching woman, Liesl looked west and knew exactly where she had to go. It was a long way to walk, though, and the straps of her shoes dug into her feet. She yanked them off and hurried barefoot across the street, through the St. Philip's cemetery where Southern statesman John C. Calhoun was entombed beneath an awning of oaks and crepe myrtles. As she skirted the grave of Dubose Heyward, whose novel *Porgy* inspired Gershwin's *Porgy and Bess*, the haunting strains of that music stirred inside her and made her run harder from the grim yard toward the cleansing currents of the Ashley River.

Soon, she hailed a cab and climbed into the grimy backseat. *Fitting,* she thought, as she glanced down at her disheveled self. The few bills in her purse weren't enough to pay the driver and buy the provisions she would need. All that mattered, though, was getting away.

When she arrived at Metro Marina, she ignored the gawking of boaters shocked by her appearance. She headed straight to the marina store and its manager, Rena Johns, who'd doted on Liesl since she was a small child. More than once, the woman had refused to let Henry Bower take his young daughter with him on one of his so-called fishing trips. Rena knew that too often they had ended with him anchoring down a creek off the Ashley and drinking himself into the next day.

Now, the woman gasped at first sight of Liesl. "Child! What happened to you?" she cried, bunching her smooth, mahogany brow and reaching for Liesl's wounded arm. "Let me see that," she ordered. Liesl had always been comforted by Rena's affections, and more than once been drawn into the woman's plump arms.

"I fell against some steps. I . . . I just can't talk about it now, Rena. I've got to get clothes and food. Is Dad's account still good?"

"Are you kidding? We're talking major nonpayment for over a year. I can't charge anything to it, Liesl. The boat wouldn't be here if your grandmother didn't pick up the dock fee." The woman dabbed at Liesl's arm with an antiseptic wipe she'd pulled from a first-aid kit behind the counter. "You want to tell me about it?" she asked cautiously as she applied ointment to the cut on Liesl's arm and bandaged it.

Liesl shook her head. "Not now, Rena. I just need some clothes, a different pair of shoes, and some food. That's all."

Rena looked at the purse in Liesl's hands. "Do you have any money at all?"

More humiliation flushed in Liesl's cheeks. "After cab fare, just a few dollars."

Rena nodded. "Wait here." She disappeared into the storeroom and returned with a faded T-shirt and a pair of denim shorts. "The girl who used to cashier for us left these months ago. I don't think she's coming back for them, so they're yours. The size ought to be about right. There wasn't much meat on her either." The woman's smile soon faded. "Where are you going, honey?"

"Just to the boat."

"Staying overnight?"

"Uh, yeah." Liesl looked down at her bare feet. "Did the girl leave any shoes? Size 9 maybe?"

Rena glanced at a rack behind her. "Tell you what, you give me a dollar or two and I'll make you a deal you won't believe." She walked over and lifted a pair of Rainbow flip-flops from a rack and handed them to Liesl. "Call it an end-of-season clearance."

"But summer just started, and these things cost, what, about fifty?"

"I knew you wouldn't believe it." Rena laughed, then nodded her head toward the storeroom. "You can change in there. And I'll get some food and water ready for you."

"One more thing, Rena. Would you call my mom and tell her I'm at the boat, and that I'm okay? Tell her I'll be home, uh . . . tell her it'll be a day or so." She paused. "I think she'll understand."

"I wish I did," Rena said, her eyes glistening.

Liesl hugged the woman. "You've always been good to me."

Rena shrugged and fidgeted with the tear in Liesl's dress. After a moment, she asked, "And you're just spending the night at the dock, right?"

Liesl pretended not to hear as she headed for the dressing room.

Later, she thanked Rena and grabbed the two food bags and her discarded concert attire. Glad to be in normal clothes again, she made her way toward her father's Grady White fishing boat.

Because many out-of-town Spoleto patrons traveled to Charleston by boat, the marina was crowded. Liesl noted a couple in tuxedo and cocktail dress step from their sleek yacht and head toward a waiting taxi. Other finely dressed visitors mingled with the boat-shoe regulars and the charter boat captains just returning from their day at sea. Liesl passed a group gathered about a stone-cold trophy marlin one captain was preparing to weigh. It had once been Liesl's catch that the dock population had admired. She'd been her dad's first mate during many sober trips to the Gulf Stream. But those times had come to an abrupt end.

At first sight of the *Exodus*, Liesl felt a lump rise in her throat. She hadn't seen the boat since the day the Coast Guard returned it to the marina. It was the day she discovered her dad had finally reached the end of himself—and taken her beloved aunt Bess with him, only she hadn't survived. The three years since had done little to dull that searing pain.

Liesl approached the boat hesitantly, looking for that place near the open stern, for the stain that wouldn't wash away. The rains had rinsed off most of the blood, leaving only a persistent dark smudge. Her dad had insisted it remain, calling it his indelible punishment.

Swallowing hard against the lump, Liesl boarded the vessel and looked around. Topside was clean enough. It appeared to have been recently hosed down, but the unlocked cabin was a wreck, foul-smelling and littered with open tins of food, empty liquor bottles, and dirty clothes. She guessed the last few days her dad had been gone from the house had been spent here, where he must have dressed for her concert. *Why did you have to do it, Dad?*

There was no time to linger over stubborn wounds that refused to heal. She found the ignition keys in a dirty coffee cup and dropped them into the pocket of her shorts. After hauling her food and clothing into the cabin, she gathered up the offending bottles into a plastic garbage bag and dropped it into a large trash bin on the dock. She was just unplugging the power cord when someone came up behind her.

"Hey, Liesl, where you going?" asked one of the dockhands. It was Jimmy Baker from her biology class.

She groaned. "Just for a ride, Jimmy. See you later."

"Well, are you sure you can handle that big boat all by yourself?"

Liesl shot him a withering look. She'd been driving boats since she was six years old. Her dad and Aunt Bess had taught her. When she was older, they'd tested her skills in the high swells and swirling currents off the jetties.

"Yeah, Jimmy. I'm pretty sure I can."

"Well, uh, does Rena know you're taking it out, 'cause she's been keeping an eye on it since your dad and aunt . . . well, you know."

Liesl didn't answer him. Instead, she climbed aboard and cranked both engines, letting them growl in neutral while she returned to the dock to cast off the lines. With hardly a glance Jimmy's way, she removed the last line off a stern cleat and pulled it on board, coiling it neatly on the floor, just like her dad had taught her. The memory that Jimmy had called to her mind stung bitterly. But she would push it back inside her own little black box where all the crash data of her life was stored.

"Well, uh, Liesl, I don't think you should—"

"Well . . . uh . . . Jimmy . . ." she mocked with only a twinge of regret. "Rena will know where I am." She paused and smiled faintly at him. "I'm sorry, Jimmy."

She revved the powerful engines a moment before easing both throttles forward. After the boat's broad stern cleared the slip, she turned into the marina channel and headed toward the Ashley River. Cruising past the other boats, she caught a few double takes from those watching the willowy teenager expertly maneuver the thirty-six-foot boat through a swift-running tide. Finally clearing a wall of yachts tied one behind the other like elephants at the circus, Liesl leaned into the twin throttles and ran with the river toward the harbor. With the sun dropping behind her and the Atlantic shining in cobalt splendor before her, she almost forgot why she was there.

Before reaching Fort Sumter, she turned north into the Intracoastal Waterway and watched for the storm-twisted live oak marking the entrance to the creek. Nothing about the aquatic wilderness of her childhood had changed since the days she'd scavenged the waters and pluff-mud banks for any living thing. In a johnboat with little more than an eggbeater for a motor, she'd drifted deep into the web of tidal creeks. The one she knew best opened before her now. She turned west then north again as she followed the muddy banks to a dock still standing strong after the battering by Hurricane Hugo two years before. She eased up to the dock, a bowline securely in hand. Moving the throttles to neutral, she flung the line against a rusting cleat, missed, flung again and lassoed it firmly. It wasn't until she cut the engines and secured the stern lines that she looked out toward the cabin. The little house rose high on stilts, not enough to clear Hugo's storm surge, though. That's why her dad had restored it after the fifteen-footer came rolling through the living room.

In the fading light, Liesl had no fears about reentering her aunt Bess's isolated getaway. If she believed in such things, she would trust her aunt's frolicking spirit to keep her company. But even though she didn't believe, she knew something good was still alive in the house. Surely it would mend her. But surely, it did not.

Soon after Liesl had returned home from that time alone at the cabin, Henry Bower had disappeared completely from her life. After serving his time for drunk and disorderly conduct, he had placed one call to Liesl's mother, congratulating the whole family on their new freedom from him.

There had been no further word from him for two years. Then one morning when the gardenia bush outside the kitchen window fanned its sweetness through the big breezy house, the call had come. Though she was already late for class at the College of Charleston that morning, Liesl stopped to answer the phone.

It was a woman from the U.S. embassy in Matamoros, Mexico. After determining that she'd reached the right party, she told Liesl that her father's body had been found on a nearby beach. The woman unleashed the remainder of the news with all the warmth and inflection of a Dow-Jones report. Liesl struggled to connect the sound bites. A fall from a fishing pier. Sharp rocks in shallow water. Massive trauma to the head and body. Two witnesses. Positive identification of the body. Ruled an accident. Victim suspected to be homeless. Will send personal effects found on him. Our sincere condolences.

Against Liesl and Lottie's wishes, a resolute Norma Bower accepted the embassy's offer to cremate and dispense of the remains, and requested only that someone cast them into the ocean.

A week later, a small package addressed to Mrs. Henry Bower arrived. Inside was a still-sodden wallet bearing a Social Security card for Henry Bower, an expired fishing license issued in Texas to Henry Bower, a water-stained photograph of Liesl at her first piano recital, and one more thing— a gold necklace with a small pumpkin charm.

When the last tear had dried, Liesl removed the remnants of Henry Bower's life from the kitchen table. Her mother and grandmother had lingered over them long enough, she'd decided. They composed silent evidence of a redundant death. Henry Bower had died too many times already. There would be no more.

At the foot of the stairs, Liesl paused and gazed into the worn treads her long legs often took two at a time, the same treads that had borne the footfalls of those she loved. She mourned the man she had listened for late at night, when he came in from the yard and dragged himself to bed. She closed her eyes. *God, if you're more than a figure in a stained-glass window, do something to heal us, please.* She opened her eyes and looked at the mangled wallet in her hand. *And if you're as merciful as they say you are, let my dad into your heaven.*

She climbed the stairs to her parents' bedroom, opened the cherry-wood wardrobe, and placed the wallet and the necklace inside the wooden box on the top shelf. The only other thing inside was the faded red cap she'd retrieved from the sidewalk in front of St. Philip's the day of her Dock Street concert. She closed the lid on the box, and the funeral was over.

She couldn't know that just a few years later, she would close the lid on yet another coffin. From the time her mother's cancer was detected, its ravenous siege took only four months to devour her life.

Chapter 20

Cade was hurriedly putting the last of the groceries into the cabinets while Ian molded hamburger patties for supper. "I don't like this one little bit," Ian grumbled. "How do we know those are really FBI agents up there? What if that young woman is being held hostage, or worse? And did you just hear that big crash up there?" He slapped the patties with increasing ferocity.

"Take it easy on the meat, Pop. It's already dead."

"There you go ignoring something you know is upsetting me. Why aren't you the least bit concerned about that poor girl? Didn't you see her cry?"

Cade was quiet, his mind spinning. No, he wasn't ignoring the pain he'd seen in her face. On the contrary. He was already planning his next move.

"Pop, now listen. I'm going out to the car for a few things. I want you to stay inside and keep that door locked, you hear?"

"What are you going to get? And why can't I come too?"

"It only takes one of us to carry a gun and a cell phone. I left both in the car."

"Now you're talking!" Ian dropped the meat onto the counter and turned to wash his hands. "But don't you think we should call the police before we go barging upstairs with a gun?"

"We're not barging anywhere, Pop. Now lock the door behind me." Cade slipped on a jacket and walked outside, immediately drawing the attention of the young man and woman who'd first confronted Ian. They were standing about ten feet apart in the driveway.

"Sir, I'd advise you to go back inside," called the young man in jeans and T-shirt.

Nothing about the two looked official to Cade. "I left my phone in my car. Mind if I get it?"

The girl was quick to answer. "If you hurry."

Halfway to the car, Cade noticed a few walkers and a jogger passing by. Traffic on the street seemed normal for midafternoon. Evidently, he'd been the only one these intruders had tried to stop from approaching the house. But how did they know he lived here or what he looked like? Or what kind of car he'd be driving? *If they're not FBI, they've got some kind of intelligence network.*

The Blazer was just where he'd left it, at an odd angle to the curb and probably an obstacle on the narrow street. "Hey," he called to the jeans-wearing woman, "mind if I straighten my car? It's a little tight through here." She signaled an okay.

They don't seem concerned that I'd take off. And how do they know that I haven't already called the police? Unless they are the police.

When Cade reached the car, he spotted the man who'd tried to stop him at the end of the block. He and another guy were standing on either side of a dark gray Crown Vic across the street and a couple of driveways down. Everybody knows that Crown Vics meant police. *Was that part of the ruse?* If this *was* a ruse. He wasn't convinced of that, despite Ian's misgivings.

Cade cranked the Blazer and eased it back into position along the curb nearest his own front door. He slid the small handgun from under his seat and shoved it into the pocket of his jacket, hoping the bulge wasn't obvious. Both he and Ian were licensed to carry concealed weapons. They had never known what they might encounter in the waters around the Florida Keys.

He grabbed his cell phone and got out, one hand shoved into the gun pocket. He nodded slightly to the man and woman, who still watched him closely. As he crossed the lawn, he looked back to confirm the locations of the other two men. It was then he noticed the same jogger he'd seen moments earlier, heading back down the street. Only now, he recognized the man, the baggy gym shorts, the thick square body. It was the man Cade and Ian had seen studying the house two days earlier.

Cade watched the man slow his pace as he passed in front of the house, looking side to side at those in the driveway and across the street. For an instant, his eyes fell on Cade, then he continued on down the street. Cade looked back at the others. They registered no concern over the man. And why would they? He was just one more in a legion of joggers fond of Charleston's historic district. Only he wasn't jogging the first time Cade saw him.

Inside the apartment, Cade found Ian pacing back and forth in front of the double windows. "Lots of noise going on up there," Ian reported, as if Cade couldn't hear the clomping of feet, opening and shutting of doors and drawers, and a female voice calling for someone named Ava.

"Pop, I need to get up there quick," Cade said, his mind sorting through a wild array of options for doing that.

Before Ian could respond, a knock came at the door. When Cade opened it, he looked down into the troubled face of Liesl Bower, her hair swirling about her head as a gust of wind blew at the door. "I'm sorry to disturb you, Mr. O'Brien," she said, pushing the hair from her face. Her wide eyes held him curiously for an instant. Then she motioned toward a couple of men standing behind her. One of them was the man who'd introduced himself as an FBI special agent. "I'm Liesl Bower," she told Cade. "These gentlemen are searching my house for something very important, and I'm afraid that includes this apartment." She lowered her eyes to the threshold of the door but not before Cade saw the fear in them.

"What's going on here?" demanded Ian, wedging himself into the doorway beside Cade, who took that moment to introduce himself and his grandfather. Immediately, Ian leaned toward Liesl in a conspiratorial manner. "Ma'am," he whispered hoarsely, "are you all right? Want us to call the police?"

"Pop, please. Let me ask the questions."

Liesl seemed strangely amused and Cade was glad to see the hint of a smile on her face, though he didn't know why he was glad.

"I assure you I'm just fine, but we are in a bit of a hurry. I have no right to ask you to submit to a search of your apartment, but I'm afraid these gentlemen do." Her tone was clipped, the smile had vanished, and Cade was left wondering how far to assert his rights.

That's when Delaney stepped forward to present his badge for Cade's inspection. Before he could get close enough to see, Ian's hand shot forward. "Let me see that thing up close. And young fella, let me see yours too," he added, sternly eyeing the other man. Apparently satisfied with the authenticity of all identification, Ian finally stepped aside and suggested Cade do the same.

"Thank you, and I hope this won't take long," Liesl offered apologetically as she led Delaney and the other agent inside.

"It would help if you told us what you're looking for," Cade said.

Delaney paused before responding. "Sheet music."

"Come again," Cade said.

"A box or file of music that my grandmother may have stored down here," Liesl explained.

"Well, as you can see, I've filled up what little bit of storage space there is. And I haven't seen any music." *Why would that be so important to the FBI?*

"Would any of you folks like some beef jerky?" Ian asked as if suddenly remembering his manners.

Delaney pivoted from a kitchen cabinet. "You mean this?" He held up an open package from which several lengths of dried jerky dangled like fly strips.

"Sure, help yourself," Ian answered.

Delaney offered no expression. "It's really tempting, Mr. O'Brien."

"Hey, don't hold back, young fella," Ian urged. "Take all you want."

And he's perfectly serious, Cade mused as he surveyed his grandfather's innocent face.

Feeling at ease now, Cade turned to Liesl and asked, "How often do you get to Charleston, Ms. Bower?" He immediately regretted his question, knowing it had sprung from his disapproval of her long absences from her grandmother.

Liesl eyed him warily. "Why do you ask, Mr. O'Brien?"

Her frosty tone took everyone by surprise. Cade stumbled. "I . . . uh . . . just wondered how often you get to see your grandmother." Inside, he winced again. *Bad to worse.*

She seemed to be mustering a reply when Delaney announced they hadn't found what they were after. He apologized again for the inconvenience, then asked Cade, "Have you seen anything or anyone unusual around the house, Mr. O'Brien?"

Without hesitation, Ian jumped in. "There was the guy staring at the house that morning, Cade."

Delaney turned to him with great interest, then at Cade, who nodded thoughtfully. "I suppose it's worth mentioning," Cade said. "It was earlier than the normal tourist traffic begins through this neighborhood. He left when he saw us return from a walk."

"What did he look like?" the other agent asked.

"Like a jogger, but kind of heavy," Ian replied. "A heavy jogger, you might say. And he wore black socks with the whitest running shoes you ever saw."

Cade chuckled. "Yeah, maybe that was a little odd."

"Did you hear him speak?" Delaney continued.

Cade shook his head no. "But there's one other thing: I saw him again just a few minutes ago."

Delaney snapped to attention. "Where?" he demanded as he lurched toward the front window and scanned the street.

"Running past the house," Cade answered, surprised by the man's reaction. "In fact, he ran by a couple of times."

Delaney whirled toward the other agent. "Get out there now and alert the others." Then he turned to everyone present. "Liesl, I want you and the O'Briens to get upstairs immediately." Then to Cade: "Sorry to alarm you, but it's for your safety. This apartment's too accessible."

"Now, I don't think you need to—" Ian began.

"Yes, I do, sir. Now please do as I say." Turning back to Liesl, he asked, "Is there a way to get upstairs without going outside?"

Cade saw fright return to her face. "Follow me," she said.

Chapter 21

Summoned on that Saturday afternoon, Ben Hafner opened the door to the Oval Office and stepped inside. "You wanted to see me, sir?"

"Sit down, Ben," said President Noland as he rose from his desk and took a seat on the sofa opposite his domestic policy chief. Outside, a blustery wind whipped a tree branch, sending its leafless, spidery shadow cavorting across the sunlit pane. It made Ben think of the shadow puppets he created for his small children, and a smile appeared on his face, an involuntary reflex because this wasn't a time to smile. He knew why he was here.

"Where are they now?" Noland asked, his voice clipped.

"Still at the house, sir. I spoke with Mark Delaney an hour ago and they were about to search the basement apartment."

"Anyone live there?"

Ben grimaced. "A reporter, I'm afraid, though he was recently laid off from the Charleston paper."

"A . . . what?" Noland shot up and started to pace. "And what's Delaney doing about that? Did he get the guy out of the house before they went in? Is Ava running interference on that?"

Ben wasn't sure which to answer first. "I don't know the status on the renter, sir. But, it seems his grandfather is there too."

Noland seemed about to erupt again, then quickly composed himself in the way Ben had witnessed often. There were few traits that garnered more respect for the president than his self-control, even when his emotions visibly battled for the higher ground.

Returning to the sofa, Noland looked Ben in the eye. "You're in this only because of Liesl. You understand that, don't you, Ben?"

"Yes, sir."

"Even though such issues aren't in your job description, you must also know that this is more than just another spy chase, right?"

Ben leaned forward in his seat. "Sir, if you'd rather I excluded myself from the matter, I will."

"There's no way you can, I'm afraid. We've led you in too deep. You and Liesl. But we need both of you." He looked down at the floor for a moment, then back at Ben. "Besides Washington, there's probably no more critical post for a Russian mole than Israel, especially a mole whose allegiance is to those operating in the back corridors of the Kremlin, with their own agenda for resurrecting the might of the USSR. The old KGB is up and running with fresh blood, Ben. And their eye is on Israel."

"They're pinning their hopes on one well-placed informant?"

"Not just hopes, Ben. They're already back in business. Russia is becoming a well-greased power broker of information. If their mole can tap into the underground stream of Israel's military strategy, deployments, arsenals, and especially into the pulse of their surprise commando operations, imagine what Israel's enemies would give for that information. Imagine the leverage Russia could wield over that part of the world. With so much upheaval throughout the Middle East, Russia is jockeying for position to take over the oil-rich fields that could fall into the hands of ragtag rebels and shadowy insurgents whose commanders hide in caves."

Ben knew there was more. "With an oil and gas cartel at Russia's command, they'd make Europe bend at the knee," the president added. "And courting Venezuela could open another hemisphere for them."

Noland got up again and moved toward one of the windows where he lingered quietly. Without turning, he said, "There's something you don't know, Ben."

Ben felt the hair on his neck move.

Noland now faced him. "In six weeks, the Israeli prime minister, the presidents of Russia and Syria, and I will meet secretly. It's taken our respective teams many months to secure the site."

Ben remained still, expectant.

"I can't tell you any more than this: when we emerge from that summit, the world will look differently to each of us." Noland bowed his head and Ben thought he saw the man's mouth forming silent words.

"Sir?"

Noland raised a strained face to Ben. "Our intelligence has picked up chatter from the Middle East, different sources saying the same thing: that a summit is coming. And one of the heads of state is marked for assassination."

Both men seemed suspended in a noiseless chamber sucked free of oxygen. But Noland rallied, as usual, to calm and reason. "You see, Ben, despite the inconvenient threat of Liesl's odd little code, the Russians will keep their mole in place just as long as they can. That's why they'll stay as close as possible to Delaney's operation. They probably see nothing but nervous agents looking for something they may never find. So why should Russia pull their mole when there's so much more for him, or her, to uncover with each passing day?"

"That would account for no suspicious disappearances of key personnel from Israel's central command," Ben suggested.

"No disappearances yet. I'm still hopeful your friend in Charleston will keep her wits about her and find what we need." Noland lowered his head again. And again, Ben saw his lips move slightly.

"Are you okay, sir?"

"I was just remembering Jesus' words: 'O Jerusalem, Jerusalem . . . how often I have longed to gather your children together, as a hen gathers her chicks under her wings, but you were not willing.'"

"What does that mean to you, sir?"

The president smiled at his trusted aid. "You're Jewish, Ben. What does that mean to you?"

Before Ben could muster a response to what he considered a loaded question, Noland tossed another one. "When's the last time you were in Israel, Ben?"

Ben hoped his discomfort didn't show. "I, uh, think about three years ago, sir. My wife's brother got married in Tel Aviv."

"He's in the military, right?"

I'm certain I never told him that. Ben remained calm, even as he wondered why and when such information about his family had been gathered. "He was, sir. Israeli army."

"Special ops, wasn't he?"

"Right again, sir." *Why is he doing this? What does he know?*

"Ever talk to him?"

Ben steadied his breathing. "Not recently, sir." He refused to give more than he was asked.

Noland eyed him carefully. "Didn't mean to grill you, Ben. That's all for now."

Ben was nearly to the door when Noland added, "And any word from Charleston reaches me immediately."

"Of course, sir." Ben closed the door and headed straight to the men's room where he splashed cold water in his face.

When Ben left the White House that afternoon, he drove aimlessly for an hour or more before finally pulling to the curb and cutting the engine on his car. He looked around and didn't know where he was or how he'd arrived in this neighborhood of dismal apartment buildings and garbage-strewn alleys. He hadn't seen much of his route, his mind's eye focused on the man he must now contact without further delay.

He reached into the center console between the front seats and fished out a cell phone he'd recently purchased. After certain modifications, he was able to place and receive untraceable calls. This one was headed to Israel.

"I'm here," came the thickly accented voice in Ben's ear.

"Then hear this. Never contact me again. Ever! You slithered up to the wrong guy."

"Your wife's brother is—"

"I don't care who or what my wife's brother is or what he's gotten himself into. You'll not get your information from me. Do you understand?"

In the silence that followed, Ben eyed a couple of hooded young men ambling down the sidewalk toward his car.

"That is unfortunate," the man finally said.

"No, it's pathetic," Ben snapped, "that he cares no more for his sister than to entangle her in, well, call it what it is: treason."

Another pause. The man cleared his throat. "Actually, Ben, it is his sister's welfare that concerns him most. It should concern you even more."

It took only a second for the man's implication to take hideous shape in Ben's mind. He felt the stinging bile rise in his throat, cutting off the raging words trying to escape. The image of his lovely Anna's face appeared before him and he wanted to scream for her to get away, to take the children and run! But no sound would come.

Suddenly there was a knocking at his window. One of the two young men he'd seen approaching called to him through the glass, "Got any money for us, mister?" The other one tapped the glass with something metallic and hard, something Ben couldn't see. Instantly, he cranked the car and launched himself from the curb and the young men screaming obscenities after him. But those weren't nearly as vile as the words he'd just heard from the cell phone still pressed against his ear.

The voice on the phone hurled Ben's own words back at him. "Do *you* understand?" the man asked fiercely.

Ben did.

Chapter 22

*L*iesl led her curious entourage into the elder O'Brien's bedroom, finding herself oddly distracted by the meticulous air of it. The bed was made crisply, and through the open door to the small bathroom, she noticed the precise arrangement of toiletries on the counter. But it was what she saw on top of the dresser that slowed her pace—an open Bible, its two exposed pages marked here and there with yellow highlighter. Liesl let her eyes linger on the book a moment before turning to the closet door.

When she opened it, she wasn't surprised to see a small assortment of clothing on hangers spaced as if by regulation, no more or less than about three inches apart. She couldn't help herself. She turned and looked past the agents and the tenant to focus on his grandfather. When the older man met her eye, he seemed surprised by her sudden attention.

"What did I do now?" he asked simply.

Liesl noted the warm crinkle of his eyes. She'd never known a grandfather. What would that be like? She glanced quickly at his grandson, catching the piercing look he'd given her several times already, then turned swiftly back to the closet. As she pushed the well-tended clothing to one side, she explained, "When my grandmother converted the lower level to an apartment, she walled it off from a staircase that runs up the other side of this closet, straight into the kitchen pantry upstairs." She sorted through the keys in her hand until she singled out one. "For whatever reason, she cut this door into the back of the closet for a secondary access to the apartment."

As Liesl worked the old, resistant lock, Ian nudged closer. "Well, I'll be," he said. "Whoever cut that door in had a bit of the trickster in him. Just paneling, hidden hinges, and a keyhole that blends in with the other knotholes. I never noticed it."

When the lock finally gave, she pried open the door. One by one, they all slipped through the closet and entered a small, dank storeroom, then followed Liesl up a flight of wooden steps. At the top, she unlocked another door and the group emerged into the back of the kitchen pantry. "Long ago," she continued, "the servants of the original owners went this way to retrieve food and provisions from the storeroom."

Ava came rushing into the kitchen. "I thought a herd of giant mice had just invaded the house," she quipped. Liesl raised an eyebrow. *Is that a sense of humor I detect?* Delaney cut off any further banter with his usual urgency. "Ava, keep Liesl and the O'Briens away from the front windows. We've got company." He motioned for his CIA associate to join him as he headed for the front door. As he corralled his team, barking instructions for locking down the house and guarding every entrance to it, Liesl looked blankly at the O'Briens, not sure what to do next. It surprised her when Cade O'Brien took the lead.

"Have you asked your grandmother where this music might be?"

Of course. Why is my mind so sluggish? Why did I wait for a total stranger to direct me? She faltered a response. "Well, I hadn't had time to . . . I doubt she would . . ." She felt suddenly helpless before this man whose eyes probed hers too deeply. Then she remembered he was a reporter and stiffened. "Your name is Cade, right?" she asked abruptly.

He cocked his head. "It is."

She couldn't stop what now welled up inside, so she bludgeoned on. "I guess your byline is Cade O'Brien or do you go by some clever pseudonym?" She didn't wait for an answer. "I suppose you'd love to get back to your newsroom and start a firestorm over this, but if you've any decency, you'll not drag my grandmother into it. She's suffered enough."

Cade's mouth fell open. "Whoa, there." His eyes flashed at her. "If you feel another one of those attacks coming on, warn somebody. For now, though, you might be quiet long enough to hear me."

Liesl wasn't used to anyone but Ben talking to her that way. Her jaw went rigid, but she remained quiet.

"Pop and I went to see your grandmother yesterday."

Something hot colored Liesl's cheeks and she wanted to cover them with her hands, but didn't move.

"She's a sweet, loving woman, who, I might add, deserves better than you give her."

Too stunned to speak, Liesl looked to Ian, as if he might intervene. But the old man seemed just as stunned.

Cade kept going. "I don't know you or the predicament you're in right now. I'm sorry for this mysterious trouble you're in, but if you can come down off your highbrow horse long enough, you'll see that some of us underlings are more than capable of decency, even us bottom-feeding reporters." He turned and walked into the dining room.

Liesl fought to hold back white-hot tears of both fury and shame. She didn't realize she was trembling until she felt the old man's gentle grasp on her arm. "Sit down, honey. He didn't mean all that." Ian bunched up his mouth. "Well, maybe he did. Cade's pretty good about speaking his mind. It seems you are too." He chuckled. "Man, I wish I had that on tape." He tugged at her until she followed him to the kitchen table, the round, oak pedestal table where she'd carved her initials with a fishing hook in third grade. He spotted them immediately after they sat down. "LLB. That's you?"

Liesl nodded. The fury had subsided, but the shame still burned. "Mr. O'Brien, how is my grandmother?"

"Just as pretty as you are," he said with a grin that lit up his whole face. "She talked a lot about you. Showed us your picture." But suddenly, his face changed. He tapped his forehead. "I just remembered something your grandmother told us." He turned to face the dining room. "Hey Cade! Get in here."

Cade came rushing back into the kitchen, anger replaced by alarm, Liesl noticed.

"Cade, remember what Lottie Bower told us about that friend of Liesl's?"

Cade thought a minute, then looked squarely at Liesl. She thought she saw a spark of regret in his face as he spoke, "She said a friend of yours had come to visit her, an old friend who wanted to surprise you. He asked where you were."

Liesl was thinking who that might be when Cade added, "She said he had an unusual accent."

No! Not Lottie! Liesl jumped up and rushed from the room calling for Ava, who soon returned with Delaney in tow. "When did this happen?" Ava asked Cade, whose grandfather stepped beside him.

"By the way, I'm Ian and this is my grandson, Cade."

Ava gazed at Ian as if he were a nuisance child. "Nice to meet you," she snapped coldly and turned immediately back to Cade. "When did this happen?" she repeated.

"She told us about it yesterday. I don't know when the man visited her."

"You were at the nursing home?" Delaney pumped.

Before Cade could respond, Liesl blurted, "How could they let that man into her room?"

"They let us in," Ian offered calmly. "Of course, all we wanted was permission to fix a few windows. You know those things are rotted clean through and it's going to take me and Cade all week to—"

"Mr. O'Brien," Ava said sharply, "would you please . . ." But she didn't finish.

"Pop, let them ask their questions," Cade urged.

"Well maybe one of us needs to be asking what in tarnation is going on here."

"Mr. O'Brien, this is a matter of national security," Delaney spat, "and that's not just movie-talk. We can't tell you the nature of our business, but—"

"Well, then, let me tell you something," Ian said flatly. "If Miss Lottie Bower is in danger from some fella she thinks talks funny, I say let's go get her out of that place. It stinks anyway."

Everyone turned wide eyes on the old man.

"Mr. O'Brien, I'll decide if that's necessary, which I doubt at this moment," Delaney said firmly. "I intend to question Mrs. Bower about the music when—"

Liesl's cell phone interrupted him. When she answered, everyone watched as her face slowly contorted. "Where are they now?" She turned fierce eyes on Delaney as she listened. "You lock down that building and get as many people as you can to guard her. We're coming immediately!" She snapped the phone shut.

"Two men just came to the nursing home and tried to take Lottie! They said I'd given them permission to take her for a ride!" Liesl's whole body shook. To the assembled agents, she cried, "I'm going to get her and you will not stop me!"

"We'll all go," Ian said. "Get the Blazer, Cade!"

Delaney intercepted them. "I'll take care of this, O'Brien. You're not going anywhere."

Cade stepped forward. "You can change your tone when you talk to my grandfather, Agent Delaney. And you might want to think about this: for whatever reason, it seems one or more people are watching this house. Do you want them to follow you out of here?"

Delaney stared hotly at Cade.

"I didn't think so," Cade said calmly. "So here's what we can do. If the FBI won't mind a little assist, we can do what Pop suggested. We'll use the Blazer. I'll move it to the street behind us. It's not the renters these people are interested in, I take it, so leaving in my own vehicle shouldn't matter to them. You can leave through the back of the house, cross through the neighbor's yard behind us, and meet me."

Ian gave Cade an approving slap on the back and announced, "I'm going to get my hat." He turned to leave, but Cade stopped him. "Hold on, Pop, let's plan this out a bit more." He looked to Delaney as if to signal it was his move.

Delaney studied the floor a moment, then looked up at Cade. "You're right. It could work, but we have to assume they're still watching the nursing home too. My guess is that the attempt to remove Mrs. Bower was to draw Liesl into the open."

Cade looked startled. "You mean, someone's after *her?*"

Liesl jumped in. "Can we get moving, please?"

Thirty minutes later, Cade, Ian, Liesl, Ava, and Delaney left the downtown peninsula in the Blazer—undetected, Delaney had assured them. He had agreed that Liesl was safer out of the house. He'd also expressed concern for Cade and Ian's safety, though he hadn't been forthcoming with any plans for them. It seemed the agent was grasping for a plan minute by minute.

Delaney had one more safeguard he'd arranged before leaving the house. He directed Cade to an emergency medical services center in North Charleston, not far from Hidden Pines nursing home. They pulled in back, parked the Blazer, and transferred to a waiting EMS ambulance, complete with two uniformed personnel. In the back, Delaney's crew rode unseen to the nursing home, where there was nothing unusual about an ambulance pulling up to the front door and loading someone on a gurney. Only this time, that someone was Lottie Bower.

When the techs gently rolled the agitated woman into the back of the truck and shut the doors, Liesl flew to her grandmother's side. "Lottie, it's me, Liesl." She clutched the confused woman's fidgeting hands. The woman looked over her granddaughter's face. "You're Liesl?" With the bone-thin fingers of her right hand, she lightly stroked Liesl's cheek and studied her face. "Yes, you are. But what's wrong with me?" She began to tug at the straps binding her to the stretcher as the ambulance pulled away.

Cade moved in to help Liesl release all the straps. Liesl met his eyes but didn't know how to read them. His motives were still suspect to her.

Lottie stared at Cade as he lifted her to a sitting position. Liesl noticed how careful he was with her grandmother's left arm.

"You . . . you're the young man who came to see me, aren't you?" It was then the woman noticed the others in the truck. She gasped. "Who are these people?"

Liesl hugged her gently. "It's all right, Lottie. They're friends of mine."

Fearfully, Lottie looked from one to the other. But when her eyes fell on Ian, she suddenly brightened and pointed at him. "I know you." She smiled bashfully. "We used to be in love."

Liesl gaped at Ian.

Ian cleared his throat. "Well, ma'am, you did tell me I reminded you of your husband."

"Yes," Lottie whispered, and her eyes glazed soft and distant. She fell silent, locked on Ian's face.

Delaney motioned impatiently for Liesl to ask the question.

She looked hard at him, wanting to take her grandmother far from them all and just love her, not interrogate her. *How dare he make me do this now.* But she knew she must. She patted her grandmother's hand and held it close to her. "Lottie, I've been looking for something that I left at the house. It's very important that I find it. I wonder if you can help me."

As if returning from a dream, Lottie took a moment to focus on Liesl. "You're home. I'm so glad you've come back. What did you ask me?"

"I'm looking for a box of music that I left in my closet, on the floor. Do you know what happened to it?"

Lottie said nothing for a moment, then, "I threw things away."

"What things, Lottie?"

"Did you say music?" the woman asked feebly.

"Yes, a boxful of sheet music in my closet."

Lottie grew agitated again. "Everyone died. So I threw it all away."

"You threw the music away?"

Her eyes now pooling with tears, Lottie nodded and said, "Yes. The garbage truck took it off." Then she turned loose of Liesl's hand and lay back down. "I'm going to sleep now." And she did.

Delaney clenched his hands in a gesture of anguished defeat. "Well, that's that," he said, putting his disappointment aside and adjusting the agenda, as if practiced in this discipline. "We'll get her to the other facility, then head to the airport."

Delaney had arranged for Lottie to be temporarily moved to another nursing facility, whether or not the sonata was found. An agent would be posted for her security. He'd suggested to Liesl that once she was no longer a target, there would be no further interest in her grandmother, and she could return to Hidden Pines. Liesl was to fly back to New York with the agents, then home to Washington with her own security detail.

"I'm not going with you," Liesl announced defiantly. "The sonata is gone. I'm no use to you anymore." She stroked her sleeping grandmother's hair. "I need to stay here awhile longer."

Delaney closed his eyes and rubbed his forehead, the image of exasperation mixed with fatigue. "You can't go back to the house," he reasoned. "They don't know we didn't find the code. They'll still come after you—for the code, for whatever you might know about it, for whatever they think Devoe might have confided in you, no matter how long ago. You can't stay here unprotected."

"They won't find me where I'm going."

"And where, pray tell, is that?" he asked irritably.

She looked at him curiously. "Odd expression, don't you think? 'Pray tell.' What do you think that means?"

Delaney clearly wasn't going to be distracted. "Where do you think you're going?"

Chapter 23

Sunday morning, a still-spritely *Exodus* left Metro Marina heading for the harbor. Liesl had kept the boat snug in its slip through the years, only occasionally taking it out for a run.

Ava and one of Delaney's agents sat near the stern watching Liesl pilot the old boat through choppy waters. They and the rest of Delaney's squad had spent the night in the security of police headquarters. Delaney had spun a secure net around the marina before Liesl and company arrived, and the *Exodus* had slipped safely away.

A distant rumble made Ava turn in her seat and cringe at the charcoal thunderheads massing behind them. Her gaze then fell straight down to the small boat running the smooth middle of the *Exodus's* wake. Beneath its Bimini top, she saw Cade and Ian O'Brien standing side by side at the helm. Delaney had convinced her that Cade and Ian were at risk remaining in a house under surveillance by Russian agents, and that the U.S. government was responsible for their safety. Because the O'Briens had been plunged into the thick of this operation and knew where the grandmother was, Delaney felt it was better to keep them close under Ava's watch, at least until her mission in Charleston was over.

"It's for their sake and ours," Delaney had answered Ava's initial objections to bringing the O'Briens along to a safe house. "Unorthodox, I

know," he'd told her. "But we've run a sweep on them both. Except for who birthed him and who married him, Cade's clean. As for the old man, he's as straight an arrow as they come. Even teaches a Bible study or some such thing right off the back of his boat at the marina in the Keys. It's best we throw them into the same protective net with the girl. Until you can get her out of here anyway." Ava had hesitantly agreed.

She believed that neither Cade nor his grandfather sensed they were under watch, federal or otherwise. As far as they knew, they were coming along for one reason: Liesl had asked them to. Ava hadn't seen that coming, but it solved the problem of how to harbor the men without them knowing. Still, Liesl's gesture puzzled Ava. Even when she'd been told that Cade had lost his job at the newspaper, Liesl had replied, "Once a reporter, always a reporter. He'll sell this story as a hot scoop to get rehired."

So what changed her mind? Ava turned to look back at Liesl, who was now studying the skies behind them and motioning Ava toward the cabin. Ava understood. She went below long enough to locate raincoats for the three of them. She handed one to Liesl and zipped herself into another. FBI agent Jeremy Tucker, a forty-something man of few words and built like a tank, had waved off the proffered slicker.

As they approached Fort Sumter, Ava noticed a tour group being hustled back to their boat as the sky grew darker. The old artillery-pocked fort crouched low at the entrance to Charleston Harbor, whose waters seemed to dance in anticipation of the advancing storm front. She turned again toward the boat following them, seeing only one person now at the controls. She noticed the other head, the younger one, hung low over the side of the boat and smiled.

The boat lurched and Ava swung back to see Liesl's strong back hover over the wheel as she dodged one swell and headed straight into another. As the boat's deep-V hull dug in for traction against the turbulence, Ava wondered at the place they were headed, at the peculiar chemistry of salt flats and tides that seemed as much a home to Liesl as the house in town. It was Ava's business to know all about her charge. She'd discovered more than she imagined one young life could bear, even more than Ava's own longer journey had encompassed—a husband who'd left her for the open road and freedom. A son who'd left to do his country's bidding in a war where the enemy wasn't clearly uniformed and corralled into forts like Sumter, but sprang like vipers from holes in the ground or hurled death from the concealing skirts of old women.

Still, Liesl's demons were just as threatening. Ava looked down at the dark splotch on the floor of the boat. She knew what had happened that summer night when Liesl was fourteen.

As if the cannons of Fort Sumter had suddenly returned to duty, a flash and boom from behind split the air, and the *Exodus* gunned it toward the Intracoastal. Braced against the wheel and calling over her shoulder for Ava and Tucker to get below, Liesl veered hard into the channel. But Ava wasn't budging. That wasn't how she'd been trained, not the mission she'd been left with. "Don't let her out of your sight," Mark Delaney had ordered her and Agent Tucker. "You know what to do if you need backup."

Ava watched as Liesl throttled back slightly then turned to check on her passengers. Getting an all's-well signal from both, Liesl glanced behind at the little runabout bobbing like a cork in the squally seas. She kept looking back at the two men struggling to stay in her wake, and Ava saw the clear concern for their safety etched into the young woman's face.

The solid downpour overtook them with no preview sprinkling. As Agent Tucker dove into the cabin to retrieve the slicker he'd refused earlier, Liesl signaled for Ava to go below too, but to no avail. Ava did join her under the fiberglass canopy over the helm, though, and held on tight. "Want me to take you back?" Liesl called over the roar of the engines and rain. Ava was surprised at the teasing smile nudging at Liesl's mouth. "It's okay, Ava." The smile turned consoling. "This old hull has dug into worse waters. It's them you need to worry about." Without looking, she nodded backward toward the O'Briens. But Ava was glad to see the little boat holding its own behind them.

"I think you're wrong about that," Ava said.

Liesl whipped around and squinted through the rain. "I guess one of them knows how to drive. Wonder which one it is."

"Probably not the one I saw throwing up in the river." The women enjoyed their first laugh together and something heavy and forbidding between them lost some of its footing.

"Pop, you want me to take it awhile?" Cade asked, his words a gurgle in the pelting rain blowing sideways under the canvas top.

Ian shook his head, widened his stance, and gripped the wheel tighter. Cade watched the old man's face lock down hard against the only thing Cade knew his grandfather to fear: aging into helplessness. Ian was seeing his years piling higher and heavier on top of him, his shoulders yielding to the weight, his joints angrily protesting the burden. Ian O'Brien, in ways no one but Cade could see, mourned the passing of time.

The little day-cruiser belonged to the same friend who'd loaned Cade the garden tools. The man had given Cade the key and permission to use the boat anytime. But its gunwales were too low for rough seas, its bottom too flat for anything but the backwaters and lakes. One more hard slap against the starboard side made Ian stumble, and though he righted himself quickly enough, he finally yielded the wheel to Cade. "I'm tired of fighting her, son. See what you can do." He stepped aside and Cade slipped behind the wheel, sensing the old man's regret.

"It's the boat, Pop. She just doesn't want to be here." Ian didn't respond and Cade hoped his attempt to mask the old man's waning strength hadn't been too obvious.

Cade throttled back and tried to ease into the rhythm of the swells. But there was no rhythm, even inside the broad wake thrown by Liesl's boat. As he struggled to maintain course behind her, he wondered why. *Why am I here? Whose plan book mapped this collision course between the world-class pianist and the out-of-work reporter?* He knew Ian would answer with something like, "God's plan book, of course."

Far ahead, Liesl was a tiny figure in a boat called *Exodus*. Cade didn't know what she was escaping from or where she was headed. He just knew he had to follow.

Liesl pointed toward the bent live oak. "That's our turn." She slowed the engines, banked broadly to the left, and eased into the center of a wide creek running west. Beyond them was a vast sea of grass whipped about by the capricious gusts of the storm. But the ribbon of water ahead lay flat, buffered by the dense growth on either side.

When it reached a sharp elbow, Liesl turned wide to the right, just clearing the shallows extending from the grassy point. In the distance, a dock ran off the right bank. Behind it rose a deep thicket of trees and scrubby growth.

"And now I understand," Ava said.

"Understand what?"

"What you told Delaney: 'They won't find me where I'm going.'"

By the time they reached the upper end of the creek, the rain had downshifted to a drizzle, the cloud line veering off to the south. But the air remained turbulent with an insistent wind pushing hard against the *Exodus*. Liesl coasted toward the dock, reversed her engines, gauged the directions of wind and current, then worked both screws forward into her final approach. It was a near flawless maneuver that snugged the boat so close to the dock, it took only a few minutes for her to hop off and secure the lines front and back, never asking for assistance. When she finally looked up at her passengers, she saw the astonishment on both faces, more like disbelief on Agent Tucker's. "You didn't think pianists were good for anything else?" she asked with marginal amusement.

Agent Tucker replied without expression, "Never knew one before." He left the boat and headed quickly toward shore.

"Hey, wait a minute!" Liesl called after him. But the agent ignored her. He drew his gun and moved cautiously up the dock. The tropical thicket rose about twenty yards from the bank, its rustic cottage perched high off the ground like something sovereign. Liesl fumed over yet another invasion of her private world. She'd never brought anyone outside her family here. Few people outside her bloodline had ever earned clearance to this hallowed spot. And now, a man she didn't even know was pushing his way inside.

"He's just trying to protect you," Ava said as she passed Liesl and hurried to catch up with the agent.

Liesl watched them mount the steps, then felt for the door key in her pocket. *They won't get far.* Then she remembered the sound of running feet behind her that night in New York, the frantic dash through the closing door of Rev. Scovall's church. She had welcomed his protection then. Why would she resent these agents now? She was beginning to feel like a tempestuous child.

She heard an engine and turned to see the small boat nudge its way around the northerly turn in the creek. Two tall figures huddled beneath the canvas top, which now drooped in the center. They were two strangers who, in less than a day, had created a stir behind her barricade. Something dormant in the dark of Liesl's inner sanctum had begun to move, like a single blade of new grass nudging against the cold crust of a long, numbing winter. It made her feel foolish and vulnerable. She knew nothing about them, except that they'd commandeered a desperate moment in her life and helped her through it.

As the boat advanced toward her, the faces of the two men grew more distinct. The old man waved at her. She could see his smile part the hedge of gray whiskers. It was the kind, soulful smile he'd shown her in the kitchen, meant to pacify and patch up the damage of his grandson's harsh reproach aimed at her. The grandson. He'd had no right to speak to her that way. Or had she deserved it? Now she watched him maneuver through the rushing current, intent on his work at the wheel. He'd come with her into a storm, willfully entangled in something he didn't understand, something that could harm him. *Why would he do that? To get the story?*

Just then, Cade raised his head and looked at her. He seemed to detect the question, as if it were painted across her face. His hand raised slowly in greeting, and though his eyes held her cautiously for a moment, they soon widened into an at-ease countenance. And inside the shadowland that engulfed Liesl, there was the faintest flicker of light.

She motioned for them to tie up across the dock from her. She watched as Cade tossed back the hood of his jacket and flicked wavy strands of dark, wet hair off his forehead. He glanced only once at her as he fought the current coming from one direction and the wind from another. The light boat with obviously poor steerage was no help, resisting its driver's every command. Ian held the bowline in his hands, but the boat wouldn't stay put long enough for him to hop off and tie down.

"Throw me the line!" Liesl yelled, shoving her own wet hair back under the hood of her coat.

In one fluid, long-perfected motion, Ian hurled a flimsy coil of line toward Liesl. She caught it firmly and pulled hard against the bucking boat, tying the line in a loose figure eight around one of the forward cleats, leaving plenty of slack until Ian could toss the stern line. When he did, she was able to finally harness the boat. Cade jumped off and further snubbed up both lines, lashing the boat tightly. He quickly appraised the tie-down job done on the *Exodus*, then turned to Liesl with open admiration. "How did you learn to do that?" His was the same amazed expression she'd seen on Agent Tucker's face, but delivered with an earnest smile. He really wanted to know, she realized. And for some reason, she wanted to tell him. But not now.

Avoiding the question, she reached to help Ian unload a few bags from the boat. He was complaining loudly. "Sorriest excuse for a boat I ever saw. That guy needs to put it back in its box and return it to Wal-Mart."

Liesl heard herself laugh out loud, something she hadn't done for a long time. She turned to see Cade staring at her, rain dripping off his chin, and something tugged in the pit of her.

"Let's get inside," she urged and hurried up the dock. She took the steps two at a time to the front porch of the house, set high atop a network of concrete pillars. She remembered what her aunt Bess had told the contractor who'd built the house: "Leave enough room under us for the Atlantic to pass through." Neither one evidently counted on a Hugo-sized storm surge.

As she pulled open the screen door, it protested with a loud screech, just like the screen door on Tidewater Lane. But of course this one would protest. It had been several years since anyone had bothered it, she hoped. Over the years, trespassers had occasionally made themselves at home in what appeared to be an abandoned cabin. As she unlocked the heavy wood door and pushed it open, she was pleased to see everything as she'd left it after her last visit. She moaned silently as if sighting a loved one after a long separation.

As everyone filed inside, she held back. Stepping back onto the covered porch, she looked farther up the creek toward the hidden dock, her aunt's favorite perch. Liesl could almost hear the penny whistle, see the dorsal fins summoned to the surface, and watch the slight figure of a woman joyfully slip into the brackish waters.

Almost. But never again.

Chapter 24

*P*avel Andreyev stood with his back to the window, his hands balled into fists at his side. The gilded apartment near the South Street Seaport smelled of broiled fish and spilled cognac. "You will return to Moscow immediately. Your work here has been a complete failure."

Evgeny Kozlov tensed but managed a passive expression, as if his ruin were but a trifling concern to him. "I request more time to carry out my duties, sir."

Andreyev slapped his hand against the marble-top table beside him, sending the crystal prisms suspended from a nearby lampshade into a tinkling flurry. "There is no more time!"

Accustomed to such outbursts, Kozlov calmly suggested, "But we can't be sure the Americans have found the code."

"True. Except for the renters, no one has been seen at the house since yesterday afternoon. The girl and her search party are gone—with or without the code. The American agents are either scrambling to pass on our mole's name or they have given up their hunt for him. He is prepared to leave Tel Aviv at a moment's notice."

"Notice from who, sir?"

Andreyev studied his subordinate. "An American. Someone we've been slowly luring, setting the hook just in time to reap his services. But never mind that. You, comrade, will be replaced by someone who will continue to hunt the girl."

Kozlov seethed with indignation, but fought to conceal it. Ignoring the affront, he plodded on. "Without proof, the Israelis won't believe there is a mole. They didn't in '96 when Devoe first warned the Americans, who then warned Israel that there was such a person. No discernible leaks, no mole, Israel reasoned. They believed Devoe was just a traitor trying to buy his way out of the American electric chair with his wild claim of a Russian informant in Israel."

"True again," Andreyev granted. "Israel believed we killed him because he'd betrayed us, not because he knew the name and was about to pass it on. But if they have the coded name in their hands, everything we have worked for is threatened." Andreyev walked to the green satin chair and sat down heavily, his eyes cast down. His fury had ebbed, or so it seemed to Kozlov.

But when Andreyev looked at him again, Kozlov realized his misconception. Andreyev's eyes burned like coals when he spoke. "You will return to Moscow tonight and take this message to our comrades: Code or no code, nothing will stop us from carrying out our mission. The time is right and we are too close. Soviet Russia *will* return!"

Chapter 25

The wet assembly of people inside the cabin stood looking at each other for an awkward moment. Only Liesl seemed certain of what to do next. She went quickly to the windows on one side of the broad room, unlocking and raising each one just enough to summon fresh air. Cade wasted no time helping her. He moved to the windows on the other side and opened them too. The room was suddenly swept with cross-currents of air so drenched and thick, the walls seemed to breathe in and out.

"Heart pine," Ian declared to no one in particular, running his hands along the heavily paneled walls and nodding approval. "Who'd you say this place belonged to?" he asked Liesl, who was following Ava and Agent Tucker into the only other room in the house.

"My great-aunt Bess," she replied mechanically, glancing from Ian to Cade over her shoulder. As she disappeared into the back room, Cade felt like he was observing her through a defense shield of plate glass. But he knew what had happened to her in the last few days. He and Ian had been briefed with the story of the sonata, if not the reasons for its urgent retrieval. Ava and Agent Delaney had allowed just enough information to "reward your invaluable assistance," as Ava had described their roles so far, "and to make you understand why exposing this mission would jeopardize the security of our country." She needn't have worried. Cade had been too enmeshed in this bizarre affair to consider it his professional duty to report it to any news medium.

Ian motioned for Cade to join him in a peek at the back room, a bedroom that ran the width of the house. Like the front living room, it was spacious, but sparsely and inexpensively furnished. The warm woods of the floors, walls, and furniture reminded Cade more of a mountain cabin than a seaside cottage.

There was a double bed and one set of bunks in the room. Cade watched as Liesl opened a closet and retrieved a stack of blankets and pillows. "You men can sleep in here," she directed. "Ava, you'll find the sofa in the living room very comfortable."

You men? Cade thought. He and Ian had no plans to stay. They'd come as escorts only. He glanced outside at the waning light. "We'll be leaving shortly, Liesl. We just wanted to run sweep behind you. Make sure you got here safely."

"Oh, I don't think leaving's a good idea," Ava inserted firmly. *Too firmly*, Cade thought.

"She's right," Liesl said. "You see that?" She motioned toward a window where a hefty wind whipped at the curtains. "This is no weather for a boat from Wal-Mart." *So, she likes Pop's humor.*

"Got that right!" Ian whooped. He and their mercurial hostess, it seemed to Cade, had initiated a thaw. But he still felt he should go. "No need to be concerned," he told her. "We'll make it home just fine. Call us tomorrow if we can help you." Cade was fishing in his pocket for something to write his cell number on when Liesl walked up to him and gently but firmly pushed two blankets and two pillows at him.

"You can go in the morning," she said with finality, training her amber eyes on Cade as if willing him to read something behind them. Her complexity was almost intoxicating, making him strangely unbalanced. The girl he'd married had seemed two-dimensional: money and drugs. Surely there had been more to her, but he was too disgusted with her, with himself, to care. He couldn't help her. Couldn't save her from her squalid death. But surely he could save someone. Was it Liesl?

He took the blankets and pillows, both hands brushing hers in the transfer. "Thank you," he said simply, then added, "But where will you sleep?"

"On the boat."

"Oh no, you won't," he objected instantly. But Ava weighed in with her usual authority.

"It's probably the best place. The unexpected place. But you won't stay there alone. I'll go with you."

Liesl shrugged resignedly and walked to a cabinet running along one wall. She pulled two kerosene lamps from inside. "We'll use one of these in each room. And, by the way, bathing is done outside in the camp shower."

"You're kidding, right?" asked Agent Tucker.

Ava smirked. "So the FBI is all tough exterior and mushy middle?" she prodded. Tucker ignored her.

"I'm sorry I have to leave you jolly folks," Ian said, "but I'd like to spread my arthritic bones out on that double bed for the night, if that's all right with you younger men."

"Not before we eat," Ava insisted as she picked up a couple of grocery bags and headed for the small kitchen tucked in the back corner of the front room.

"By the way, we use solar energy here," Liesl noted to the group. "There should be enough for your stay." She looked pointedly at Ava. "If that's not too long."

Ava regarded her compassionately but said only, "We'll do what we have to do." Then she busied herself with preparing the evening meal: subs, chips, and sweet tea from the marina store. "Tomorrow's fare is even less impressive," Ava admitted. "It was the best I could do before casting off. Sorry."

Ian hurried to help her pull food from the bags.

Later that night, Cade slipped from his bunk, pulled on his windbreaker, and eased quietly toward the front door. He didn't feel good about the women sleeping outside by themselves. He felt certain no one had followed them here, especially in the storm. Still, he needed to check on them.

Then he remembered the shrieking screen door, enough to wake the dead. He searched for another way out and noticed a side door off the kitchen. He slowly opened it, grateful for its compliant hinges, and reached for the flashlight he'd pocketed before going to bed. Once outside, though, he put it back. The thunderheads had scattered, leaving a bright moon to light his way. He skirted the grassy boundaries of the house and headed for the dock. Halfway down its weathered, uneven boards, he stopped to listen. There was only the rhythmic lapping of the tides against the hulls of the two boats, and nothing stirring inside the *Exodus*.

He walked to the end of the dock and watched moonbeams dance like pixies on the water. Above him stretched a velvety gray canvas from one marshy horizon to another, spattered with pinpricks of light. He found himself barely breathing, not wishing to dispel the majesty. He looked toward the bend in the creek he and Ian had navigated that afternoon. Nothing but the tide and breeze-ruffled grasses moved. It wasn't until he turned to look upstream that he saw the figure, dark and still against the bright sky. It was seated on a small platform over the water. His heart beat wildly until the figure slowly stood. The moonlight caught her full in the face and Liesl lifted a hand toward him, then let it drop.

Something's wrong! He rushed toward her, picking his way along a narrow, sandy path overhung by dense palmetto rimming the bank. Uncertain of his footing, he reached again for the flashlight in his pocket and flicked it on.

"Turn it off," she called in a whisper carried on the wind.

"Are you okay?" he responded.

She didn't answer, and he quickened his pace, pushing back wild clumps of fronds until he emerged into an open glade. He turned toward the creek and found her sitting again on the edge of a tiny dock he hadn't noticed when they arrived that afternoon. Her back to him, she sat cross-legged and still.

He hesitated, not the rescuer, it seemed, but the intruder in this midnight moment that had been hers alone. Then she turned around. Her hair blew in her face and she didn't remove it, let it billow in the sea air.

"Come sit with me," she said softly.

It was a moment before he could shift gears from observer to participant in her strange world. Is that what she was asking him to do?

Liesl moved over. Cade lowered himself beside her on the narrow dock, and they both swung their legs over the edge.

After an awkward moment, he repeated, "Are you okay?"

She tucked her hair behind her ears, not shifting her gaze from the water. "This afternoon you asked how I learned to handle a boat."

Cade remembered her swift, confident moves on the dock. "Go on," he urged, opening the door for whatever she wanted to tell him.

"Then Ian asked who the house had belonged to," she continued. "The answers to both questions are the same: Aunt Bess." She lifted her long, sinewy arms and stretched, her fluid moves like a cat. Cade wondered if she knew the drama she projected, if it had been groomed into her upon the world's stages, or if it just sprang naturally. There was so much he wanted to know about her. But why? He remembered the things he'd told his grandfather about the house in town, that it was a stranger he wanted to know. Could he have imagined it was the girl who'd grown up there that would captivate him more?

"She used to sit here at dawn," Liesl said, "playing that old penny whistle she'd bought in Scotland. And in a little while, she'd see the first dorsal fin approach, then another. Soon, there'd be two or three dolphins circling in front of her and waiting."

"For what?"

Liesl turned an amused grin on him. "For her to join them."

His eyes grew wide with surprise, and that seemed to delight her more.

"She swam with the dolphins up and down this creek. You should have seen it. Not many ever did. We were very private back here."

"We?"

Liesl nodded. "I spent a lot of time here with her."

"Tell me about her."

Liesl's bright mood paled and it took a few moments for her to answer. "She was my grandmother's younger sister and my refuge. She and this house."

Should he ask? Why not? "Refuge from what?"

She fixed him with an uncertain eye, as if questioning how far she should take this. Then, abruptly she asked, "Have you ever known an alcoholic?"

Go ahead, tell her. "Both my parents."

There was just enough light for him to see the open mouth, the hard blink. Then the softening began. The thaw. "Both?" she asked, her voice strained.

"Yes, for as long as I can remember." He paused. "My wife, too."

"Your . . . wife?"

"Ex-wife, now deceased. She did alcohol and drugs. A bad batch of meth ended it for her."

He didn't look at her but could feel her eyes drilling into the side of his face. Then she did something he couldn't have seen coming. She reached with both hands and turned his face to hers. With tears shining in her eyes, she pulled him to her and kissed his cheek. "I'm so sorry," she whispered, her lips so close to his.

Then suddenly, she released him and pulled away, as if tumbling back to her senses. And Cade knew she was, once again, in full retreat. She turned stiffly toward him. "I didn't mean to embarrass you. I'm sorry."

Embarrassed? Are you kidding?

"Look, Liesl. What you just did was show compassion for someone who, evidently, has suffered as you have. Why should that embarrass me? Or you?" She seemed startled by his bluntness, but he was just gaining speed. He'd observed too much. "Yeah, you've been through something more. This whole Russian thing is enough to make anyone run off and hide."

"Is that what you think I'm doing?" she snapped.

"Yeah, I do. I think you're hiding inside yourself and have been for a long time, turning away everyone who wants to help you, like that offends you. And you know what? I did the same thing. I just closed up my shell and dared anyone to come near."

Even in the dark, he could see her tremble and wanted to reach for her. But not now.

He had more to say. "It was Pop who realized the state I was in." *Should I say it now? Yes, especially now.* "But it was God who saved me from myself."

He sensed her body grow rigid, a fierce silence engulf her. Finally, she spoke, her words a low rumble. "God let my mother, my father, my aunt, and the teacher I loved die horrible deaths." Her voice broke and she quickly put a hand to her mouth as if to restrain what might escape from inside. Cade was quiet, letting her gather herself. "There has been no saving in my family. Not even Aunt Bess, who worshipped God her whole life. She read her Bible, prayed, never harmed a soul, loved everybody. And did her God save her that day in the boat? That vile, evil day?" When her voice broke this time, there was no stopping the tears that followed, though she swiped furiously at them.

Cade reached for her and gently pulled her to him. She yielded at first, and he felt the warmth of her as he tucked her close to his side. He closed his eyes and willed her to stay, to listen to the things he wanted to tell her. But too quickly she pushed away and stood up. "No, I won't do this."

Without another word between them, he followed her back to the boat. He watched until she closed and locked the cabin door behind her, no more eye contact with him. He lingered on the dock, letting this ponderous thing wash over him. What was it? As hard as he had worked to throw off the burdens of his past, like heavy covers on a hot summer bed, something more was falling upon him.

Liesl climbed into the front berth of the *Exodus*, pulled the covers up high and waited. He was still out there. She stared into the low ceiling of the boat. *Go away, Cade. Go look for a story somewhere else, or whatever it is you're doing. I shouldn't have asked you to come.* She still wondered at her own motives for doing that.

A board creaked outside the narrow porthole high on the boat's hull, and she wondered if Ava could hear it too. How was the CIA agent sent to protect her sleeping so soundly through this night? Or was she?

After a moment, Liesl heard Cade's footsteps fade toward the house, and only the scent of him lingered. The touch of him. His arm around her, his shoulder firm against her cheek, his voice deep and soothing. She shook herself as if from a dream that promised things not real, that would disappear with the waking. *Cade O'Brien isn't real*, she told herself. *Nor his God.*

Chapter 26

The next morning, Cade awoke just after dawn and hurried toward the dock, anxious to know the two women were still safe inside the boat.

"She's gone," Ava announced, emerging from the cabin of the boat and pointing upstream. "She pulled a kayak from under the house and launched a few minutes ago. Short of brute force, there was no stopping her."

Cade moved to the end of the dock and looked up the creek. In the distance, the kayak slid silently against the current, its rower dipping her paddle side to side with perfect timing. He watched her image diminish with each stroke and lifted a silent prayer. *Go with her, Lord.*

"It's an island, Cade. No one here but us." She joined him on the dock, zipping herself into a light jacket. "Though there's an abandoned fish camp on the other side of the island. Liesl says it's fallen in and uninhabitable."

Cade didn't shift his focus from the kayak.

"She promised to be back soon. Said she just needed time alone." After a moment, Ava added, "You two must have had quite a chat last night."

He looked but couldn't read her, and wanted no misconceptions about his late-night encounter with Liesl. "And that was all we had," he said crisply.

"Easy there." Ava smiled.

Cade resumed his vigil on the kayak, which was just disappearing around a far bend. He felt it slip off his radar, just a transient blip in time, a life that had stormed his world then suddenly withdrawn. People did that. Then he thought of the ones Liesl had lost. He turned toward Ava. "What can you tell me about her aunt?"

Ava sighed and looked down into the swirling current. "She was quite a character. Much livelier, more expressive than her older sister, Lottie. Bess Avert was a religion professor at the College of Charleston, very popular with the students but constantly in trouble with the administration. She was a devout Christian. It seems she too often used her curriculum as a springboard for sharing her faith."

Cade listened intently.

"She was widowed at a young age and never remarried. She built this place out here mostly to dry out her nephew."

"Liesl's dad?"

Ava nodded. "She treated him more like a son than his mother did. Seems Lottie Bower never approved of him, not even as a little boy. She saw too much of her husband in him.

"Horace Bower had made a fortune in the stock market before drinking himself to death. They would have lost the big house if Lottie hadn't squirreled away as much of his money as she could lay her hands on."

"How do you know so much about the family?"

Ava held his eyes a moment. "When the stakes are high, we have to know every last nuance of a subject's life."

"Liesl's a subject?"

"Has been since Devoe's murder. We know she had nothing to do with that, but what she knows, and isn't aware that she knows, could be critical on many fronts."

Cade looked up the empty creek. Still no kayak.

"Come with me," Ava told Cade as she returned to the *Exodus* and climbed aboard. Cade followed her to the stern of the boat, where she pointed to a faint stain on the fiberglass floor. "It's mostly worn away now," Ava said, "but this is where it happened."

Cade braced for the story he felt coming.

"Henry Bower had taken his aunt offshore to spear fish. They did that quite often, according to the woman who ran the marina store at that time. It seems Bess always made sure there was no booze on board. But that day, she must have missed the flask of vodka the Coast Guard later found in Henry's tackle box.

"Apparently, during one of his dives, he was running out of air and trying to surface slowly to avoid an embolism. As he broke the surface gulping in air, he was grabbing for his buoyancy compensator to inflate it and hold him up. He couldn't find it and panicked. The mix of alcohol and fear led to an unfortunate chain of events. He tried to ditch his weight belt while fighting to keep his head above water. He yelled for his aunt to take the speargun while he struggled with his gear. Without latching the safety on it, he hoisted the spear toward her. In his thrashing about, the trigger caught on something. The gun fired into her abdomen."

Cade flinched. "Is that a drunk man's story?" he asked more harshly than he intended, remembering the lies his own father told so easily.

"No, it's hers. Henry was sober enough to operate the marine radio and call for help. A medivac team flew from Charleston. When they arrived, Bess told them—very clearly, I understand—what happened. She bled to death en route to the hospital. But right up to the end, she kept repeating 'was accident.'"

Cade pondered that kind of devotion. Unconditional and selfless. He'd tried it with his parents and wife, but couldn't sustain it. Self-preservation had overruled it, and he had fled to the Keys, where the winds and tides swept his life clean. Or so he had thought.

"It would take more than Henry Bower could consume to anesthetize him against that kind of pain."

"And Liesl?"

Ava squinted up into Cade's face, the sun now strafing them with its first, sharp bursts of light. "She was fourteen, sitting at the kitchen table with one ear tuned to the marine radio. About the only place that would hire Henry was Metro Marina, where he was a dockhand. He was more at home there than anywhere, except the water, I'm told. The radio at the house was sort of a lifeline. He kept it on all the time."

"Let me guess," Cade said grimly. "Liesl heard her dad's call for help on the radio."

Ava nodded. "She and her mother were at the hospital when the helicopter landed. Liesl barged through security and had to be restrained from running onto the helipad. Can you imagine?"

Cade turned and walked away because, yes, he could imagine it, and he wouldn't let Ava see how much. He hurried along the path to the little dock, sat down hard on the end of it and mourned for the young woman whose life was slowly embedding itself in his. He didn't will it to and didn't understand why it kept coming.

And here it came again. Paddling back with the current, her hair a burnished gold in the early sun, her face a lovely mask. He ached for the tragedies she'd endured, as much as he ever had for himself. Why?

She must have seen him. Before she reached the small dock, she dug her paddle deep into the current and veered sharply to the left. He saw the resolute set of her face as she paddled briskly toward him, ramming the bow into the soft, muddy bank beside him. Not until she stepped out and pulled the kayak from the water did she look up at him. "Is something wrong?" she asked with little expression, as if doubting there was any other reason for him being there. Cade tried to see behind the mask, but it was on tight. He shook his head in answer to her question and looked down at the mud around her feet, clad in rafting shoes. "So they call this pluff mud, huh?" It was a lame attempt to shift into neutral territory, but after last night's contentious parting and the story he'd just heard from Ava, it was time to just drift.

Still, he was surprised by the shift in her mood, subtle but distinct. Perhaps the run up the creek had uncoiled the tempest inside her. She poked a rubber-toed shoe at the dark, spongy scalp that rooted the marshes around Charleston. "You get used to the smell and the feel of it if you wallow in it long enough."

"And you have?"

"Head to toe. Aunt Bess and I used to get on all fours and chase fiddler crabs along here until we reeked like dead fish. Then we'd just roll into the water and let it ooze off."

Her voice lifted with the wind, and Cade wanted to hear more. But after the story Ava had just told him, he knew he had to be cautious. "So you swam the creek too?"

"Oh sure."

"No sharks back here?"

"There's a shark hole on the other side of the island where the Intracoastal and the creek merge again. But I've only seen one around here."

"Go on."

She grew more animated, her hands waving to illustrate the telling. "We saw a manta ray fly out of the water one day. We didn't see them much around here, especially flying like that one did. So Aunt Bess and I stopped to marvel at it. Then we looked about ten feet behind it and saw the dorsal fin rising. It wasn't a dolphin's. You can tell the difference. The thing surfaced long enough for us to see its freaky head. It was a hammer-head, about twelve feet long and ready for lunch. To sharks, the manta ray is a delicacy. The poor thing finally took one desperate leap sideways and flattened itself against the bank, as high up as it would go. I don't know how long it would have lived out of water, but I think it might have preferred suffocation to mutilation. I thought Aunt Bess would come out of her skin with excitement. She ran to the house and got her gun. With just a couple of shots, she scared the shark away but didn't hurt it. The ray flipped back into the water and disappeared in the opposite direction."

Liesl paused for too long. Cade feared he'd opened an old wound. If he had, it seemed she'd grown adept at patching over them and moving on. "My aunt loved all living things, no matter how harmful they were."

Including Henry Bower, Cade thought, and wondered if that had occurred to Liesl too. Determined to keep the conversational gear in neutral, though, Cade suggested, "What do you say we get some breakfast. I can almost hear Pop rattling around in the kitchen now."

Liesl looked oddly at him for a moment, then seemed to dismiss whatever had crossed her mind. "Sure." She started pulling the kayak over the bank.

Cade sprang to help her. "Let me do that."

She seemed to grapple with that offer a moment, then shrugged and stepped aside. He hoisted the narrow, single-seat fiberglass hull over his head and started down the path. She was just a few steps behind him. Seconds later, he dropped the kayak and lunged for Liesl, pulling her to the ground.

She screamed, but his hand flew to her mouth and muffled her outrage. "Shh!" he ordered. "Listen!"

She squirmed violently in his grip, then suddenly went still. She too heard the engine. Through the loose cover of the undergrowth, they saw the bow of an approaching boat take the downstream turn in the creek and head their way, slowly. His hand came off her mouth. "I'm so sorry," he whispered close to her ear.

Then came Ava's sharp command from the house: "Get down!" Someone was now running full tilt toward them.

Agent Tucker burst through the palmettos, gun drawn.

"Stay with her!" Cade told him, as if forgetting which of them was the FBI agent. But it didn't matter. He wasn't going to cower in the bushes if someone was coming for her or any of them.

The agent protested. "You'd better—"

"No time to argue, man! I said stay with her." Cade released Liesl, jumped to his feet, and shot down the path to the boat dock, running low behind the creek-side screen of wild shrubs. As he approached the dock, he saw Ava crouched in bushes nearby, her sidearm aimed at the creek.

Cade took an out-of-sight position on the opposite side of the dock from Ava. He wished he'd pocketed the handgun he'd stored on the boat, though he guessed the federal agents with him wouldn't allow him to brandish a gun anywhere near Liesl, concealed-weapon permit or not. Though the weapon was small, he knew the damage it could do, having once blown a mortal hole in a marauding shark bearing down on a few swimmers in Florida Bay.

He and Ava crouched low as the boat approached. It was an open fisherman with no cabin. The two men inside exhibited the normal complement of gear. The early-morning hour was appropriate for chasing fish up the tidal creeks. Cade was about to dismiss the anglers as exactly that when their boat slowed and both men turned their full attention on the *Exodus* and the house, neither man uttering a sound. When the driver cut the throttle even more and the passenger grabbed a line as if preparing to tie up to the dock, Cade didn't wait for a go-ahead signal from Ava. He stepped into the clearing at the head of the dock and called, "Got a problem?" he barked. Ordinarily, he would have been more cordial, but the events of the past two days were anything but ordinary.

His sudden appearance seemed to take the men by surprise. They didn't immediately respond. But when Ava emerged from the bushes, the driver blurted, "Hey, what's up with you two? Playing hide-and-seek this early in the morning?" The other man snickered.

"Steady," Ava cautioned Cade in a hushed breath. He noticed her hand shoved into a pocket with a gun-shaped bulge in it.

"Unless you've got a problem, you won't need to tie up here," Cade informed the pair. "This is private property."

"Well this here creek sure ain't, young fella," the driver shot back. "And if we want to, we can set out here all day and night 'til we're good and ready to leave."

It was then Cade noticed the empty beer cans littering the boat, and his pulse slowed. *Just a couple of good ole boys with an early jump on the brew,* he figured. He glanced at Ava, who didn't seem ready to stand down yet.

"What are you fishing for?" Cade asked, his tone more friendly. But there was a reason for the question. An answer that signaled unfamiliarity with these waters would mean trouble.

The men appeared confused by Cade's change of tone, then rallied. "Well, now," began the driver, "me and my son-in-law are gonna get us some redfish and sea trout. You a fisherman, fella?"

"Got that right!" came a voice from behind Cade. "When he's not throwing up!"

Cade groaned out loud.

"Oh boy," Ava echoed the groan. She and Cade both turned to see Ian coming down the porch steps.

"Well, why don't you folks join us and we'll all just have a good time."

The driver patted the top of a nearby cooler. "We got enough beer for everyone."

"I believe you do, sir," Cade allowed.

"Oh, now it's 'sir,'" said the younger man. He didn't seem as eager to take on guests as the driver, supposedly his father-in-law.

"Mind if I see what kind of rigs you're using?" Ian asked as he headed for the dock.

Cade wasn't comfortable with his grandfather getting any closer. "Pop," he said as Ian passed him, "don't go down there."

"Better me than you, son," Ian mouthed over his shoulder.

"Pop," Cade cautioned, but Ian just waved him away with a hand behind his back, and kept going.

For the next fifteen minutes, Cade and Ava stood like sentries on either side of Ian at the end of the dock as the old man traded fish tales with the two strangers, their boat in a near-idle against the now-sluggish current. More than once, Cade looked toward the upstream dock, glad to see no movement from where he had left Liesl and Agent Tucker.

As Liesl lay still on the sandy path between the two docks, Agent Tucker knelt protectively beside her, his focus locked on the two fishermen in the creek. It was the man crouched about fifteen yards behind him that Tucker couldn't see.

They have no idea how close I can get, the man thought, pulling the hood of his camouflage jacket farther over his balding head. Flat on his stomach, he trained his binoculars on Liesl's face.

But it's not time.

Chapter 27

After the two fishermen left and headed up the creek, Cade rounded irritably on his grandfather. "What did you think you were doing, Pop? You had no idea who those guys were. Have you forgotten why we're here?"

"Have you forgotten that you're a news reporter and not Rambo? And by the way, you'll never make it in the diplomatic corps either, not the way you went charging into those guys. Somebody had to run interference, especially with that young one getting all heated up." He folded his arms over his chest and stood his ground. "Yep, that's what I was doing."

"Well don't do it anymore. You scared the wits out of me shuffling up to two guys who might have blown you away."

"I don't shuffle," Ian snapped, his arms still clamped in place.

"I'm afraid you've both forgotten that Tucker and I are the law enforcement around here," Ava said. "So next time a situation arises, let us handle it, okay?" She looked quickly at the two heads bobbing down the path just over the palmetto blind.

Agent Tucker appeared first, glancing harshly at Cade. Coming toward him, Tucker growled, "If you don't mind, I'll do my job without further assistance—or orders!—from you." He brushed past Cade and boarded the *Exodus*, taking a position facing upstream, binoculars about his neck, gun in hand. To Ava, he called, "Better report those guys now. You never know." She drew out her cell phone and walked toward the cabin.

Cade resented the double-barreled scolding. He was about to make a sarcastic comment like, "How foolish of me to try to stop those guys from hurting anyone. Why, I don't even have a badge." But before he could spew his mounting anger, Liesl came up beside him and laid a hand on his shoulder.

"Thank you for what you did," she said with a sincerity that disarmed him.

"I, uh . . . I'm sorry for shoving you to the ground like that. I—"

"You were pretty rough on me." She made a show of brushing sand and briars from her fleece vest, then lightly ran a finger under her top lip, withdrawing a smear of blood.

Cade reacted instantly. He grabbed her shoulders and bent to inspect the injury. "Did *I* do that?"

"No, Rambo did," Ian quipped as he passed behind Cade and trailed Ava to the house.

Cade watched him a moment. "Stop shuffling!" he called.

Liesl laughed at them both. "You're the odd couple, you know that?"

"He's odder than I am," Cade replied distractedly. He was far more concerned about her lip. No, it was more than that. He looked down at her, wanting to touch the wound he'd inflicted and treat it. But what about the other hurts, the ones he couldn't see?

"It's not that serious, Cade." She squinted one eye at him and was about to add something, when the front door flew open.

"Liesl, better come here," Ava instructed. She was holding her cell phone.

Liesl looked back at Cade. "I'd like for you to stay another day," she said. No reason given. None needed, Cade decided as he watched her go.

"They're still out there," Ava told Liesl when she reached the porch. "Delaney says a couple of guys showed up at Metro Marina last night asking questions about the *Exodus*. He'd left instructions for the dock master to report any inquiries about you or the boat to him. You know what this means."

The two women looked at each other as if the sleeping monster at their feet had suddenly stirred. "It means someone must check on my grandmother immediately," Liesl insisted.

"I've already asked the local police to do that. They're also standing by if we need help out here." She looked intently at Liesl, not knowing how much more of this the young woman could take. She was too quiet, as if the weight of being prey had snuffed out her voice. Ava watched as Liesl mechanically slipped out of her soiled vest and pushed up her sleeves, her eyes intent on some spot on the ground, some out-of-focus spot Liesl now drilled with her unspoken fear. But Ava saw it in the glazed eyes, the shadow of sunken cheeks. It suddenly occurred to her that Liesl had grown noticeably gaunt. Though her beauty was indelible, its polish had faded in just days. Her hair unkempt, makeup missing, clothes too loose on her long frame.

Then, as Ava had watched her do before, Liesl yanked herself up from the drowning, swilled the oxygen of defiance, and declared, "They'll have to leave. There's nothing for them to find. They'll just slither back into their little holes and it'll be over. Won't it?" It wasn't a question but a pronouncement.

Ava hesitated to hurl anything else her way, but Liesl needed to know. "There's something else, Liesl." Sharp eyes bored into Ava as if she were the predator. "Juilliard has reported a persistent caller asking for you and your whereabouts. Someone at the school had the good sense to record the most recent call. My office ran it against a handful of other calls regarding anything to do with you, and we got a match."

Liesl waited.

"The Juilliard caller is the same man who reported the break-in at your house—the man who claimed to be a neighbor out for a jog. At two in the morning."

"I don't understand. What's the implication?"

Ava sighed. "Not sure. He still might be just a concerned neighbor wanting to know you're all right. But he could be someone working an opposing camp."

"I still don't understand."

"And I'm trying desperately to, so bear with me," Ava implored. She looked toward the *Exodus* and drew a hand under her chin, thinking through the tangle of dangling information. "Someone opposed to Evgeny Kozlov's mission might be running a counter op to head him off."

"By jogging at night and placing a few phone calls?" Liesl's voice betrayed what Ava sensed was a growing discontent with the job her CIA and FBI handlers were doing. But Ava could offer no clearer answers at that time.

"For now, let's concentrate on keeping you and your grandmother locked down securely. As you say, the trail these people have been barking down has grown cold for them. No sonata, no code. It's taking them longer than I expected to discover you have neither." Though Ava feared the Russians might want Liesl for reasons that hadn't yet surfaced.

"Let's just stay out of sight," Ava continued, "and I'll let you know as soon as I get a report on Lottie. I'm sure she's fine." But Ava wasn't sure at all. They'd tried once to snatch Lottie Bower. They'd try again if they felt she was the key to Liesl.

Voices from the dock made both women turn to see Cade, one foot propped on the *Exodus*'s gunwale, talking to Agent Tucker. "I believe that's Cade making amends with Agent Tucker," Ava observed. The women looked at each other and, once again, reached a subliminal common ground. Though they couldn't make out the words, they listened quietly to the distant voices, drawing both a distraction from their combined worries and, at least for Ava, an admiration for a very uncommon young man.

Stealing a glance at Liesl, who still watched the two men on the dock, Ava said, "He came to the boat soon after you left this morning." Liesl turned, her eyes questioning. "Just checking on us, he said. He was concerned that you had left by yourself, as I was."

Liesl looked back toward the dock. "Did you talk?"

Ava knew what she meant. "Yes." She paused. "I told him about your aunt Bess, about the accident. I thought he should know. If that upsets you, I apologize. But he seems to care a great deal."

The two were silent awhile. "I wonder why," Liesl said.

"You don't trust him, do you?"

"Do you?"

"Surely you don't think you're the only one we've checked out. He's here, isn't he? That means his background has been combed and cleared by us. His and that funny old man's." Ava chuckled and Liesl turned with a glimmer of surprise on her face.

"Yes, I find the elder O'Brien very amusing," Ava admitted. "Now, I have more calls to make. I suggest you—"

The porch door banged open loudly behind them. "Oh, sorry," Ian mumbled. "Liesl, I'll fix this thing if you've got any tools. In fact, there's a whole lot needs fixing around here. But what I came to ask is—" His attention swiftly turned to Cade, who was just approaching from the dock. "Son, you got to see what's out back." Ian looked at Liesl. "That's what I came out here for," he continued. "What's up with that big cross behind the house?"

Is there nothing private? Liesl struggled to compose her thoughts, her words. This kind old man means no harm. *Get hold of yourself.* She answered dismissively, "Something my aunt put up just before she . . . died." She swallowed hard. "It blew down soon afterward." *That's a lie and you know it.* "I just left it lying there."

Ian shook his head. "No. The cross I just saw is standing straight up."

It was as if an ice-cold hand had just gripped her throat. Liesl felt the color drain from her face. Her mind raced to comprehend. *No, it can't be! I knocked it down myself! It was still on the ground the last time I was here.* It didn't matter that they were all staring at her now. She turned and ran around the side of the house, down the winding path to a small clearing ringed by native shrubs. There in the dappled shade of a nearby scrub oak was the cross, about six feet high, rising straight and tall from the weedy soil. Her knees buckled and she dropped to the ground.

Seconds later, she felt strong arms lift her and heard a faraway voice. "Open the back door, Pop!"

He carries me like a child.

She felt as if she'd slipped into paralysis, her limbs not responsive. Still, she tried to move inside Cade's embrace. But he just held her closer. He was now lowering her to the double bed, plumping a pillow beneath her head and pulling a blanket over her. She watched his face, though her own felt inanimate, unable to form an expression or issue a word. She didn't see or hear anyone else in the room.

Then he sat on the bed and looked into her eyes. He picked up her hand, which to her, seemed to belong to someone else, though she could feel his warmth. It had to be *her* hand. Gently, he stroked her hair, then whispered, "You've had a shock. I don't know why. I guess I don't need to. But you need to stay in bed and stay warm. Try to sleep, Liesl."

She didn't have the words to argue. When Cade left the room, she closed her eyes, but not to sleep. Instead, she watched herself kick and push against the cross until she uprooted it from the loose soil. It was her battle with God. How could he let her aunt die that way? Why her and not the man who killed her? And what was Liesl supposed to do? Kneel at the cross and worship? For years, her aunt had tried to teach her the ways of the cross. But Liesl had dug in her heels and resisted the notion of a loving God in control of all things. He couldn't seem to control one drunken man. And later, couldn't stop the spear.

Without stirring beneath the covers, Liesl looked around the bedroom at the paneled walls her father, the skilled carpenter, had installed in the house, at the iron light fixture he'd found at a garage sale, at the framed photograph hanging on one wall. It was her family gathered around the little house he'd built in the backyard for her, the one with the surprise steeple he'd copied from St. Philip's.

She squeezed her eyes shut and remembered something else. When he died, she came back to the island, to the place where he'd once been whole and well, hoping to carry away something good from him. But when she wandered back to the clearing and the toppled cross, Liesl felt a callous chill overtake her. Instead of raising the cross again in her father's memory, she left it in the dirt, where it had remained all these years.

Who did this? Was it trespassers like those her aunt had found staying in the house a few times? But why would strangers bother to raise the cross? Maybe it'd been some of her dad's old drinking buddies from the marina. Before he'd left for good, they'd all come out for parties. Maybe some of them had recently returned. But why disturb the cross? The hunt for an answer grew tedious. Sleep tugged at her until she finally yielded.

When she awoke that afternoon, Cade was sitting in a chair beside her. Through the partially open door, she could hear Ian and Ava talking quietly in the kitchen. As Liesl stirred, Cade leaned over and took her hand. "Feeling better?"

She found her voice. "Why do you care about me?" she asked. "Am I the headline that will get your job back?"

He abruptly released her hand and sat straight up. "That again, huh?" He looked out the window behind the bed and shook his head. "I think it's time for me to take my shuffling grandfather and go home."

As he stood up, Liesl grabbed his hand and held onto it. *No!* she cried silently. *Don't go!* With her other hand, she threw off the covers, then swung her legs over the side of the bed and tried to stand. She wobbled just an instant before he caught her up in his arms and pulled her to him. "I'm sorry," she whispered. He didn't answer. Instead, he ran his fingertip lightly over her wounded lip. The touch of it made her shiver. When she closed her eyes, his lips came down gently on hers. He nearly lifted her from the ground as she leaned into his kiss. And for those few moments, her perilous world disappeared.

Agent Tucker motioned for Ava to follow him outside. When the two reached the front porch and closed the door, Tucker asked, "Does it seem odd to you that there's been no attempt to break into the Bower house? I mean, if the Russians are watching the place and wanting that sonata as badly as we do, don't you think they'd be in there by now? Especially since we cleared out two days ago."

Ava nodded slowly, then turned troubled eyes on Tucker. "Unless they already knew the sonata wasn't there. That our search had produced nothing."

"But how would they know we . . ." He halted his question as if suddenly figuring the answer.

"Yes," Ava repeated, "how would they know?"

Chapter 28

*A*fter a late dinner scooped from various containers Ava had brought from the mainland, Liesl and Cade slipped down to the little dock, but not without ample cautioning from Ava. Though there had been no more visitors to the creek, Ava had learned that CIA intelligence had picked up a surge of cyber chatter from the field. Something distinctly Russian was building, and spy masters at CIA headquarters in Langley, Virginia, were hunkered down over an undulating map of pirated transmissions, trying to read them like fortune-tellers over a lava lamp. "We might need to leave soon," she'd warned them both.

Liesl followed Cade onto the dock. A veil of dark clouds to the west was rimmed with fire from a sunset struggling to be seen, if only in silhouette. Liesl closed her eyes and raised her face to the sulfur-laced thermals rushing over the marsh. She willed them to lift her beyond Ava's constant warnings and the inconstancy of life. She needn't have. As Cade slipped his arms around her waist and turned her toward him, it was all the escape she needed. She yielded so completely to his embrace, almost limp against his chest, she wondered when the barricade had tumbled from around her and if she would survive the exposure.

But when Cade kissed the top of her head and tightened his embrace, a strange and uncertain peace washed over her. She was afraid to speak in case it might dispel the closest thing to happiness she'd felt since . . . when? Suddenly, a torrent of sensations sprang at her from different directions. From the afternoon her family gathered at the new playhouse; the careless adventures up and down the tidal creeks and eddies of her childhood; the wild applause after her first Carnegie Hall performance; the sound of a penny whistle from this very spot. She wrenched herself from Cade's grip and looked up at him. His dark eyes pierced hers with an intensity that made her catch her breath.

"What's wrong?" he whispered. "Do I make you uncomfortable? I don't mean to. I just—"

She touched a finger to his lips, then lifted a strand of the dark hair spilling over his forehead. She cupped his face and kissed him so lightly it seemed like only a breeze that passed between them. He buried his face in her hair and whispered, "Liesl, trust me."

She pulled back and studied his face, surprised by the flash of unguarded pain she saw there. The temptation was to smother him with kisses. But something stopped her.

You don't know him, she warned herself.

She disengaged from him, walked to the end of the dock, and sat down. He followed her. After a moment, she said, "Do you mind if I ask about your ex-wife?"

He stared into the rippling creek. "No, Liesl. You should know. But I'm only going to tell this once."

Without looking up from the water, Cade began. "Bonnie Lorence was every frat boy's dream. Good-looking and easy to come by." He glanced sideways at Liesl. "You know what I mean." He looked up at the sky and seemed to mumble something to himself. Liesl thought it odd, but kept quiet. "She was going to be a nurse until an internship at Grady Memorial in Atlanta opened a different path to her. Someone there with access to the pharmaceutical closets led her from her usual straight vodka to a smorgasbord of dope. It became a habit she managed to conceal pretty well."

Liesl watched his jaw muscles tighten.

"My parents knew it, but it didn't bother them. They were partiers too, rarely caught without their own brand of intoxicant in their hands, usually swirling around in expensive crystal glasses. And they were crazy about Bonnie. Her family was old Atlanta. Mine was new. And when new Atlanta wanted passage into the pedigreed side of town, you married into it. That was my lot."

"They forced you to marry her?"

Cade shook his head. "I really cared about her. She was sweet and gentle when she wasn't high. I thought I could save her, so I did what everyone wanted me to do and married her, right out of college. Pop was furious with me. But Dad had impressed upon me how good it would be for his real estate business to have Lorence connections. And since I was to join the family firm and make a zillion dollars like he had, I should bring a 'dowry' with me: a five-foot-five, platinum blond contribution."

"How long did it last?" Liesl asked, not sure how much more she wanted to know.

It took awhile for Cade to answer that one. "Until the night I flew home from a fishing trip with Pop in the Keys and found her entertaining a male guest in our bedroom. They were both stoned and buck naked. Bonnie and—my dad."

Liesl gasped, but Cade kept going.

"I ran out of the house, drove straight back to the airport with my duffle bag of dirty fishing clothes, and flew back to the Keys. To Pop."

The knot in her throat kept Liesl from doing anything but listening.

"He's always been my safe harbor. Through the divorce, Bonnie's overdose and death, my parents' divorce. Just Pop and God."

Liesl found her voice. "God?"

Finally, Cade turned toward her. "He's as real to me, as close to me, as you are right now. He's the only way I could forgive my dad for what he did."

"You forgave that man?" Liesl was incredulous.

"If I hadn't, my hate for him would have eaten me alive."

Now it was Liesl who stared into the waters.

Cade took her hand and held it gently. "I carried a lot of bitterness around with me, Liesl, like you do."

Liesl knew it was true. She had woven a braid of distrust and melancholy into a ligature bound so tightly about her that it threatened to cut off all circulation. Was she, even now, only slightly alive? Was this man who implored her to trust him just another apparition of hope? A match that would flame brightly for a short time then snuff itself out despite her frantic attempts to sustain it? She looked into the marsh but didn't see it. Instead, the familiar, old, flickering newsreel, played too many times, jerked along its haunting continuum before her, its images blotting out all else. They came quickly now, as they always did: the father who'd loved and drunk so fiercely, then died. The mother who'd been helpless to save her family, then succumbed to cancer. The grandmother who'd given music to the child and gentleness to the home, then wandered away into dementia. The aunt who'd offered refuge, tried to show Liesl a Savior, then perished at the point of a spear. The nurturing professor who'd endorsed her giftedness, then unwittingly lured her to his execution.

Mercifully, the images finally diffused into the marsh, taking all the faces with them. Liesl knew they'd return, though, feeding their old, cellulose litany of hurt into the projector again. She was so tired of seeing them. She squeezed her eyes shut and silently pleaded for relief. For a new beginning.

She had fallen so deep into herself, she barely heard Cade calling her name. Barely felt his hand on her shoulder until the warmth of it drew her to the surface again. "Look at me, Liesl," he urged. And she did.

"You have no reason to think of me as anything but an intruder in your life. And maybe I have no business being here at all. I'm not sure why I am, except that I was certain you needed my help and that I needed to give it."

Words wouldn't come to her. They weren't necessary. But at this moment, in some strange answer to her plea for help, *his* words seemed very necessary.

Cade ran his fingers through his hair as if massaging his thoughts. He looked at her with a palpable longing. "Right now, I could hold you and kiss you for the pure pleasure it would bring me, with no thought of tomorrow. I just asked you to trust me, but neither one of us knows what will come tomorrow or the next day."

Liesl hardly breathed.

"But God never changes, Liesl. He never forsakes, never abandons. He is your future."

Liesl blinked hard. *A new beginning?*

"I once clung to Pop for dear life. Still do in a way. But he's so human." Cade chuckled lightly. "So powerless. And one day he'll be gone." He glanced at the clouds advancing over the marsh, then back at her. "And so will I. Hopefully not tomorrow."

He got up and pulled her to her feet. With both hands, he tucked her long, wind-tossed hair behind her ears and smoothed it over her shoulders. He lifted her chin and gazed down so tenderly at her. Liesl felt as if the world had closed over them, and they were standing on the only spot left on earth. He brushed his lips over hers, then again until she slipped her arms around his neck and drifted deep into the kiss, sensing the purity of its passion, the unselfish honesty of it. When it ended, neither one spoke. Liesl felt as if she'd just surfaced from a long, underwater swim and the rush of pure oxygen was all there was to know.

Arm in arm, they started back for the cabin. It was just past ten when Cade saw her safely inside, locked the door behind her, and headed for his own berth aboard the *Exodus*. Since the marina's report of strangers looking for the boat, the sleeping arrangements on the island had shifted. He and Agent Tucker stationed themselves at the boat, Ian took the couch and the women the bedroom.

Halfway down the porch steps, though, Cade stopped. He'd heard a sound from somewhere to his right, from where he and Liesl had just come: the rustling of autumn-dry fronds, the soft but unmistakable thud. Something fallen, now up and running into the dense hammock behind the cabin. Cade's hand closed over the pistol he'd slipped into his pocket before he and Liesl left for the dock, and he took off after escaping feet he couldn't see. "Stop!" he called.

In seconds, Ava burst through the front door and Agent Tucker leaped from the *Exodus* onto the dock.

"Cade!" Ava called, but he didn't answer. He was trained on the retreating sound and nothing would stop his pursuit. Except Liesl's voice, begging him to come back. He slowed to listen for his prey and her urgent cry for him.

"Cade, don't go back there!" Liesl called.

Just then, Agent Tucker caught up with him. "What is it, man?"

"Someone's out there!"

Both men turned to see Ava sprinting toward them, flashlight in one hand, gun in the other. "Don't go any farther. Liesl says there's quicksand and rattler nests farther back."

"Are you sure you heard someone?" Tucker asked.

"Positive, but it was much closer at first," Cade said, squirming at the implication. "Closer to the small dock."

"Where you and Liesl just were?" Ava asked.

Cade nodded. "Yeah."

"We're out of here!" she declared. "We'll pack up and leave immediately."

"Where will you take her?" Cade asked, his voice tight.

"We'll talk later. Let's hurry back to the cabin. I left Ian locked down with Liesl."

Before they turned to go, all three paused to listen once more, but the night was at rest again.

The years had taught the man the art of disappearing. After tripping over the stump and scrambling to his feet again, he had fled as far as he dared into the swampy hammock, then simply slid beneath a layer of rotted leaves and pulled a cover of fronds over him. The man who chased him would have reached the sinkhole before he found the hiding place. He was so close, this one Liesl called Cade. And now, hidden just feet from where his pursuers stopped, the man could hear every word. They were going to flee with Liesl Bower, as if he and the others wouldn't find her again.

But he would get to her first.

Chapter 29

*T*hrough the downpour, two hazy, glowing orbs grew brighter as the Mercedes navigated the rutted lane to the dacha. From an upstairs window, Vadim Fedorovsky watched the approaching car, considering his options for dealing with the castigated yet doggedly loyal KGB veteran inside it. Though sent home as a failed operative, Evgeny Kozlov had suffered worse from more ruthless superiors than Pavel Andreyev. Fedorovsky could retire the agent altogether, but sometimes, Fedorovsky had found, it was the rebuked subordinate bent on restitution who was most valuable to a cause, especially a cause with such an urgent deadline.

The car stopped near the tree line of aspens surrounding the dacha. It was a large, sturdy home of rock and rough timbers, not outwardly impressive, but its reasonable proximity to a good fishing lake, the Moscow Conservatory, and the Kremlin made it a strategic dwelling for a man whose covert credentials far surpassed his laurels as a music professor.

When Kozlov stepped from the driver's side and opened a black umbrella, Fedorovsky hurried down the red-carpeted staircase toward the front door. It opened to find Kozlov removing his boots as was customary to do even in dry weather. He deposited his dripping umbrella and raincoat onto a porch table before embracing Fedorovsky and kissing both of the man's florid cheeks. "You are well, I hope," Kozlov offered, though stiffly.

"Yes. Yes. Come in." Fedorovsky led the way into the rather overdressed comfort of his country home. His late wife's collection of Victorian furniture, ornate silver services, embroidered tablecloths, and ruby glassware made the home look more like an English tearoom than the outpost of a formidable Kremlin veteran.

Entering the dining room, Fedorovsky pulled two chairs from the dark walnut table and invited Kozlov to sit. The host then poured two cups of black tea from a small but elaborately etched, bronze samovar, one of many from yet another of his wife's expensive collections.

Kozlov gazed admiringly about the room. "Your service to the country has been rewarded handsomely," he noted. Fedorovsky knew the man was taking liberties with their longtime association, but didn't react to what any other subordinate would have been forbidden to say.

"I asked you to come, Evgeny, because I, unlike Pavel Andreyev, don't believe your service to us should come to an end, especially at this particular moment." His guest didn't stir. "It's unfortunate you failed to capture Miss Bower." He paused to reflect. "And to think that it wasn't too many years ago that I entertained both her and Schell Devoe in my Moscow apartment."

"I venture to say that ordering Devoe's execution was most difficult for you, was it not?" asked Kozlov.

Fedorovsky grew testy. "You must trust me a great deal to say such things to me, comrade."

"'Comrade?'"

Fedorovsky eased his tone. "Still comrades, yes. Our loyalties to Russia remain on common ground."

"That's why I trust you now to help resurrect our country from its tomb," Kozlov said.

Fedorovsky drew a full breath. "Nothing resonates deeper inside me than the fight to restore our nation to Soviet dominance."

"And certainly, no one at the Kremlin would ever suspect how you and the others intend to do just that. I only regret that it has to be done this way."

Fedorovsky pounced. "How *much* regret?"

Kozlov bristled. "You misunderstand me. I have no affection for our president—and certainly not Syria's. But . . ." he hesitated.

"But what?"

Now plainly guarded, Kozlov offered, "The council rules. If they say it must be done, then so be it."

Fedorovsky almost regretted his challenge to this man. "Evgeny, I share your distaste. But this is our moment in time. The assassination of the Russian *and* Syrian presidents at the summit with President Noland and Prime Minister Shulman will turn the world on its head. Who would ever believe we killed our own president? Or that the Americans would be so overt. But the world will have no trouble believing the Israelis did it. After all, it's Israel who believes Russia and Syria are in alliance to annihilate them. Our mole in Tel Aviv is preparing documents—grand forgeries—that will be the indisputable evidence that Israel, out of self-defense, struck first. And how sly of them, the world will think, to do so in the presence of their own prime minister, thereby deflecting blame from Israel."

Kozlov seemed transfixed as Fedorovsky surged into the broader scope of the plan. "The Americans will be so outraged, they will turn their back as Israel is wiped off the map. But meanwhile, Comrade Kozlov, while our nation mourns its slain president, we will take over the Kremlin. Our numbers are many, including Ambassador Olnakoff, who aided our pursuit of Miss Bower. Make no mistake. We are equipped and ready to mount another revolution!"

As if crystallizing the complexity of the mission into one pure element, Kozlov said, "And it all hinges on the performance of your one man in Tel Aviv. He must stay in place long enough to learn the logistics of the summit. And he must finish the documents that will condemn Israel."

Fedorovsky looked out the window at the aspens and birches swaying in the rainstorm. *How tossed about by circumstance they are*, he thought. He refused to be. "That's why you're here today, Evgeny." Fedorovsky hoped he was making the right decision. "I am sending you to Tel Aviv immediately. We have just discovered that besides the threat of the Americans finding the code to the mole's identity, he might be compromised by someone in his own household."

Kozlov's eyes narrowed.

"You know who I'm talking about, don't you?" Fedorovsky asked.

Kozlov nodded grimly. "Long ago, I had warned of such a thing."

Chapter 30

It was now clear that Liesl was still in Russian sights. With the two men hunting for the *Exodus* at Metro Marina and one or more tracking her to the island, Ava didn't want to waste another second getting Liesl out of Charleston. But there was a bigger obstacle than the KGB. Liesl herself. She had refused to leave until she'd seen that her grandmother was securely tucked away in the new nursing facility. It wasn't enough that she was listed under a false name, a guard posted outside her door and another in an unmarked car outside, or that ties with all her former doctors had been temporarily severed. Liesl insisted on seeing Lottie Bower first thing Tuesday morning.

It was going to work like this: before daylight, Ian would leave first, taking the *Exodus* back to Metro Marina. Followed by a plainclothes police surveillance team ensuring that no one else was tagging along, Ian would drive the Blazer to a remote landing far up the Ashley River and wait for the others. Cade would drive the small cruiser to the landing with Liesl, Ava, and Agent Tucker hidden below in the cuddy cabin.

"Can you handle that?" Liesl had teased Cade, who hadn't realized the matter of his weak stomach had become common knowledge. He assured her the calmer inland waters would pose no problem for him or, more importantly, his passengers.

Transferring to the Blazer, they would arrive at Riverview Senior Care before Lottie was even awake. Everything about the plan worked out fine, up to that point.

With Agent Tucker stationed alongside the guard on duty at the nursing facility, and Ava and Ian outside Lottie Bower's door, Liesl stole quietly into her grandmother's room. Cade hung back a few feet from the bed.

"Lottie?" Liesl whispered. Her grandmother's eyes fluttered open then closed again.

"It's Liesl. Lottie, wake up. I've come to see you."

The small head, matted with soft gray down, turned toward the voice, and the eyes opened wide. Lottie Bower's frail right arm withdrew from the covers and floated toward the face before her. The old woman's hand drifted through uncertain space in search of the sound. "Liesl?" came the childlike voice. "Is that you?"

Liesl felt a tug of elation. *She knows me!*

"Oh, Lottie." Liesl gently clasped the wavering hand and pulled it to her chest. She leaned over her grandmother and wept softly. Cade moved in and placed a supportive hand on Liesl's shoulder. "I've missed you so much," Liesl said, flicking away tears. "I'm so sorry I haven't been here for you."

The woman looked calmly at Liesl, but said nothing.

"Is there anything you need?" Liesl asked, stroking the soft hair that curled about the withered face.

Lottie shook her head slowly, smiling as if Liesl's presence was all she wanted.

Cade bent low over the bed. "Mrs. Bower, do you remember me? I'm Cade O'Brien. My grandfather and I would like to keep visiting you, if that's all right." He and Liesl had agreed they shouldn't announce that she was leaving Charleston.

"Why, yes, that would be fine," Lottie said with unusual clarity. Her gaze lingered on Cade a moment, then she added, "Are you the one looking for the music? Did you find it in the secret place?"

Liesl gaped at her. "Wh . . . what did you say?"

"The music, dear."

Words piled up in Liesl's head but the shock blocked their exit.

Cade moved in closer. "Where is this secret place, Mrs. Bower?" he asked with deliberate calm.

A mischievous glimmer skittered over the old woman's face. "Oh, you'll never find it."

Liesl's mind flashed with vivid images of the house and all its rooms. Could she have lived there so long and not known of such a place? Or was this just more nonsensical wanderings of a doomed mind? Finally the words broke through and Liesl tried to issue them with calm, not wanting to alarm her grandmother. "Lottie, please tell me where this special place is. I'd like to visit it and, uh, make sure everything's all right."

Lottie pushed back the covers and tried to sit up. Cade lifted the thin body to a comfortable position. As he did, he caught Ava's curious glance through the open door and motioned for her to stay put.

Sighing with some irritation, Lottie warned, "Child, you must never tell your grandfather. He'll be so angry that I hid things from him."

"Is that where you hid my music?"

The woman touched Liesl's cheek. "I would find you there, wrapped in my red cashmere cape. You always loved the smell of that place."

Liesl released the breath she'd been holding, disappointment flush on her face. The cedar closet. She'd already watched one of Delaney's men search it and find no music. Still holding Lottie's hand, Liesl sat back in her chair and smiled sadly at the woman. "So, your secret place is the cedar closet?" she asked in a voice she hoped wasn't too patronizing. It was the voice she'd regretfully acquired to respond to the aimless thoughts her grandmother so often spoke.

"No, child," Lottie replied with clear exasperation. "Under it."

Liesl looked quickly at Cade, who held up a cautioning hand. "Mrs. Bower," he began, "someone with great skill built your beautiful home."

Lottie turned from Liesl to Cade and nodded gratefully at his compliment. It hurt Liesl that she and Cade were now manipulating the broken mind this way, to cajole it for their own purposes. In Cade's face, though, she saw something genuine and caring. As he looked down at the innocent Lottie, his eyes warmed with a fondness that Liesl read as real. As trustworthy. And something inside her leaped. Just then, the code didn't matter. Only the nearness of Lottie, and this kind, gentle man.

"Did the builder make a special way to get inside your secret place?" Cade asked.

Lottie grew wary, her voice rising. "I won't tell you! It's my secret." She pushed back against her pillow and began to fret, her words mumbling together now.

Reaching with both arms, Liesl embraced her grandmother. "Shh, it's all right," she whispered, her face close to Lottie's, her hand patting the sunken cheek. "It's still your secret. Still your house." Without hesitation, Liesl closed her eyes. *Don't let us hurt her. Don't let anyone hurt her.* Then she realized she'd just prayed.

When she opened her eyes, she was surprised to see the old woman relaxed and smiling again. Liesl couldn't bear to upset her anymore. If there were a hidden compartment beneath the cedar closet, she knew Cade would find it. But there was one more thing she needed to know.

"Lottie, why did you hide my music?"

The old woman looked at her as if the answer should be obvious. "It was all I had left of you."

Chapter 31

*B*en Hafner was bent over a spreadsheet of health care projections when his door opened and Ted Shadlaw, his aide, stepped in and closed the door behind him. "What have you got?" Ben asked, a nervous edge to his voice.

"They're headed back to the house, sir. Mark Delaney just reported a *development*, he calls it. A lead on where the code might be. He wouldn't say more, but promised to keep us updated."

"Where did this development come from?" Ben asked tersely.

"The grandmother."

Ben frowned. "Not very reliable, is it?"

"Maybe not, sir. But we'll know soon."

"Anything else?"

"That's all he said, sir."

Ben stared down at the spreadsheet without really seeing it. Finally, he glanced up and dismissed the aide. "Hurry back when you've got something. No phones, remember."

"Yes, sir," Shadlaw said. "Uh, sir. Are you all right?"

Ben glanced quickly at him. "What do you mean?" he asked too abruptly, instantly regretting his lack of composure.

"Well, uh, you just seem upset," Ted said hesitantly. "Maybe you just miss your family, right?"

Willing his voice to steady itself, Ben turned a calculating eye on Ted. *Easy*, he warned himself. *His concern is only natural. Of course I miss my family. But he can't begin to know my fear for them.*

A smile made a brief appearance on Ben's face. "I appreciate your concern, Ted, but all is well. Anna and the kids have only been gone a couple of days. They'll be home soon enough." *No they won't! Not until this is over.* "They're having a wonderful time in Florida." *And oblivious to the reason I insisted they go.* "I've just been working too late. Not enough sleep. You know what that does to you." He studied Ted's open face, the high forehead and eyebrows that slanted up in the middle, giving the man a look of perennial surprise. Ted Shadlaw had been the consummate public servant and Ben's go-to man for the nitty, administrative details that Ben abhorred. *He deserves better*, Ben thought.

"So how's *your* family, Ted?" Ben offered in hopes of quelling the tension.

Ted brightened. "Oh, Julie and I have our eye on a bigger house. When the kids spotted the pool in the backyard, it was all but a done deal." He smiled broadly at Ben, who nodded enthusiastically.

"That's great, Ted. You need a bigger place with all those kids you keep having. What is it now, four?"

"I never knew what a huge number that was," Ted joked. "Well, I've kept you from your work long enough. And thanks for asking about the rest of the Shadlaws. I'll keep you posted on Delaney's updates from Charleston." He smiled thinly and returned to his small, glassed-in post outside the door.

Ben buried his face in his hands. *How much longer?* he brooded.

He reached for the phone and punched the single digit for the president's secretary. Within minutes, she showed him into the Oval Office. Travis Noland stood quickly behind his desk. "And?"

Ben told him all that Delaney had just reported.

Noland shook his head. "We hover and wait for news, and all they give us is a hint of a development, whatever that means. Ben, I want you to get Mark Delaney on the phone this instant and . . . well, never mind. Let the man do his work."

Noland studied the presidential seal woven into the carpet before him, his hand fidgeting about his chin. "CIA briefed you about the chatter?" he asked Ben.

"Right after Ava did, sir. No clear indications yet?" Ben knew how closely the CIA monitored communications pinging the airwaves of hostile countries.

Noland shook his head. "Something Russian. Something Middle Eastern. So what's new? One thing's for sure, though; it's too late to change the site for the summit. And we're not moving back the date. It's going to happen. There's too much at stake with an arms race run amok and warships ramming Israeli blockades. It's got to stop now. And everyone at that table has to be focused on the world's security, not their own hides."

"Is the site still secure, sir?" Even Ben didn't know where it was.

The president nodded affirmatively. "Many of those working the location this moment don't even know what's going to happen there. They think it's a . . . well, they have no idea. I would venture that even the Russians' Tel Aviv mole doesn't know the location—not yet."

Chapter 32

The man wandered outside into the morning sunshine. He punched in a number on a cell phone and uttered a password. Inside the Russian embassy, an operator received the call and immediately routed it to Pavel Andreyev at the Kremlin.

"They're going back to the house," the man said. "Something happening. Stand by."

"My people are there." It was Andreyev's only response.

The caller pocketed the phone and returned to his office.

When told Lottie Bower might have hidden the music and where it could be, Ava's first impulse had been to order heavy backup and race to the house. She thought better of it, though, when Mark Delaney warned that the house was still "hot." The local agents keeping an eye on it had spotted observers cruising the street.

Not wanting to touch off an international incident with agents of Russia and the United States squaring off on a quiet, residential street, Ava reasoned they should wait for the cover of dark. But there was a more critical reason. Langley and Israel wanted to catch the mole before he could flee, if he hadn't already. If Russia believed the code had not been found, it was best they continued to think so, and keep their agent in place. "But I don't like waiting all day," Ava said. "If the music's there, I want it now."

The five of them were in the Blazer, still parked at the nursing facility. "Well, why don't I just go in and get it," Cade said from behind the wheel. "I live there, don't I? Anyone out there shouldn't think much about the renter entering his basement apartment like he's been doing ever since they started watching the place."

"Yeah," Ian chirped. "The big old CIA can leave this little op to me and my boy here. So let's get going."

Ava stared at Ian. He stared back. "If it's there, Miss Mullins, we'll get it for you. No charge for the services."

"Mr. O'Brien, you don't—"

"Oh yes, I do," Ian cut in. From the backseat he tapped Cade on the shoulder and ordered him to drive. "I know just what to do."

After leaving Liesl, Ava, and Agent Tucker at a Charleston police station, Cade and Ian headed for the Bower house. Driving onto Tidewater Lane, they quickly scanned the area, spotting what they hoped were Delaney's watchers who had hovered about the house for days now. Cade spotted two men parked in a dark sedan across from the house.

He and Ian parked the Blazer in their usual spot by the curb and hopped out like they'd just returned from an everyday errand. Once inside the apartment, they locked the door and hurried into Ian's room. "Grab your tool belt and a flashlight, Pop. We'll need both."

With the key Liesl had given him, Cade worked the rusted lock on the camouflaged door at the back of Ian's closet. The tool belt now strapped around his waist and a flashlight in hand, Ian murmured over Cade's shoulder, "Secret doors, secret places. You got a secret too, Cade?"

"What do you mean, Pop?" Cade wiped sweat from his eyes as he struggled with the lock.

"Anything you want to tell me about you and Liesl?"

Cade tugged hard on the heavy lock. "Not now, Pop. Let's do this job and we'll talk."

When the old lock gave, Cade shot through the doorway and up the stairs. At the top, he paused to open another locked door. By that time, Ian had caught up with him and they filed into the kitchen pantry. From there they moved into the wide entrance hallway, now flooded with morning light, and took the stairs to the third-floor landing and the cedar closet that opened onto it. When they flung open the door and inhaled their first gulp of cedar, Cade reached for the pull cord dangling above him and turned on the bare bulb that so poorly lit the closet. He pushed back the few woolen clothes hanging inside and knelt to the floor, which also was cedar. "Hand me the flashlight, Pop."

Ian crouched beside Cade as he guided the bright beam of light to all four corners. They studied the smooth, wide planks of wood running lengthwise on the floor. They were old and dry, and the spaces between them had grown wide with the years. "See anything?" Cade asked.

"Hand me the light, son." Ian stroked the beam along the baseboards running around the three walls. "Yeah, I see something. These three baseboards are a lot newer than the floor. And something else: they're awfully thick. But this one here's about twice as thick as the other two. He ran his hand down the length of that board, then stopped. "There's a seam here," he announced. He felt farther down and stopped again. "And one here, about eighteen inches apart." He sat back on his haunches for a moment, then leaned over and thumped the board between the seams with his fist. It gave. Ian looked up at Cade. "Give me that long flat-head."

Ian wedged the slim edge of the screwdriver behind the loose span of baseboard and pried. The board popped loose from two clamps holding it in place and fell onto the floor. The wall side of the upright board had been hollowed out to conceal a hand-pull bolted to the floor.

"Check for a hinge on the other side," Ian instructed.

Cade moved to the opposite wall, and after more thumping and prying, removed another span of baseboard to reveal two long hinges. When

Ian pulled the handle on his end, a section of floor lifted along two of the wide cracks running between the floorboards.

The first thing they saw in the dark recess beneath the floor was a red cashmere cape laid over a shallow cardboard box. Cade carefully removed the cape, allowing himself only a moment's glimpse of Liesl the child wrapped contentedly in its plush softness. With Ian peering over his shoulder, Cade carefully opened the flaps of the box, fingered through the stack of sheet music inside, and looked up at Ian.

"Better call it in, son. Tell 'em we've got it, then let's get that stuff out of here."

Chapter 33

Cade and Ian were heading for the kitchen pantry and basement stairs when Cade glanced out a living room window in time to see two shadows moving over the side lawn. "Hold it, Pop." He set the box down and went quickly to the window, concealing himself behind the heavy drape. "I don't know if it's Delaney's guys or not, but there's two men headed for the backyard."

Ian flung open the door to the basement. "Let's move!"

A few minutes later, Cade emerged from the front door of the apartment. He was carrying a tackle box and fishing rods, hoping their little charade fooled the right people, still not knowing who the two guys in the sedan were. Behind his sunglasses he quickly surveyed the property and street. The men he'd seen in back of the house weren't visible, but Cade knew they had to be near. Traffic flowed as usual as he approached the Blazer, noticing that the dark sedan across the street appeared to be empty. Cade guessed—hoped—it was Delaney's men he'd seen in the yard.

He turned and signaled to Ian, still inside, where Cade had made him stay until it was safe to come out. As Cade moved swiftly to the Blazer, Ian followed, pulling a wheeled cooler behind him. For anyone watching, they were just off for a bit of fishing.

Cade continuously watched the street and yards as he lifted the music-filled cooler into the back of the Blazer. As he and Ian pulled from the curb and started down the street, Cade glanced in the rearview mirror and saw two men rounding the side of the house at a full run toward the Blazer. Instinct told him they weren't Delaney's men, and he floored it. As they gained speed past the dark sedan, he looked inside and the Blazer swerved almost out of control. One man was slumped at an unnatural angle in the front seat. Cade was certain there had been two men in the car. He could only guess where the second man—or his body—might be.

"What's the matter?" Ian shouted.

"Hang on, Pop!" There was no need to further alarm his grandfather with news of what he'd just seen in the sedan.

Locked on his rearview mirror, Cade prayed. *Get us out of here, Lord!*

Just before he sped around the next corner, he saw a small van shoot from an alley behind him and head his way. "We've got trouble!"

Ian whipped around in his seat and Cade heard him speak under his breath. He knew the old man was praying.

Before the van appeared again in the rearview mirror, Cade turned sharply onto a short residential street offering no place to hide. He took the next turn toward the center of town. *Better to lose them in heavy traffic,* he thought. But at the next intersection, the van ran a red light off a side street and skidded in behind the Blazer. "Pop, get down!" Cade yelled. When he swung the wheel violently, nearly flipping the Blazer, the van attempted the same maneuver, but was cut off by a delivery truck and a column of pedestrians strolling toward the old Slave Market. With a lead of only seconds, Cade dashed into a one-way alley and emerged onto a different street, heading back the way they'd come.

There was no sign of the van, but Cade knew he had only seconds more to disappear. Coming up ahead of him was his chance. The small parking garage was dark and crowded, but Cade shot up one ramp after another until he wedged the Blazer onto a top floor spot and grabbed his cell phone, quickly punching in Ava's number. Her instructions had been to meet her and Liesl at the College of Charleston music department, since it wasn't safe to work out the code on the Bower piano. Liesl was to secure one of the college's practice rooms.

Ava picked up immediately.

"We got the music! But two guys tailed us from the house. We're hiding in a parking garage. You'd better get here fast. And by the way, I don't think you want a gunfight in the middle of a college campus, so find another place to do your work." Cade gave her directions to the Blazer.

"Roger that. Look for a white Suburban."

"Oh, and Ava, it might be too late, but you'd better send an ambulance to the house. I think you've got two men down, one in a car out front. You'll have to hunt for the other."

There was a silent gap before her response. "I'll take care of it."

Fifteen minutes later, the Suburban stopped behind the Blazer, Agent Tucker at the wheel and Ava next to him. Cade swung his backpack, which now housed the music, over his shoulder and he and Ian plunged into the backseat next to Liesl. He handed the backpack over to her. "It'd better be in there."

As Tucker raced from the parking garage, the others watched Liesl thumb quickly through the music. In just seconds, she pulled Tchaikovsky's *Grand Sonata in G Major* from the stack. They stared at the innocent-looking pages as if they were laced with anthrax. Cade wondered if even Ava knew what would happen once the mole was uncovered. But he was more concerned about the present. "Where are we headed?" he asked.

"The Naval Weapons Station," Agent Tucker reported over his shoulder.

"You're kidding," Cade said.

"Nope," Tucker replied flatly. "Fort Sumter didn't have a piano."

Ava frowned at the agent, then looked back at Cade. "They're ready for us. They're not believing our request but they're ready for us. There's a rec area on base with an old piano they assure us is in good working order."

"So you called the U.S. Navy and asked if you could bring some ragtag bunch of folks onto their maximum-security weapons base just to play their piano?" Ian asked incredulously. "And they just said okeydokey?"

From the backseat, Cade could see Ava's cheeks bunch into a grin. Then, she cleared her throat and answered, "No, Ian. The White House called them."

By the time the Suburban reached the gates of the navy base, there was another vehicle in tow, full of extra security. The van that had tailed Cade and Ian hadn't reappeared, but Ava ordered more support anyway.

Clearance didn't take long, once the identification of everyone in the car was verified—and once the confirmation call to Ben Hafner's office was made directly from the gatehouse.

The Suburban followed a guard detail to a low-slung building nudging the Cooper River north of Charleston. The main rec hall had been cleared of all personnel and the outside doors locked. The guards waited outside the main entrance as Liesl flew to a fairly new upright piano tucked in a corner of the large, dusty room.

Ava pulled a chair close to Liesl while the others waited in another room. They were sent there by Ava, given the classified nature of the name she and Liesl were about to uncover. "Remember what I told you," Ava began. "He added dots and rests where there shouldn't be any, mostly on the last movements. Do you remember where you found the mistakes before?"

"Just the fourth movement, I think." And she began to play. After only a few measures, she stopped. "Here! This B-flat half note should not be dotted. I'm certain."

Ava applied the B-flat to a letter grid Devoe himself had devised. After a few calculations, she announced, "The corresponding letter is A."

Liesl continued to play, then halted again in the middle of a run. "Two more wrong notes; a C and a D-flat."

After a few moments, Ava announced, "That means an X and a U. Keep going."

But something had already begun to stir in Liesl. In the next bar, she discovered that Devoe had blackened the center of a whole note and added an upward stem. When that decipher yielded an M, Liesl stopped and stared openmouthed at Ava, who seemed to ignore her.

"I think we missed something," Ava said. "Stop here and back up. That's not the beginning of the name." The agent kept her eyes on the music. "Pick it up halfway through the third movement."

Liesl swallowed hard and did as she was told. Not until the end of that movement did she discover the same mistake that had just yielded an M, and the stirring inside her suddenly ran cold. "Maxum?" She could almost see the workings of Ava's mind, no doubt sorting rapidly through names connected to Israel's central command. But that particular name connected to only one person Liesl knew.

"Anything between that and the first A?" Ava asked.

Liesl deftly fingered the conclusion of the third movement. "No."

"Pick up where you left off in the finale," Ava instructed, still focused only on the page.

Liesl felt the sweat run to her fingertips as she slid into the next mistake. M again. *No, it can't be!* She glanced at Ava, who still allowed no expression but sternly waved her on.

The coded letters came more swiftly now. By the time *Maxum Morozov* sprang from Ava's grid, Liesl was frantic. Though Ava had warned her to hold the name revealed to them in confidence, Liesl now jumped from the piano bench. "It's a horrible mistake!" she cried to Ava. "It can't be Max! You know him!" Liesl remembered Max's visits to Harvard when Ava was still teaching there. "You know his music. It isn't possible!"

Ava quickly ushered Liesl from the piano into the small kitchen nearby and closed the door. She hushed Liesl with just a few words. "It's his *father*," she said in a low, strained voice. Liesl had never known Max's father's name.

"The man works in the office of Israel's Ministry of Defense." Ava quickly pulled the information from a mental file. "He's a very high-level official, though one of many with access to sensitive files. I knew his son was your friend, but that was no reason to suspect the man. It could have been anyone in his or another department. There was no connection between Max's father and your accidental possession of the code, nothing to lead us to him." She looked down at the name scrawled across the grid in her hands. "But he's our mole."

Liesl watched as Ava hastily pulled a different cell phone from her bag.

"You're calling it in *now*?" Liesl asked, her voice shrill.

"That's why we're here!" Ava snapped. "Have you forgotten?"

"But, Ava, what will they do to Max? What if the Israelis round up the whole family? What if—"

Ava raised a quieting hand, her other tight around the phone. "Liesl, calm down and think!" The agent was almost shouting through a whisper. "This is critical information. You have no idea how critical." She glared at Liesl. "Remember what I once told you about information? It's this country's greatest weapon."

Liesl wondered what Cade would say about that. Would he declare that God was their nation's greatest defender? Still, didn't God instill wisdom and might in his people to use in their own defense? Instill information?

"Now, wait for me here," Ava ordered, then left the kitchen by an outside door. She returned a few moments later.

"You already called Langley?" Liesl asked with surprise.

"All they needed was the name. Now, they're waiting to debrief us. We'll leave immediately."

"Wait!" Liesl pulled her cell phone from her pocket. Ava looked at the phone as if it were a live grenade. "I . . . I have to warn Max."

"You'll do no such thing!" Ava barked and reached for the phone. But Liesl pulled it away.

In seconds, Agent Tucker burst through the door, his eyes darting between the two women. "What's going on?" he demanded.

"Stand down, Tucker. I just reported the name to Washington. We'll leave as soon as . . . as Liesl is ready."

He looked severely at Liesl, then down at the phone in her hand. "Do we have a problem here?"

"No, Tucker," Ava answered. "Now leave us alone for a few more minutes." When he was gone, she rounded on Liesl. "Listen to me. Your friendship with Max does not override national security. And it certainly isn't going to preempt this operation! Now give me your phone."

Liesl glared at her. "Are you serious? You don't trust me?"

"I don't trust your emotions. Now give it to me or I'll have to take it from you. And, if I think you're about to jeopardize the capture of this informant, I'll have to sequester you and let other authorities decide your fate."

Shaken by the verbal affront, Liesl was about to rail against yet another assertion that she might betray her country, when the phone in her hand rang. She looked down at the caller ID, then stumbled backward.

The signal blazed across the man's screen and he knew he'd have to act quickly. He opened his briefcase and pulled the phone from beneath the false bottom, then got up and walked outside. First the number, then the password. After a brief patch-through from the Russian embassy, Pavel Andreyev picked up in Moscow.

"They have it!" the man announced.

"When?" Andreyev asked.

"Maybe twenty minutes ago."

A pause. "You know the escape route, if you need it."

"And the Israeli?"

"We pulled him after your last call. Too risky to stay longer. He's leaving immediately."

"With the documents?"

"Yes, he has them," Andreyev answered. "Now, you know what to do." The call ended.

Before reentering the building, the man paused at the sound of a helicopter. Marine One was just landing on the South Lawn. President Noland emerged and headed up the lawn at his usual trot, looking past the crush of media and noticing the man just outside the West Wing. When the president waved at him, the man returned the friendly gesture, then stepped back inside.

Chapter 34

Max Morozov thought he would come out of his skin before the rehearsal ended. As the Israel Philharmonic glided into the delicate passage of a Beethoven symphony, Zubin Mehta's baton stroked the air as if it were fine silk. But Max's bow fairly strafed his violin's strings, drawing a harsh glare from the legendary conductor.

Max couldn't rein in the fear, though. Not this time. Something at home was terribly wrong. Though home, for Max, had never been right. Not with the abuse his father had heaped on him and his mother through the years, the man's frequent and unexplained travel, his scathing disapproval of his gentle, artistic son. And certainly not with the phone calls and visits from strangers in the middle of the night. Max had demanded to know who they were only one time. The brutality of his father's response had ended any further inquiries.

Soon after, Max had tried to log on to his father's home computer, searching for evidence of the man's late-night activities. It must have tripped a security-breach alarm somewhere, because moments later, his father tore into the room and struck him repeatedly.

In the last few months, his father's perennial scowl had grown even darker. He rarely left his office in the basement of their elegant Tel Aviv house. He'd even begun to sleep nights in the subterranean suite of rooms he'd fashioned for himself many years ago. He'd rarely allowed anyone into his "chambers," as he called the gloomy detachment, even insisting on cleaning the area himself. He'd excused this behavior to his wife as a necessary escape from his stressful position with the government.

In the last week, though, Max had seen something in his father he'd never seen before. Alarm. It was hard to believe anything could frighten the aggressive, physically imposing man whom Max had never called anything but *father*. But something had happened to the man. The conversation Max had overheard the day before confirmed it.

Yesterday, two of Max's students had canceled their afternoon violin lessons, and he'd left his studio early. He looked forward to a few leisurely hours with the house to himself. His father would be at work and his mother at the art classes that seemed to sustain her within the fractured marriage. It was because of her and her failing resistance to his father's cruel tyranny that Max had moved back into the family home. Reluctantly, he'd sublet his high-rise apartment overlooking the Mediterranean, forsaking his blessed separation from his father for whatever comfort and protection he might provide for his mother.

When he reached his car in the parking lot, he discovered a flat tire. Rather than waste a free afternoon, he decided to fix it later and welcomed the long walk home on this bright autumn day.

He'd just settled into a living room chair to catch up on some reading, when he was surprised to see his father's car pull into the driveway, hours before he'd normally be home. He listened as the outside door to the basement opened and closed. It occurred to Max that since his own car wasn't in the driveway, his father wouldn't realize Max was home. That shouldn't have mattered. But when he heard a phone ring downstairs and the tone of his father's answering voice, something told Max to remain undetected and pay attention.

He slipped off his shoes and moved slowly toward the door that led to the basement, the heavy soundproof door his father had installed "to block the noise of that cursed violin," he'd claimed. The door wasn't often ajar, as it was now. Through the slight opening, Max clearly heard his father's staccato responses to an unknown caller:

"No code yet?"

"When will you know?"

"If that happens, how long will I have?"

"No, I'll be ready."

"Family?" He chuckled. "What family?"

Max's stomach tightened, but he didn't move, afraid the floor would creak.

After a lengthy silence, his father's voice spiked.

"You don't threaten me, Pavel! I've got backup files on everything I know about the summit op. You'll never find them, but I'll make sure others will."

Another long silence. "That's better. That's what I want to hear. You call me the instant you know something."

There was no good-bye, just the pounding of a fist against a wall below. Moments later, Max heard boxes dragged across the floor and file drawers opened and slammed. Soon, a shredder cranked up and sliced through what must have been a great many papers.

Then another call, this one outgoing.

"Saeed," his father said, "get the boat ready."

"No, just me."

"Wait for my call. Maybe soon."

Who is Saeed? Max wondered. *What's happening?*

Max finally heard the basement door below open. When he was reasonably sure his father was outside, Max moved cautiously toward the window overlooking the drive. He watched as his father placed an aluminum briefcase in the backseat. Before the man could return to the house. Max raced upstairs to his room, scolding himself for hiding like a child. But this was no time to encounter his father.

A few minutes later, though, the car and its driver were gone. Max sprang from the bedroom and headed toward the basement, thankful that the door was still open. *He must have been in a terrible hurry to have overlooked the door.* At the bottom of the stairs, Max stopped and looked around. He hadn't seen the place in almost a year, not since his father had invited him down there to open Max's birthday gift. It had been a pair of boxing gloves, a cold slap at the masculinity the elder Maxum Morozov found lacking in his "fiddle playing" son. Max shoved the pain back into the dark hole inside him and pushed off into the forbidding room.

On the surface, it appeared as usual, bereft of anything familial. No photos of father and son on a fishing trip or any other trip, none of a smiling wife. Everything was neat and orderly, except the laptop was missing, along with whatever had been shredded. And a couple of open file drawers were empty. Others, though, still held an assortment of papers that Max now searched hurriedly, not knowing when his father might return. Nothing jumped out at Max, not even the confirmation of a recent flight to Rome. Maxum, the father, was always spending money, the source of which his wife dared not question. But Max knew his mother snooped whenever she could. She'd confided in Max often enough about receipts she'd found for five-star hotels in far-flung places. And expensive jewelry that she'd never seen.

So the flight to Rome raised no flags. But the small slip of paper bearing next-day confirmation for the air hop from Rome to Corsica gripped Max like a vice. *He went back?*

When Max was a teenager, he and his parents had vacationed in Calvi, Corsica, one summer, staying in a small seaside hotel. It was rare the family went anywhere together, so the details of the trip were still vivid. At a local gallery, Max and his mother met a potter, an elderly man who lived in Calvi but kept a studio in the remote, mountaintop village of Sant'Antonino. When he invited the three Morozovs to spend a day with him there, Max's father went begrudgingly, much preferring to fish. But soon after they arrived in the village, Max witnessed an indisputable uncoiling in his father. As the four of them roamed the ancient hamlet and the wind-swept fields that ambled away from it, his father's enchantment with the place grew palpable, the metamorphosis incomprehensible. Max heard his father laugh at the silly games of a few village children. He watched as his father tried his hand at the potter's wheel and reacted like a gleeful child, himself, when the clay responded to his touch and a small bowl took shape. Later, their host took them just outside the village wall to an abandoned olive press inside a mountain cave. Nearby was the stone cottage once occupied by the family who'd run the press centuries ago. It stood vacant, but habitable.

To everyone's surprise, Max's father asked if his family could spend a few nights in the cottage. The potter arranged for it, and it was done. It was an idyllic time for them all. There were no arguments, no shameful outbursts, only adventure and sweet isolation from the things that usually tore at them. Years later, young Max returned alone to the little cottage. Then again, and again, searching for his own peace and contentment. He'd once invited his father to come along, but the man seemed to have forgotten his earlier affection for the place. In time, Max, too, stopped his sojourns to the village.

As he held the small paper in his hands, he wondered what had drawn his father back there, and how many times he'd returned. He couldn't afford to wonder long, though. He heard a car wheel sharply into the driveway and the engine die. Max flew into a frenzy. He slammed the file drawers shut, turned off the light and raced up the stairs, uncertain whether to leave the hall door open as he'd found it, or closed as his father usually kept it. He decided to close it.

When he heard the basement door below open, Max flew out the back door of the house, ran down alleys, and exited the neighborhood on foot. He wanted no questions about his whereabouts that unexplainable afternoon. He would return to his car, fix the tire, and arrive back home at his usual time. When he did, he found his mother cooking and his father ensconced, as usual, in the basement—as if nothing unusual had occurred that afternoon.

But now, nearly twenty-four hours later, Max was desperate to leave the auditorium and get home. His mother had called during a break in rehearsal, pleading for him to come right away. His father had taken a call during their early dinner, then immediately bolted upstairs, she'd reported. He soon returned with an already-packed suitcase and spewed instructions for her not to speak to anyone about him without their lawyer present. He assured her that she and Max would be all right, but they shouldn't expect to see him again for a long time. He'd hugged her lightly, then said, "You're free now."

The instant Mehta dismissed his orchestra, Max rushed from Mann Auditorium to his parked car. He sped through downtown Tel Aviv toward an artery running to the exclusive neighborhood the Morozovs had lived in since Max was a small child. Twilight had ebbed by the time he arrived home. He found his mother in the upstairs master bedroom. "He'll never come back," she sobbed, unfolding her hand to show Max his father's wedding ring. "He left it on my night table."

Max folded her into his arms as she wept. He could almost feel the break in her, and realized how much she'd loved her husband. Max knew he should stay and comfort her, but the germ of suspicion, planted in him the day before, now spread with dreadful certainty. His father had fallen, or marched willfully, into something he now had to escape from. And Max and his mother were about to pay the price. They had to get away.

"Mom, listen to me. We have to leave. Right now!"

"But why?" she asked, her voice cracking.

"Something I overheard yesterday. But there's no time to explain." *As if I could.* He looked at her tear-swollen eyes and regretted frightening her, but he had to make her understand. "Something's about to happen, Mom. I'm not sure what, but we've got to get out of here. I'm taking you to the airport." He paused to think. "You go to Aunt Neva's in New York and stay there. I'll join you later."

"Why can't you come with me?" she wailed.

Because I need to know what my father has done. But he answered, "I'll come soon, Mom. Now, pack a suitcase quickly and be ready to go when I get back."

"Where are you going?" she almost shrieked. "Don't leave me!"

"Just to the basement. Now hurry!"

He rushed down two flights to the basement, not knowing what he was looking for. Something, anything to make sense of this.

The room appeared as Max had left it the afternoon before, though his father had worked there late into the night. Doing what? *What did he ever do down here?* The computer was still missing, the two file drawers still empty, and the others much as he'd left them. But he would look again. Of the three remaining drawers, he searched the first and moved on to the second, opening its first manila file. As he had with the others, he flipped quickly through the pages, lots of them with Ministry of Defense letterhead, but nothing that looked classified or forbidding. He read a letter from the ministry director to his father commending him for his careful documentation of armament purchase and movement. There was a note from his secretary, dated two weeks ago, reminding him of an appointment last week. Just an ordinary memo in her neat, boxy hand. Max flipped the small note over and was about to slip it back into the file, when his father's large, scrawling letters jumped out at him. Letters of a name that didn't belong. Not here. Not Liesl's name! His mind spun like a roulette wheel waiting for the ball of reason to drop into place. For what possible reason would his father write her name, especially on a note he'd just received two weeks ago. Though Max had phoned her a few months ago, he hadn't seen her in over a year, at a concert she gave in Jerusalem. They'd had dinner and talked long about their careers, but nothing more. There had never been anything more, and never would be.

This is crazy! But he couldn't linger another moment. He shoved the note into his jacket pocket and raced upstairs to his bedroom. He paused at his mother's door and was relieved to see her scurrying to pack.

Fifteen minutes later, mother and son locked the house and climbed into Max's small car with their suitcases.

As he pulled out of the neighborhood, he noticed a set of lights behind him but they soon merged with countless others on the highway to the airport.

At Ben Gurion International Airport, Max was alert to anyone taking undue interest in them. With no plane reservation, he considered it a minor miracle that the El Al flight to New York, leaving in an hour, had a few empty seats, even after all standbys were accommodated. After a rush of documentation and a sprint to the gate, he kissed his mother's cheek and watched her disappear into the passenger corridor. Though it wasn't his habit to pray, having long forsaken the faith of his fathers, he issued a silent petition to the God he hoped was somewhere near, asking that no one would be waiting to apprehend his mother at JFK in New York. And that, as his father had told her, she would be free, indeed, of his menacing reach.

The prayer still lightly on his lips, Max realized he'd stood in one place too long. He glanced quickly about but saw no one taking obvious note of him. Still, he had to get somewhere and just . . . think. How did the pieces fit? What was the whole he needed to see?

He spotted an empty table in the back corner of a nearby coffee shop and headed for it, making the obligatory beverage purchase on the way. Hunched protectively over his father's Rome and Corsica flight confirmations and the note with Liesl's name on the back, his mind whirled through possible scenarios. He could see her in the Moscow apartment of Vadim Fedorovsky, when they'd overheard the conversation with Devoe, one that had included the words *our friend in Washington*. He remembered Liesl telling him about the CIA questioning her after Devoe's murder. To the mix, Max added the key words he recalled from his father's conversation the day before: code, threaten, summit op, backup files, and someone named Pavel. A Russian name. And suddenly, the roulette ball dropped with resounding clarity into the wheel. Max wished it not to be true. *Not my father. Not a spy!*

Then *backup files* returned to mind. Something his father had hidden, something he used as a weapon when threatened during that overheard conversation. Max looked down at the flight ticket to Corsica and he suddenly knew where, if not what, the backups were. As appalling as it was, he was now convinced his father had hidden something critical on the island of Corsica. Instantly, the image of the cottage loomed before him, alternating with the lovely face of his longtime friend.

What's happened to Liesl? What does she know about this? He instinctively reached for his cell phone, then dropped it back into his pocket. *Not here.* He got up, left his untouched coffee, and slipped into the current of travelers on the concourse. He hadn't gotten far, though, when he caught the eye of a man watching him from the doorway of a nearby store. Nothing about him was familiar to Max, not the slicked-back black hair, the flat-cheeked face. It was the abrupt movement the man made toward him that now launched Max into full stride down the concourse.

This can't be happening! But a stolen glance over his shoulder was all it took to convince him otherwise. The man was now weaving quickly through the crowd, his eyes locked on Max.

Surely the guy knew he was in one of the most heavily guarded airports in the world. Maybe he was one of the guards, but Max didn't think so. Still, even Israeli security posed a threat to Max, who didn't know the nature of his father's predicament or the price possibly on Max's own head. There was no one to trust but himself. And maybe Liesl, if he could stop long enough to call her.

Not wanting to risk a full run and attract the attention of the guards, Max speed-walked through the crowds. He was thankful he'd left his cumbersome suitcase in the car. Another glance and he saw the man was closing the distance quickly. Max rushed around the next corner and immediately ducked into a bookstore that appeared to have a front and back entrance. He was wrong. It was a dead-end alcove, except for one thing. A storeroom. Grabbing a book from the shelf and holding it to his face, he inched toward the door and tried the knob. It turned and in seconds he'd slipped inside and closed the door behind him. He held his breath and waited, half expecting either a clerk or his pursuer to fling open the door. But that didn't happen. He looked around the crowded room full of unopened boxes and stacks of newspapers. Then he noticed a narrow spiral of stairs. He climbed them quickly to an even smaller room above. He collapsed his thin frame into a squat behind more boxes and pulled out his phone.

Chapter 35

*I*nside the kitchen at Charleston's Naval Weapons Station, the two women had squared off yet again. After Ava's blistering reprimand, implying, as Liesl interpreted it, that she cared nothing for her country's security, Liesl had been ready to hurl an angry retort and flee the room when her cell phone rang. The caller ID replaced that anger with shock.

Now leaning against the wall for support, Liesl looked at Ava. "It's Max!"

"Switch to speakerphone and answer it. I warn you to tell him nothing about this, Liesl."

Liesl summoned her breath. "Max!" she said too forcefully.

His words tumbled with urgency. "Liesl, listen to me. I can't talk long. Something's happening here. Someone's chasing me. It's got to have something to do with my father and whatever trouble he's in. I found your name in one of his files. Why, Liesl? Why would he have your name?"

Without taking her eyes from Ava, Liesl avoided the question and asked one of her own. "Max, what kind of trouble is your father in?"

There was silence on the other end. Then, "I'm not sure, but he's left my mother and told her not to talk to anyone without a lawyer."

"Are you safe where you are?" she asked.

"No. I can't stay and whoever that guy is has probably doubled back to look for me."

"What does he look like, Max?" Her question drew a cautioning hand from Ava.

Another pause. When he spoke again, he was guarded. "Liesl, tell me you can't possibly know who this guy is."

"Just tell me, Max," Liesl pressed.

"Skinny. Maybe fifty. Black hair plastered to his head. What's going on?"

Liesl squeezed her eyes tight and didn't answer.

"Liesl, are you there?"

"I'm here, Max. Tell me why you think your father's in trouble."

"I heard something yesterday," he said hesitantly. "A conversation he had when he didn't think I was home. He's hidden files or something that must be awfully important. And I think I know where they are. It's got something to do with a summit."

Suddenly, Ava took the phone from Liesl's hand. "Max, this is Ava Mullins of the U.S. Central Intelligence Agency. Please listen carefully to me. Are you using your own phone?"

There was no response.

"Max, it's okay," Liesl assured, hovering near the phone. "You can trust Ava." Just then, Liesl realized how foolish she'd been not to. She met Ava's eyes.

Still no answer from Max.

Liesl knew she had to keep him on the line. "Max, they're hunting for me too!" she cried.

"What?" Max blurted.

Ava jumped in again. "Max, answer me. Did you call us from your own phone?"

"Yes."

"Then do not—repeat—do not tell us where you are. Do not say anything else about your father on this phone. You're in great danger. You need to get to a phone that isn't yours and call back to Liesl's number as quickly as you can. After the first ring, it will reroute to a different number, as this call just did. Wait and I will answer. Can you manage this?"

"You mean ask a stranger for his phone?"

"If you have to. It's important that my next instructions to you aren't intercepted, as our conversation, even now, might be."

Max ended the call and quietly took the steps to the lower storeroom. He listened at the door, his mind furiously scanning for a plan of action. *I can't stay here. Someone's going to open that door any minute and scream for the police.* With his hand on the knob, he was conjuring an excuse to give whatever clerk might see him emerge, when his eye caught sight of a cord dangling behind some stacked boxes. He pushed them aside and discovered an old wall phone.

He picked up the receiver but heard no dial tone. He started punching different numbers until one launched the tone. From the contacts list on his cell phone, he pulled up Liesl's number and punched it into the wall phone. Just as the woman whom he hoped was truly a CIA agent had said, the first ring shifted to a series of beeps and buzzes. In seconds, though, she answered. "Identify yourself, please," she instructed.

"I'm still Max Morozov, the fiddler. Now tell me how to get out of here."

"Where are you?" Ava asked, back on speakerphone.

"In a storeroom at Ben Gurion International."

"Be specific."

He hesitated. "Hey, uh, can I talk to Liesl?"

"Max, I'm right here," Liesl said. "You've got to trust us. I'm pretty sure the man following you is a Russian KGB agent."

"A Russian . . . what?"

"Max, we don't have time to explain," Ava said. "You have to stay where you are. I'm going to arrange for airport police to come to you. They're not arresting you, though it will look that way to others. Put up no resistance. They'll safely escort you from the airport to a place you probably won't recognize. You'll be questioned by officers of Mossad. Do you understand?"

"Shh!" Max warned.

The door to the storeroom opened and Max clamped his hand over the receiver. He compressed himself even tighter behind the wall of boxes and held his breath. He glanced up at the empty cradle of the wall phone and willed its missing handset to draw no notice.

Near the door, someone slit open a box. He heard the slap of hardcover books stacked one on the other, and soon the person left and closed the door.

"It's okay," he informed. "But my legs are going numb. And, did you say Mossad?"

"Yes. Now tell me exactly where you are."

Over the next twenty minutes, Max stretched his limbs as much as he could without toppling the shield of boxes. Twice more, someone visited the storeroom and left. The cramps in Max's legs were growing severe. He had to stand up now or he wouldn't be able to later. Just as his head cleared the top layer of boxes, a commotion erupted outside. He could hear people exclaiming and the movement of many feet. Before he could drop to the floor again, the door burst open and two gun barrels froze him to the spot. Two fatigue-clad officers rushed toward him. "Mr. Morozov, come with us."

Max couldn't speak, but there was no need for conversation, it seemed. The men immediately pushed the boxes aside, strapped a bulletproof vest on Max, secured a helmet on his head, and led him into a scene he could never have imagined. The bookstore had been evacuated and a platoon of armed soldiers with automatic weapons—off the shoulders and positioned to fire— formed a semicircle around the entrance, all of them facing out from the store. His two escorts hustled him into the center of the human shield and the whole unit moved as one to the nearest exit, where two vans waited.

Evgeny Kozlov left the Ben Gurion terminal by another exit. Hurrying to his car, he reached for his phone.

"The Israeli army just made off with our boy. You told me to keep an eye on him, and it was just luck that I arrived at his house in time to see his car leave. What's going on?"

"Did he see you?" Vadim Fedorovsky demanded.

Kozlov knew he had, that he'd frightened the younger Morozov, who'd obviously called for help. But soldiers? What could he have told the authorities to warrant a military response? "Of course not," Kozlov lied. "But this proves your suspicions. He knows far more about his father's business than we thought. Evidently enough to make him extremely valuable to the Israelis. But how did they know where he was?"

"Perhaps Washington can answer that."

It was nearly eight that night when Max was driven to a walled bunker outside of town and led into a sweep of austere rooms, each one, it seemed, outfitted with as many uplinking, downloading communications devices as he'd ever seen in photos of space shuttles. He was finally relieved of his protective gear and directed to a seat inside one of the rooms.

Soon, he had recited the whole conversation he'd overheard between his father and someone named Pavel. His audience was a General Lapin and two other officers of Mossad. After the lurid picture of his father's treason against Israel had been painted for him, Max felt sick. It was the same chronic illness of isolation from his father, a brokenness he'd suffered for so long that this latest evidence of his father's treachery seemed just another waypoint along the path. Max's music and an acquired levity toward life had sustained him so far. But now, how did one process such betrayal and mask its odor? He couldn't do it anymore.

And then, the boom of reality fell hard upon him. He suddenly thought of the young men he'd grown up with, those who'd gone to war for Israel, and those who never returned. Had his father's subversion caused their deaths? Could he bear knowing it had?

Max lowered his head into his hands and wept. He didn't care who witnessed it. His father would have slapped him, as he'd done before. "No son of mine will shed the tears of a girl," he'd sworn before each blow to young Max's face.

But there was no time for comforting the distraught musician. As quickly as Max composed himself, the Israeli officers' questions fired rapidly. Max struggled to answer each one as best he could. No, he'd never suspected his father of spying. Yes, there'd been late-night visitors to his house. No, he'd never seen them, but his mother had. Yes, he'd put her on a plane to New York.

The questioning became more intense. No, he had no further knowledge of anything about a summit or the backups his father had said no one would ever find. But yes, he felt certain he knew where they were.

Chapter 36

By 2:00 PM Washington time—8:00 PM in Israel—the Oval Office had become an intelligence camp with Noland's Chief of Staff Hank Bessinger, CIA Director Eric Stone, Deputy Secretary of State Lorraine Mercin, FBI Special Agent Mark Delaney, and Ben Hafner huddled over incoming reports from Israel. The discovery of the Israeli mole's identity had ignited a furor, mostly from what the man's son had overheard. The word *summit* had tripped alarms on three continents. American and Israeli intelligence were now scrambling to uncover the "summit op" Maxum Morozov Sr. had spoken of in his secret chambers. This confirmed the assassination chatter the CIA had picked up earlier.

At that moment, the White House was seeking clearance from the French government to land an Israeli military transport on Corsican soil, more specifically, the northwest port of Calvi. From there, the mountain village of Sant'Antonino was just a short helicopter flight.

Rushing back to his office to retrieve more files from his safe, Ben Hafner stopped in Ted Shadlaw's doorway. "You'd better pull up all we've got on Calvi, Corsica. Have it ready for me as quickly as possible." He looked into the grave face of his longtime aide. "Is something wrong?"

"Not at all, sir. I'll get that for you."

Ten minutes later, Ben thought of something else he needed and headed back to Ted's office. He was surprised to find the aide gone. Rather than wait for him to return, he started searching through a pile of file folders stacked on top of the desk. Near the bottom of the pile, Ben found something that shouldn't have been there—a dossier on himself. Ben flipped through pages of reports on every school he'd ever attended, grades he'd made, old girlfriends, club memberships. And there it was. The thing he'd once carefully buried: that turbulent time in a secret society of young communist sympathizers who liked to call themselves the Boston Bolsheviks. During his freshman year at Harvard, Ben had fallen hard for one of its members, Evie Siegred, whose pounding mantra was the reformation of the United States into a land of collectives and shared wealth. He'd even moved into her Boston commune where he'd encountered his first taste of subversion. He'd narrowly escaped the group's midnight assault on a downtown federal courthouse, falling to the rear of the raucous assembly and fleeing before the violence began.

Ben turned another page of the file and found a handwritten letter from that same girl, dated just two months ago. In it was a rambling, almost incoherent account of Ben's earlier association with her and her organization, even his "involvement" in the courthouse raid that had landed her and two others in prison.

Clipped together at the back of the file were a handful of photographs: his brother-in-law protesting outside Israel's Knesset, bloodied and running from police, leaving an Israeli courthouse in the custody of a military escort. And one more: Ben and his brother-in-law arm in arm, both in camouflage and holding automatic weapons.

Ben lingered as long as he dared over the dossier, then slammed it shut and hurried away from Ted's office. There wasn't a moment to lose.

He called the president's secretary and excused himself for the next hour, assuring her he'd be close by should the president need him. Quickly, he launched a flurry of phone calls from his office, then dug into his staff's personnel files. One of the last calls he made before returning to the Oval Office was to Evie Siegred.

The first drops of an afternoon shower splattered the man's shoes as he stepped outside his office and dialed the number. When Pavel Andreyev answered, the man said, "It's Calvi, Corsica. That's all I know for now." He pocketed the cell phone and hurried back to his task.

Later that afternoon, Ben left the Oval Office and returned to Ted's glassed-in cubicle, finding him bent over his computer keyboard. "There's been a new break in intelligence from Israel," Ben told him, glancing at the pile of folders still stacked where Ben had left them. "It seems our mole might have hidden another set of backup files in a seaside house just north of Haifa, Israel. Here's the location." Making minimal eye contact, Ben handed a memo bearing the house's coordinates to Ted. "See what you can find out about the area. We'll be launching another search party there."

When Ben reentered the Oval Office, President Noland was just ending a call from the French president's office and issuing a silent go-ahead signal to the room. CIA Director Eric Stone immediately authorized his team, already on the ground in Tel Aviv, to join the Israeli commando unit on their mission.

"Sir, I'd like to return to Langley, where I can more closely monitor developments," Stone said.

"Of course," Noland replied. "You may all go, but keep me informed at every turn." He waved them on to their duties.

"Except you, Ben. I need to talk to you."

Chapter 37

When Liesl and Ava finally emerged from the kitchen, Cade, Ian, and Agent Tucker were standing outside talking with the navy guards. At first sight of Liesl through the window, Cade hurried back inside.

Liesl reached for him and he embraced her. "This just isn't going to end," she groaned.

"What do you mean?"

"The burden has passed from me to—"

"To someone else," Ava jumped in, fixing Liesl with a warning eye.

"So you can't tell me," Cade said to Liesl. "That's okay. All I need to know is that you're safe now."

"Let's just say that there's much more we have to learn about developments in Israel," Ava informed them.

"What does that mean?" Cade asked.

"It means I need to get Liesl back to Washington immediately and continue security for her until . . . until certain events have passed and we feel reasonably sure she's no longer of interest to—"

"Come on, Ava," Cade broke in impatiently. "Spit it out. Is she in danger or not?"

Liesl's attention ricocheted from one to the other until she could stand it no more. "Whether I am or not isn't what matters now, is it?" She looked directly at Ava. "I have behaved like a spoiled, whining child, unable to see anyone's needs but my own. I'm sorry for that."

To Cade, she said, "Someone I care about, a good friend, is in desperate trouble at this moment. There's more to this whole thing than we knew, and now he's stepped innocently into the midst of it, whatever 'it' is." She turned back to Ava. "I'll do whatever I need to."

Ava looked as if she'd witnessed a birth. Liesl understood the reaction, but couldn't explain the seismic shift in her focus from her own wounded self to others. Many, many others. She'd just glimpsed a global impact of what Max and those now surrounding him were desperate to find. Something larger than her world. Something disastrous, she sensed, and imminent. Just then, though, she remembered what her aunt Bess used to quote to her. It was the Lord saying, "In this world, you will have trouble. But take heart! I have overcome the world." *Lord, are you here?*

She looked into Cade's eyes and sensed a peace that made no sense to her. In the midst of all this, how can there be peace? "I have to go back to Washington," she told him. "Will you come with me? Ian too?"

"I don't think that's advisable," Ava said, looking long and hard at Cade. "However, it seems we've already recruited you, haven't we? So, come if you want. But tell me now. I've got a plane ride to arrange."

Cade searched Liesl's face. "Are you sure?" he asked.

She slipped her arm around Cade and rested quietly against his side.

"I'd call that an affirmative," Ava said dryly.

"But, Ava, I have to go back to the house before we leave," Liesl said, her arm still snug around Cade.

"That's not possible, Liesl. I'm sorry. We just lost two officers at your house. We're not losing anybody else." She looked quickly at Cade. "They found the other guy in the backyard. They'd both been shot at close range; silencer, no doubt."

"As for gear," Ava continued, "I'm afraid whatever you left in the boat will have to do you for the trip."

Just then, the door opened and Ian lumbered in, followed by Agent Tucker. "How come you leave us standing out there with two of the most boring young fellas I ever met? They didn't have enough words between them to fill a thimble. So, what's up?"

Ava shook her head and laughed. "How'd you like to go to Washington, Ian?"

"Well, I don't think you and me have known each other long enough, do you?"

Ava threw up her hands. "Cade, you handle this one. I've got phone calls to make, then we'll head back to the landing. Oh, and you'll need to call your friend to pick up his boat after we leave. That ought to go over well." She grimaced.

After following the small cruiser from the island, through the harbor, and up the Ashley River before dawn that Tuesday morning, the man had watched the foursome transfer to a waiting Blazer. When they'd gone, he'd beached his boat against a sandy bank around a turn in the river, and walked back to the landing to wait for their return. He touched the wound to his arm through his camouflage jacket and winced.

Many hours later, he was about to forsake his vigil when he heard the crunch of tires on the dirt road leading to the landing. He crouched behind a thicket of wild shrubs and lifted his binoculars. She was the last one to emerge from the second of three unmarked cars. She'd pulled a denim cap over her hair, and dark glasses covered much of her face. He adjusted his lenses and let them linger on her as she moved between the armed men surrounding her.

They were all in a hurry, and, to his surprise, seemed to have no intention of leaving in the boat. Instead, they removed gear from inside it, climbed quickly back into their cars, and in a fit of dust, disappeared down the road.

He slammed his fist into the ground.

Chapter 38

Just before daybreak on Wednesday, the small Israeli jet approached Calvi, Corsica. Hunched over inside the plane, Max was reeling with the speed at which his life careened far from the predictable, metronomic rhythm of a Beethoven symphony. From the moment the landing gear thumped back inside the jet on takeoff from Tel Aviv, he felt as though he were hurtling into a realm from which he would never return. But he dared not exhibit a breakdown in composure before the gritty soldiers on board.

Mercifully, it wasn't long before the lights of Calvi appeared on the horizon. At first sight of them, he pushed aside his fears to reach back for the days he'd wandered aimlessly along the cobbled paths that veined throughout the scenic fortress. Soon, Max could see the town's rocky promontory, which rose in stark contrast to the sleek yachts stretched sleepily in the marina below.

After landing, Max was immediately hustled onto a helicopter for the short hop to Sant'Antonino. *I shouldn't be coming back like this*, he brooded. It should be with a sanguine heart and a Stradivarius, not a chopper full of Uzis. It had been nearly ten years since he'd visited the windswept village that perched so contentedly above the Mediterranean. Its red-tiled rooftops strung with laundry as colorful as ships' flags, Sant'Antonino didn't care about propriety or the things of the world. Up here where vapors of time never evaporated, it was always yesterday and never tomorrow. Always Medieval windowsills cradling geraniums. Always the uneven, granite thresholds as inviting as warm hearths. But now, this enchanted place had been violated by his father's treachery.

Max had no idea why his hunch about his father's hiding place for the backups to a "summit op" was enough to launch a middle-of-the-night bolt for this mountaintop. What summit? What op? It wasn't for him to know, evidently. No one had bothered to explain the urgency, only implement it. He did know that the French president himself had authorized this joint Israeli-American mission, at the risk of alarming the villagers and whatever tourists had wandered into peace-loving Sant'Antonino. He also knew that arrangements had been made to search the old stone cottage.

Like a monstrous dragonfly, the helo alighted on a barren field outside the walled village, which capped the granite dome of the mountain. To the east, a new day had just pushed off the horizon, tossing light beams like candy along its parade route. Max gazed forlornly at the spectacle that had always lifted him with its promise of something new and good. But not now. Today, he believed, the sun would drag him crashing into the west with no hope of resurrection. How could he survive bearing the deeds, the very name, of a traitor?

The rotors still slashing into the innocent morning, Israeli Capt. Moshe Stiegle signaled for Max to stay put as the soldiers sprang to the ground and secured the area. There remained the possibility that the Russians had learned the location of the elder Morozov's hidden files, if this, indeed, was their resting place.

Stiegle returned for Max, tugging him down into a crouched sprint from beneath the spinning blades. Once clear, Max led the soldiers away from the village, down a rugged path toward one of many olive groves rooted in rocky soil that seemed impossibly fertile.

As the sky brightened, the path took a turn around a bald knob and delivered the party straight to the small cottage. "This is it," Max announced, not taking his eyes from the simple little refuge.

Capt. Stiegle's men fanned out as he tried the door and found it locked. The man who owned it had instructed him to find the key lodged in a crack of the foundation. Capt. Stiegle located the key quickly and went inside, Max on his heels.

"Where do we begin?" he asked Max, his words hurried.

Max looked around, pleased to see that little had changed. He wondered if his father had stayed here on his recent visit, but decided that was unlikely. The beds in the corner of the only room were both missing mattresses. Dust covered the primitive, rough-hewn tables and chairs. The kitchen sink was rusted. The curtains with the hand-tatted lace trim that his mother had found so charming had shredded in the harsh, unfiltered sun.

His eyes rested on the fireplace, now black with soot. He walked to it and ran his hands over the loosely stacked stones. "Short of dismantling the place, I guess we'll just have to poke and pry into every crevice we can," he advised. And so they did, inside and out, but found nothing remotely close to classified documents, CDs, photos, tapes, or whatever receptacle Maxum Morozov Sr. had used to store the evidence that would guarantee safety from his Russian handlers, those who might be inclined to trap and kill their pet mole after his services ended.

"There's a stable of sorts out back," Max informed. "The owner used to keep a donkey there." He caught Capt. Stiegle's raised brow. "People still ride donkeys up to the village," Max explained. "Cars aren't allowed inside the walls. The owner left his at the base of the mountain and donkey'ed up. I've done it too. Not a bad mode of travel."

"Show me the stable," Capt. Stiegle urged impatiently, showing no further interest in donkeys.

The shelter, like the cottage, had been long abandoned. There was little to search but the rafters above and the ground. Two of Capt. Stiegle's men scouted for any sign of freshly turned earth, anything lodged in the rafters or slid under a trough. Growing uncomfortable with the silent, questioning darts from Capt. Stiegle's eyes, Max sank to the ground and stared into the dry, fall-withered grass. He closed his eyes to see his father in this place, if this was, indeed, the terminus of his recent flight to Corsica. *It's got to be. He came here. I know he did. To hide something. Where?*

His eyes still closed, he envisioned that summer when his family had been happy in this place. For just a short while, his father seemed to have left his demons behind. Max remembered him running each morning, up and down the lane to the cottage as if reveling in a freedom that he knew couldn't last. On one of the rare occasions when his father had invited him to come too, Max had run alongside the man. It had begun to rain, and his father led him into the . . .

Max shot up from the ground. "This way!" he called to Capt. Stiegle. His legs now charged with renewed certainty, Max tore into the lane, just as his father had done. As he ran even farther from the village, the remainder of that long-ago morning played out in his mind. He saw his father running ahead, drenched in the cool rain, heading straight for the ancient cave that housed an olive press—the cave now dead ahead.

As if running alone, Max was lost in the memory. He saw his father run into the cave, all the way to the back where the massive crushing mill had been installed centuries ago. Max saw him stop and lean over the pit inside the mill, run his hand over the millstone that had once rolled like a leaden doughnut over the crushing stone, squeezing the oils from the fruits of the olive groves outside.

As the phantom video kept playing in his mind, Max watched his father pant, out of breath but strangely exhilarated by the carefree dash through the rain. He'd even clapped a hand on young Max's shoulder and drawn the boy into the only hug Max could recall receiving from his father. Then the man released him and turned his attention to the ruins of the press. He'd explained how it worked to Max, how the wooden axle slipped into the hole of the millstone, then was harnessed to an animal, probably a donkey. As it walked the millstone around its orbit, the first sweet oil of the fruits flowed through the spout. *The spout.*

Leaving some of his men at the entrance to the cave, Capt. Stiegle and two others looked on as Max approached the broken stones that formed a smooth, flat spout.

"I came here once with my father," Max said as he removed half of the cracked spout. "He tried to figure out what had caused the spout to break in two." Max removed the other half of the spout and stood back. The sand beneath was smooth. Too smooth. Capt. Stiegle saw it too.

"Shovel!" he shouted to one of the men outside. Moments later, the sound of metal on metal pinged through the cave, and Capt. Stiegle withdrew a flat, stainless steel box from its recent burial spot.

Chapter 39

At the same time Max led the search party into the cave on Corsica, a speeding car bore down on a seaside house on the outskirts of Haifa, Israel. The five armed men inside had been given the same orders as those in the cave: find Maxum Morozov's summit-op files. Except for one thing: the men in the car had received their orders from Pavel Andreyev in Moscow.

The sky was barely tinged by morning when the car slowed to its cautious approach. The driver cut the engine, and the men sat quietly for a moment, scanning the grounds of the modest, concrete-block house sitting alone on this scarcely populated beach. There was no light inside or out. No sound or movement from any direction.

Four doors opened and the men fanned out to scout their surroundings. After severing the lock on the back door, three of them stole quietly into the house, leaving the other two to patrol outside. Simultaneously, though, the outside guards fell to the ground, a tranquilizer dart embedded in each neck.

Inside the house, flashlight beams hatched through the darkness as the men began their hunt, much like their brethren had done at Eugenia Devoe's house in Canada. The clamor of their search grew so intense, they didn't hear the first creak of the attic floor above an upstairs bedroom, nor the ensuing footsteps down the stairs. The stealth of their attackers was so complete, the Russian agents had only an instant to pivot before the first darts hit.

Only after the five sedated agents were loaded like logs into the back of a van, did the Israeli commando leader report to Tel Aviv.

At that point, it was almost midnight in Washington, where President Noland waited alone in the Oval Office for the call. When it came, a spokesman for Israeli Prime Minister Yoni Shulman notified the president that five Russian agents had been captured inside the house in Haifa.

When the call ended, the president turned off his desk lamp and sat back in his chair, still and mournful. It was nearly one in the morning before he finally returned to the residence.

Later that Wednesday morning, when the West Wing first stirred with life, President Noland summoned Ben Hafner to his office and told him what had happened at the Haifa house, that someone had tipped the Russians to the possible location of the mole's files.

Ben's whole body felt leaden, his mind drained of defenses. He knew what would come next.

A team of security officers assembled discreetly outside the Oval Office. Inside, Ben sat on a sofa staring at a surveillance photo of the Haifa beach house. The president sat in a nearby arm chair. And they waited.

Soon, Noland's secretary opened the door and ushered Ted Shadlaw into the office—Ben's trusted aide and frequent confidant, the one who'd gathered the damning evidence on his boss.

"Sit down, Ted," Noland instructed.

Ted moved to the sofa opposite Ben, who found it odd that he couldn't read his aide's face, the familiar eyes, which now avoided Ben's.

"Ted," Noland began, "you should know that Russian agents just broke into the house near Haifa, Israel, in a frantic search for something. The Morozov files, no doubt."

Ted seemed to wait for the rest of the report, but finally concluded on his own, "So the mole must have confessed to the Russians that he'd hidden them there."

"That's not likely," Ben said calmly, his eyes riveted on Ted.

"Why not?" Ted replied, his focus now hot on Ben.

"It's not likely, Ted, because Maxum Morozov has never been to the house in Haifa. You see, it's *my* house. My Israeli family's vacation home." He paused to search the stricken face before him. "No one would have directed the Russians to that house . . . but you."

An ashen cloud swept over Ted's face. He uttered no sound.

"We fed you a lie because we had to know if it was true, Ted," Ben continued. "True if all those weighty deposits we just discovered in your bank account had come from Moscow. If all along, you'd been alerting the Russians of our every move. Of when the sonata wasn't found. When it was. And where the Russians should search for Morozov's files."

Ted was deathly still.

"And by the way," Ben pressed, "I found the dossier you prepared on me. A lot of trouble for nothing. The president knew all about that brief madness of mine at Harvard. And if you thought a letter from Evie Siegred would amount to anything, you missed the significance of her return address. It's a halfway house for people who've lost their mental bearings. She's been there for years.

"Were you going to frame me for your crime, Ted? Did you know they'd tried to recruit me too? They would have played us both, and neither of us would have known about the other." Agony turned to surprise on Ted's face. "But the president knows all about that too," Ben added. "I immediately reported their first contact with me. And now, the FBI is having to protect my family." Ben paused to let that soak in. "They threatened my wife and kids, Ted. Do you think they wouldn't have done the same to yours if you ever refused them?"

Ted's hollowed eyes barely lifted toward Ben. "It was all the money Julie and I would ever need." That was all he said.

President Noland walked to his desk and pressed a button on his phone. "Mr. Shadlaw is ready to go."

Chapter 40

The helicopter lifted high over the thistled fields outside the walls of Sant'Antonino. From the air, the village looked like a mosaic of tile rooftops grouted by pebbled paths. Max wished to stay and heal, if he ever would.

He looked at the metal box cradled in Capt. Stiegle's arms. The soldier held it so stoically, as if it were a sarcophagus of priceless antiquity. It was a casket, all right; one holding the ashes of his family. Max knew that something inside it, though, was critical to his country, maybe others. He couldn't imagine what his father had brought down on them all. It seemed that Capt. Stiegle didn't either. After prying the lock from the box, he'd only glanced through the contents before ordering everyone back to the chopper. Max hadn't seen him open the box again.

When they landed a short time later at U.S. Army Garrison Livorno in Italy, they were met on the tarmac by two armored vehicles and whisked away to a low-profile building one might mistake for a small warehouse. Once inside, though, they took an elevator down to a subterranean command post every bit as imposing as the one he'd just left in Israel. Max wondered at what havoc could be wreaked from such a place, a situation room, they called it—a place surely wired to the nerve endings of the world. What was a mild-mannered violinist doing here?

As Capt. Stiegle was led into the inner sanctum of the place, Max was instructed to wait outside in a small anteroom. When the door closed in front of him, he could hear nothing from inside. A tray of soft drinks and packaged crackers was brought to him by an American soldier with a kind face. "Better fortify yourself," the man said simply and stepped away.

"Thanks," Max answered, wondering what lay ahead for him and his mother. He moaned inwardly for what she might be enduring at this moment. There had been no word from her, and no one could tell him if she'd arrived safely in New York, if she'd been met by his aunt Neva or the FBI. Was she resting in the familiar, cozy kitchen of the Brooklyn apartment with a view of the harbor, or dungeoned in some hellish precinct and forced to tell things she couldn't possibly know?

Max gazed at the cheerful red can of soda on the tray before him. *Why couldn't my father have been an advertising copywriter who dreamed up soft-drink jingles for a living? None of this would be happening.*

He looked up at the soldier and nodded, then popped the top on the can and let the syrupy effervescence quell some of the churning inside him.

Over an hour later, the door in front of him opened and he was ushered into the situation room and shown to a seat at a long, nearly empty conference table. A uniformed officer who introduced himself as Army Col. Drake Hendig sat opposite him along with Capt. Stiegle and one of his men. Max was alone on his side of the table.

"Mr. Morozov," Col. Hendig began, "your country and ours are both indebted to you for leading us to the information we now have. Though we can't divulge the contents of the box you uncovered for us, be assured that you have helped save many lives." He met Max's unwavering stare. "It has just come to our attention, though, that your own safety has been compromised. It seems someone close to this operation has been feeding updates on it to those your father works for. It is our belief that they know it was you who led us to your father's documents in Corsica. Therefore, we'd like for you and your mother to be our guests in America, in a place where we can guarantee your safety, at least until we feel you are no longer in danger."

Max leaned forward and tried to read the man's face. "How would you know that?"

"Know what?"

"That we're no longer in danger."

The colonel hesitated, then leveled a straight-eyed gaze at Max. "We may never."

Max nodded, considered this, then turned from the ominous implication altogether. "Is my mother all right?"

"Yes," the colonel replied crisply, as if glad for the change of subject. "She's waiting for you to join her."

Max looked about the starkly lit room, at everything and nothing in particular, then back at the colonel. "May I ask a question, sir?"

"Of course."

"Do you know what's happened to my father?"

Col. Hendig addressed the others in the room. "I'd like to speak privately with Mr. Morozov, please."

When they were alone, Col. Hendig pulled a file from a briefcase sitting near his feet. He placed it on the table before him, then looked steadily at Max. "Just before you arrived, we received an intelligence report from one of our operatives inside Russia. Immediately after your father fled Israel for Moscow, he was taken to a dacha outside the city. It is owned by a man we've been watching closely for years, a man we believe to be the head of an underground movement to resurrect the Union of Soviet Socialist Republics."

Something leaped in Max's memory. "Who is he?"

"That information is highly classified."

"Did Schell Devoe know this man? Was he, by chance, a music professor like Devoe?"

The colonel's eyes grew wide. "How could you know . . . that?"

"Colonel, you're not reading your mail. Surely some CIA type assigned to tap into Liesl Bower's memory bank on Devoe would have passed on the findings that she and I both knew Vadim Fedorovsky, if that's your man."

The colonel blinked several times but said nothing.

"I mean, it's just a hunch, but Liesl, Devoe, and I did have dinner with the man in his Moscow apartment. Liesl and I overheard some strange things spoken privately between the professors. Fedorovsky owns a dacha near Moscow, and rumor has it he's an unofficial insider at the Kremlin. Just connecting a few dots, sir."

Max knew the man was ill at ease now.

"You seem very sure of your hunch," Col. Hendig said tersely.

"I'm not sure of anything right now, colonel." Max regretted any disrespect he might have shown the man. It was clear the colonel was bristling.

"But, sir, if you don't mind, I must ask again, what's happened to my father?"

Col. Hendig carefully gathered the papers before him and slid them into a binder, his face impassive once more. "We don't know. We'll notify you when we do. It shouldn't be long now."

Max read something different in those words. He didn't know if it was the clenching of the colonel's jaw or the shadow of regret in the man's eyes that signaled something else. But Max knew. "What you mean is, he's now a threat to them. And it won't be long before they end that threat."

Chapter 41

The contents of the metal box spilled, figuratively, all over the Oval Office, leaving its stunned occupants awash in the stench of the uncovered plot. Israeli intelligence had just relayed the details of the one CD, the tape recording of Maxum Morozov's voice, and the sheaf of copied documents found inside the box. The report now rested on the president's desk.

At a secret summit with President Noland and Israeli Prime Minister Yoni Shulman, the presidents of Russia and Syria were to be assassinated. The mole Maxum Morozov had learned the location of the summit, the travel plans of those attending, and the logistics of all the meetings. As a highly placed official of Israel's Ministry of Defense, Morozov had forged documents "proving" that Israel was responsible for the deaths. It would be disclosed that Israel feared Russia was aligning itself with Syria and other Middle East allies in an axis so powerful, Israel would be helpless to defend itself.

In reality, the assassins were hired by Pavel Andreyev, Vadim Fedorovsky, and their shadowy network inside the Kremlin, which included members of the KGB and high-ranking military officers. For years, they'd padded the palms of those who, in the chaotic aftermath of the president's sudden death, would clear the way for the new party to swiftly and brutally assume power.

Meanwhile, the torrent of outrage over the Syrian president's murder would sweep over the Middle East and channel its monstrous force to just one place. Israel.

Noland had just summoned the ambassadors of Syria and Israel to the White House, but not Ambassador Olnakoff. "I can't trust that even the Russian ambassador is innocent of this conspiracy." The president's secretary had placed a direct call to the Russian president. Now, Noland waited to speak to him, to deliver the staggering news from Morozov's metal box.

Though others waited with him, he chose a solitary position near a window, his customary thinking post. Outside, autumn leaves quivered in the breeze, scattering their brilliant colors over the morning. He turned to those in the room, the same heads of national security that he'd summoned the day before, and asked, "How does man look upon God's gifts of creation, of life, and repay him with such evil?"

Ben knew his boss wasn't looking for an answer. There wasn't one, Ben believed.

There was only reprisal for the evil deeds, especially those against Israel, his ancestral home. That had been the sum of Ben's faith, not the faith of his fathers but of his own despair over a world gone mad with crimes against itself. How much longer, he'd wondered, would God, whoever he was, allow mankind to feed on itself before he put an end to it? How much longer would Israel survive? And did God really hear the cries of his people? Ben longed to know those things.

"Sir, the larger concern right now is containing this news," Deputy Secretary of State Lorraine Mercin said, diverting attention from Noland's rhetorical question. "The Russian president will need time to clean his house, so to speak, before the media bursts open with news of insurrection at the Kremlin. It's in our best interest that we help him do that."

"As much as he will allow us, you mean," the president noted.

"Yes, sir," Mercin replied. "But there is one variable that's already forced our entry into Russian affairs."

"Ted Shadlaw," answered CIA Director Eric Stone.

"Correct," said Mercin. "His arrest has been leaked. A Russian mole in the White House? We might as well be sitting on the lid of an underground silo whose rocket is already rumbling."

"But we can't be forced to divulge the nature of classified information he slipped to the Russians, or the plot attached to it," White House Chief of Staff Hank Bessinger countered. "We can do more damage control than you think."

"But Lorraine's right," Noland conceded. "This will come to light in time. And it should. The American people need to know what's underfoot in the world."

The door opened and Noland's secretary stepped inside. "I have the Russian president on the line, sir."

Noland glanced down at the blinking red light on his phone. "If you will," he said to the room, "I'd like to speak privately with this man."

Now alone in his office, Ben mourned the tragedy that was Ted Shadlaw. How pitifully he'd fallen, toppled by the thing that had narrowly missed Ben. How narrow was that margin? Would Ben have yielded if the price, or threat, had been greater? A shudder sped up his spine and he feared what lay at the base of him. Or didn't. What exactly was it that steeled him against this covert Russian assault on him. Was God with him or not? It suddenly mattered a great deal to Ben.

He opened a drawer and removed the convincing dossier Ted had hidden. *He would have tossed me into the shredder for the big house with the pool.* It occurred to Ben that even as he and Ted exchanged pleasantries about each other's families the day before, Ted had already plotted Ben's ruin. But what tore most savagely at Ben was the source of all that now lay in his lap. Only Jeremy Rubin, Anna's brother, could have supplied it. The reports about Harvard, the Boston Bolsheviks, and Evie Siegred. And the photos of Jeremy's own ruin. But the one of him and Ben had been taken in the woods with a group of paramilitary guys Ben and Jeremy had met on a hunting trip many years ago. The weapons were real, but the intent pure farce. *How would I have explained that one?* Ben thought.

Jeremy Rubin, a Harvard dropout, also had been a member of the Boston Bolsheviks and fallen under Evie's provocative spell. Unlike Ben, though, Jeremy wallowed in the aura of the subversive potion. It fed him. It ran him to every rebel-rowdy hot spot in the world, eventually to Israel where he ranted and protested against that government too. Soon, though, Jeremy fell into a den of anarchists who wouldn't let him leave even when he wanted to. Ben guessed that Jeremy's value had rocketed when his handlers discovered he was related to a White House insider.

Anna hadn't heard from her brother for years now; before that, just the occasional letter, oddly phrased and troubling. No one in the family knew where he was.

Ben thumbed the viral documents and photos before him. *What did they do to you, Jeremy? How did they coerce you to betray your family?*

Chapter 42

$\mathcal{A}$va had secured a CIA safe house called "the ranch" well outside the Beltway in Washington where she, Liesl, Cade, and Ian were settling in late Wednesday afternoon. It was an unremarkable house at the end of a winding road surrounded by open fields. There was a high-walled garden in back and, at present, entirely too many security guards to suit Liesl.

She had wanted to return to her Georgetown home, but Ava wouldn't allow it. "Not yet," she'd told Liesl. "I'm afraid we're here for a while until things calm down."

Liesl still didn't know what those things were, and Ava wasn't telling. "For your own sake," she'd told Liesl. But Liesl was certain it involved the summit, the one now canceled. Ava had told her that much, also that Max and his mother were under heavy guard somewhere in the United States. If she allowed herself to, Liesl could spiral into a reclusive non-existence, removed from a world that hurled too much at her. She would just leave it all behind.

Except for Cade. She closed her eyes and remembered the feel of his arms around her, the touch of his lips on hers, and she felt the welling up of an inexpressible, incomprehensible joy inside her—even in the midst of turmoil. She sat on the bed and stared into the sunburst pattern of stitching on the downy comforter, and long-ago words came rushing to the surface of her mind, something her aunt Bess had taught her. She'd spoken of a one-on-one personal relationship with Christ, which had seemed impossible to Liesl. Then her aunt had quoted something from the Bible, one of the few verses Liesl had memorized. And now it returned to her: "The Lord is near. Do not be anxious about anything, but in every situation, by prayer and petition, with thanksgiving, present your requests to God. And the peace of God, which transcends all understanding, will guard your hearts and your minds in Christ Jesus."

She used to repeat it often, trying to convince herself it was true. But every time something slashed into her world shattering her peace, she withdrew her trust from God and ran from him, angry that he hadn't stopped the hurting things.

She opened her eyes and looked out the window of her upper-story room, across a field where crops sprang uniformly along neat, orderly rows. She yearned for order, was desperate for it. For a place where she could live in peace. As she stared into the golden fields, she suddenly knew what she must do. The thing she'd kept seeing from the corner of her mind's eye for days now sprang in front of her with shining clarity, and there was no deny-ing it was good. She was going home. She would move from Washington back to the old house on Tidewater Lane. She would throw open the win-dows and fill the house with light and life. She would bring Lottie home to live out the remainder of her days, with all the care she needed. There was money to do that. Liesl had earned handsomely and lived frugally.

Liesl's mind sailed beyond these closed and guarded days, down the coast, into the harbor, and onto the shaded lane. Cade would be there with her, with that sweet old man who made her laugh. She dreamed of ocean breezes billowing curtains at the windows. She would paint and scour and polish. She would restore the house she loved, then let it restore her and her grandmother. She promised herself it would be so.

But reality stole like a virus into the waking dream. *My promises to myself are useless. They always have been. I have no such power.*

Odd that the face of Rev. Francis Scovall would come to mind at that moment. It seemed years ago, not days, that she had burst through the side door of his church in a blind panic. Weak with fear and desperate for help, she'd found such comfort in his kindly manner, and in his words. "I don't know what kind of trouble you're in," he'd told her, "but God knows. He's your Father, Liesl. The only one you truly need."

Her breath quivered. She closed her eyes and sought, with no holding back this time, God's own face. *I think I've seen you near me, Lord. Am I right? Did you hold the door open for me to escape into the church that night? What else have you done that I didn't see? Refused to see? Will you forgive me for that, for all the ways I've failed you and those around me?* She clutched the comforter in tight fists and drew it around her, feeling its warmth. But it was just cotton and feathers, soothing for a while, then it would wither and rot. Was there a comforter that was everlasting?

And she knew. *The reverend was right. I can't do this alone anymore. I need you . . . Father!*

Liesl wrapped the comforter into a cocoon around her and leaned back against the pillows. As the sun's rays grew horizontal, painting a soft, gossamer sunset on the western canvas, Liesl drifted into a peaceful, dreamless sleep.

When she awoke, light from the hall filtered into the room. A man's figure stood in the open doorway. She knew the at-ease shape of the silhouette instantly, the lanky arms and legs, the thick, tousled hair. "Cade," she whispered, "turn on the light." She pushed back the comforter and stood up, stretching slightly.

But Cade just opened the door wider and moved closer. "I kind of like it like this," he said, reaching for her in the half light, gently enfolding her into his arms. She nestled her head against his chest and drew a deep, sleep-sweet breath. They stood quietly together, resting against each other. Then Liesl pulled back to look at him. She caressed the side of his face, toyed with a wavy lock over his forehead. And there was no stopping the kiss that engulfed them, plunging Liesl into the purest, quenching emotions she'd felt for another person for so long. Is that all it was? Feel-good emotions? Were they just two lost people in need of tenderness, vulnerable and searching for someone to hold on to? Would it end with the turn of a day, a month?

Cade looked longingly into her eyes. "Liesl, this isn't supposed to happen."

She didn't understand. Was he rejecting her? She pulled away, but he caught her hand and drew her to him again. "What I mean is," he continued, "you and I aren't a likely story." He softly stroked her cheek.

She pulled his hand into hers and held it close. "What story is that?"

He grinned down at her. "The hapless, jobless reporter—in whose lap has dropped the biggest story he'll never write—falls for the beautiful heroine. But you see, she lives in the high-brow realm where men wear tuxedoes and talk about dead composers. While the reporter of little means is fresh from the world of dead fish."

She dropped his hand in feigned annoyance, barely suppressing an out-loud laugh. *Lord, who is this person you've brought to me? He is from you, isn't he? Because I sure do like this man.*

Reaching both arms around him, she squeezed hard. "Let's just write this story one page at a time." She looked coyly at him. "Then we'll see about that tux."

Chapter 43

The next morning, Ava woke Liesl early. "Get up and get ready. We're going to the White House."

"The . . . what?" Liesl slurred, her tongue thick with sleep. She'd returned to her room shortly after dinner the night before, noticing that Cade had made himself scarce after their time alone. "We're what?" Liesl repeated.

"Ben Hafner called after you went to bed last night. President Noland wants to speak with you. And he specifically asked to see Cade and Ian too." Ava rolled her eyes, but her smile gave away a growing fondness for the pair, as Liesl had observed.

"He who?" Ian asked, just turning the corner in the upstairs hall.

"The president," Ava shot back.

"Of what?" Ian passed Ava in the hall and kept going, as if the answer didn't matter.

"The United States," Ava called after him, then looked back at Liesl and winked.

From her bed, Liesl didn't hear an immediate response, but Ian suddenly reappeared in the doorway, focused only on Ava. "Travis Noland wants to meet me?" he asked, his voice rising.

"Cade too. But he mostly wants to talk to Liesl. I doubt you'll get more than a handshake." Liesl knew Ava was messing with him.

"Doggone if that's so. I've got a thing or two to ask him."

"Such as," Ava prodded with good humor.

"Such as why they wouldn't let me go to Iraq with the rest of the troops. I could shock-and-awe as good as anybody."

Liesl had wrapped herself in a bathrobe and now approached the doorway to the hall. "You wanted to enlist?" she asked Ian, half grinning as she tied the sash on her robe.

"Sure did," Ian answered firmly.

"At age what, seventy?" Ava chuckled.

"Sixty-four at the time and a lot more dispensable than some young fella with little kids. Why couldn't they let me go in his place?"

Liesl caught Ava's suddenly sobered eye, certain she was thinking of her son, whom Ian couldn't have known about.

"Besides," he continued, "I know how to use a weapon and, well, I still look pretty good in uniform." He scratched his scruffy beard. "I would have even shaved this off."

He studied the women's open stares for a moment, then, hearing no response, turned to go. "I can see I'm leaving you two speechless. Happens to me a lot." Halfway down the hall, he called over his shoulder, "I'm assuming the dress for today is fishing casual."

Ava didn't answer, but watched him turn into his bedroom and close the door behind him. She looked back at Liesl. "I should warn the White House."

Later, Liesl stared glumly at her meager choice of clothes. There'd been no time, or security, for returning to the Charleston house for more than she'd first carried with her to the island. She'd have to speak to Ava about gathering what she needed from her Georgetown house. Meanwhile, the best she could muster was the now-rumpled gabardine pants and jacket she'd worn on the plane to Charleston. At least the morning shower had revived her spirits and produced a clean head of hair, which she now brushed into submission.

Where is he? All her thoughts soon fell into one basket labeled "Cade." *Why is he avoiding me?*

Now dressed, she stepped into the hall and nearly collided with him. "Oh," she said with surprise.

He smiled silently at her for a moment, then asked brightly, "Sleep well? Ready to meet the president?"

She tried to see past the cheerful veneer, if that's what it was. "What happened to you last night? You disappeared."

"Just giving you some space." He placed both hands on her shoulders and eased her close to him. "I shouldn't have loaded you down with anything else, not now."

She was about to assure him that he had everything to do with "now" when a door down the hall closed loudly. They both jumped and disengaged, whirling toward the sound.

"Thought I'd give you a warning before you embarrassed me." Ian stood before them in jeans, a vented-back fishing shirt under a bright orange vest, and the floppy hat that sat too low on his head. "I don't know how you do that before breakfast. Let's go. The president's waiting." He breezed past them and headed for the stairs.

An hour later, two dark sedans arrived at the White House. When Liesl stepped from the backseat of one, she saw Ben Hafner quickly heading her way. It seemed a lifetime since she'd seen him last, the night of the East Room concert, the night someone followed her limo home. Reflexively, Liesl glanced toward the street, beyond the gates where security guards would now hold back the intruders to her life. But what about later?

Ben reached her quickly and hugged her with big-brother affection. "Anna and the kids told me to give you one for them too." So he hugged her again.

Liesl noticed how weary he looked, and the reality that others also had suffered through this ordeal tore at her. *All you've thought about was you,* she scolded herself. "Maybe this is all over now," she offered.

"Yeah, maybe," Ben answered lightly, too lightly, then turned to the others. He shook Ava's hand and whispered something quick and almost unnoticeable into her ear. Then he took Agent Tucker's hand and thanked him for his service to the others. When he finally turned to Cade and Ian, he studied them a prolonged moment before warmly gripping their hands. "Besides Liesl, I can't remember when civilians have played such crucial roles in a guarded operation like this. But I mostly thank you for taking care of this wild-child piano player." He avoided eye contact with Liesl and ushered them all into the West Wing.

With Liesl directly behind him, Ben led the group to his office. Entering first, he immediately stepped aside, giving Liesl an unobstructed view of the man now rising from his chair. Young Max Morozov took only one step forward before Liesl flew to his open arms. "Max!" She pulled back and looked at him as if he were an apparition. "You're supposed to be, I mean, should you be—"

"Here?" Max supplied. "Instead of hiding under a bed somewhere?" He beamed at her. "Maybe, but I thought it was a good day to climb to the top of the White House and play *Fiddler on the Roof.*" Then he looked past her, scanning the other faces, his eyes returning to Cade's. Liesl saw the inquisitive light in Max's eyes.

Before she could introduce the two, Max extended his hand. "Are you Cade O'Brien?"

"I am," Cade said, meeting Max's firm grip. Liesl was glad that Ava had finally shared some of Max's story with Cade and Ian. It had brought Max into the fold of their peculiar fellowship.

"Careful there," Ian warned Cade. "There's no telling what those hands of his are worth."

"And you have to be Ian," Max said.

Ian stepped forward and clapped Max on the shoulder, clearly taking him by surprise.

"Always have been, and we're happy to see you safe and sound, young man."

Max grinned. "Thank you, sir." He looked from one O'Brien to the other. "I've heard about the adventure Liesl led you on. But I hope . . ." he paused, "that every one of us is safe now."

Something in his voice gave Liesl a start, something she wasn't used to hearing from the redheaded prankster—caution. What terrible thing had he found in Corsica? Did he even know?

"Max," she said softly, "I'm so sorry for your father's . . . uh . . ."

"Treason? Exile? Possible execution?" He shrugged. "At least my mother won't lay awake nights waiting for him to come home."

Liesl cringed at the pain lying beneath the brittle sarcasm.

Max seemed to think better of his answer. "I'm sorry, my friend," he told Liesl. "You deserve better than that. I guess I'm not handling this very well."

Liesl went to him and gently touched his arm, counting yet another victim besides herself.

Ben's phone rang once and he picked up. "The president's ready for us," he reported.

After the round of introductions, Liesl, Cade, Ian, Max, Ava, and Ben were all seated comfortably in the Oval Office. President Noland stood before them, the elegant statesman who just now, like Ben, looked drawn and grim. "Thank you for coming," he began. "Forgive me for standing, but, as my staff will attest, if I sat, it wouldn't be for long." He looked hard at the floor then back at his guests. A smile made a brief appearance, then vanished quickly. "You have no idea what disastrous thing you have prevented," he said boldly.

Liesl didn't move, but glanced at the others to see each one, even Ben, locked on the president's somber face.

"I can't divulge what that is to you now, not exactly, but I expect that one day you will be told—given the persistence of the media." He looked directly at Cade, who didn't react.

Noland began to pace, one hand at his chin. "For years, a powerful substrata of a foreign government has been weaving a plot of murder and world upheaval in order to seize control of their country and as many others as they could." He stopped and looked back at his guests. "This awful tapestry was almost complete and tied off when one little thread worked its way loose. Liesl Bower didn't know she held the end of that thread in her hand." He paced some more, head down, then turned to address Liesl directly.

"I don't know your spiritual beliefs, Liesl. But I'd like to tell you what *I* believe: that God used you to unravel this deadly scheme."

Liesl caught her breath. *Me? God used me?*

Noland continued. "From the moment you first encountered Schell Devoe, I believe God led and protected you throughout the task he gave you." Liesl's mouth was dry, her hands clenched and still. "You didn't ask to do it. You just fell innocently into it, having no idea where it would lead."

Noland looked at the others. "Presidents don't often say such things. They aren't politically acceptable." He chuckled. "But imagine the one who sits on this tiny little throne here in the White House banning the God of the universe from its little doors." He slowly shook his head, then turned again to Liesl.

"With the aid of everyone in this room, Liesl, you led us to the code that gave us Max's father." Noland looked compassionately at Max. "From there, Max took the loose thread from you and, as God led *him* to do, pulled until this plot lay undone."

To Max, the president said, "You have done this for Israel. Your prime minister waits to honor you, not shame you. It is understood that the son had to betray his father to right the grievous wrong he'd done. Max, do *you* understand that?"

Max nodded slowly, but said nothing. Liesl caught Max's eye long enough to transmit her support. But there was more she couldn't convey because it was just now taking shape. The notion that God's own hand had steered her, that her small broken life had been of value to him was almost too ponderous to process. Yet her mind spun rapidly through the pieces and parts of her life, the hurts and triumphs. And God had been there for each one?

Noland's voice broke through her thoughts again. "As you will soon hear from the news networks, this administration also suffered a betrayal. One of our own turned against us to join in this plot—for money. For his family, he said. Now his children must visit him in prison." The president's voice grew strained.

"Sir," said Ian, who had removed his fishing hat and held it bunched in his rough hands. "God knew this man you trusted would do that. And maybe God's already chosen someone to go into the prison and restore that man. Maybe that someone doesn't even know it yet. Maybe it's you."

All eyes darted to the president for his reaction, which was slow in coming. Then Noland threw back his head and smiled. When he looked back at Ian, he nodded as if confirming something to himself, then said, "Mr. O'Brien, I need you at the State Department."

"Oh no you don't, sir," Cade responded instantly, drawing voiced agreement from Ava.

"But I welcome wisdom, even a challenge, from whoever wants to give it," Noland insisted. He pulled a chair closer to his guests and sat down. "And that leads me to the main reason I asked you here." He leaned in and rested his forearms on his knees, clasping his hands tightly. "Because of things beyond your control, beyond your private worlds, each of you has endured your own kind of pain and fright throughout this affair. I apologize to each one of you—you too, Ben—for what you've encountered. Throughout history, the power grab of a few has always victimized the multitudes. In this case, the actions of a few—each of you—saved the lives of at least two heads of state and possibly the population of an entire country." He looked pointedly at Max. "Yours," the president told him.

Max recoiled, and Liesl was certain he hadn't known the full scope of what his father had hidden in Corsica. She wondered if they'd ever know.

"My concern today is that each one of you looks at what's happened to you through the right lens." He worked his hands together, gripping and ungripping. "However man intends to harm you—or me or anyone we love—God can use it for good." The hands went still. "I want each one of you to find the good he left just for you.

"In the wake of this terrible time," Noland continued, "is something pure and restorative for you, something different for each. Find it and let it comfort you."

The president stood and walked to the back of his chair. He leaned toward his listeners. "If you were soldiers, I'd pin a medal on each one of you. But it would tarnish. You might even lose it. But you can never be separated from God. He's all the badge of courage and honor you need." Noland straightened and stepped back.

Ben rose first, the signal that this special audience with the chief executive was over. Noland stood at the door and shook hands with each guest. When Liesl approached, he motioned for her to stay.

Now alone with the president, she followed him to one of the tall windows, its panes swathed in gauzy light. "Look out here, Liesl." She moved beside him. "See that high fence at the foot of the South Lawn?"

"Yes, sir." She remembered a class trip in eighth grade when her teacher had to almost drag her from that same fence. She'd been that determined to catch a glimpse of President Reagan, the man who'd stood up to Russia and demanded they tear down a wall, the symbol of a reign of terror. *How ironic*, she now thought.

"We can't protect you very far beyond that fence," the president said. "So I'd like for you to stay where you are for a few more weeks. Those involved in this plot are being rounded up at this moment. I'd like to give you a broad cushion of security for as long as we can."

An unfamiliar ease spread itself confidently into all the dark places in Liesl's mind. She smiled warmly at the elder statesman beside her. "But Mr. President, you forget what you just told us."

He looked at her curiously.

"God intended it all for good, and we must find what that is. I'm pretty sure I know already. I'm going home to Charleston as fast as I can get there. "

Chapter 44

When Liesl left the Oval Office, she found Cade and Max in conversation. They seemed to be enjoying each other's company and she hesitated to interrupt that, but Ben caught her arm and gently pulled her toward them. "I wanted you to hear what I have to tell Max," he said.

When Max turned toward them, Ben informed him, "We just received clearance to release you from our protection, if that's still your wish. You and your mother are free to return to Israel, where, I trust, you'll have to endure another round of tight security." Ben smiled regretfully at him.

Ben's attention was suddenly drawn away, and Liesl followed his eyes just in time to see the briefest signal pass to him from Ava, who was just ending a phone call. When Liesl looked back at Ben, he averted his eyes and shifted his conversation to Ian, who'd been strangely silent since leaving the president.

"So tell me what kind of fish you chase down in the Keys," Ben began. Liesl let the conversation run on without her, since Ava had now pulled her aside.

"The cars are waiting," Ava announced. "We'll go straight to Langley for debriefing. It shouldn't take too long."

"Um, Ava," Liesl began, "I need to get some clothes and things from Georgetown. Can we do that first?"

Ava considered this. "I can arrange that, but you'll need to be quick."

"I will. And one more thing. I'm going back to Charleston. Tomorrow."

Ava was clearly startled. "That's not . . . advisable, Liesl."

"Look, Ava. I appreciate all you and the others have done to keep me safe. But I'm not going to hide anymore. I'm going home. There's a noon flight to Charleston and I plan to be on it. I'll have my car and what little furniture I have in Georgetown packed up and shipped down later." That's when she noticed that all conversation around her had stopped.

Ben cleared his throat. "Ava, may I speak with you privately?" They excused themselves and moved into Ben's office. He shut the door behind them.

Liesl met Cade's troubled gaze. "Had you planned to announce this to anyone else?" he asked. Liesl saw the irritation in his face.

She regretted not telling him sooner. "I just decided yesterday." She took his hand, not caring who watched. "I hoped the three of us would leave together."

Liesl was pleased to see Ian and Max reabsorbed in conversation. Ian was telling him that he could play the fiddle too and that Max should consider doing bluegrass.

Cade pulled her away from the lively conversation. "Liesl, there's nothing I want more than to have you back in Charleston. But if Ava thinks it's too soon, there must be a reason, and you should listen to her. I can't stay here any longer. I've got to start looking for a job, but you need to remain here."

His sweet, handsome face so close to hers, the concern in his voice made her even more determined to be near him. "I'm coming home, Cade," she insisted. "May I reserve three seats on tomorrow's plane?" Her face felt hot.

Slowly, he nodded agreement, and she resisted the urge to hug him tightly in front of everyone, especially Max. She glanced over to see her old friend watching her and she ached for whatever hurt she'd ever caused him. *Lord, bring him someone to love.* The feel of a prayer on her lips was so oddly comforting. Empowering. Why had it taken her so long?

Just then, she saw Ben and Ava leave his office and approach her. "Pending the outcome of this afternoon's briefing," Ben told her, "we're okay with you going back to South Carolina—under one condition. We're going to continue security at the house."

Liesl frowned.

"For a while," Ava added. "We just need to be sure."

Reluctantly, Liesl agreed.

Before leaving the White House, she was allowed a little time to say good-bye to Max. "How can I help you?" she asked him.

"By giving a concert with me in Tel Aviv next year. It was Zubin Mehta's idea. A fine one, I think. Will you come?"

"Of course I will."

"And bring Cade and Ian." He smiled broadly at her. "I'm happy you've found someone, Liesl. Now it's my turn."

"Oh yeah?"

"Well, there's a new violinist in the orchestra. Sometimes her bow and my bow almost touch. It's true love, I'm sure of it." He winked.

She grabbed him by the shoulders and gently shook him. "Will you be serious for a moment."

He took her hands and held them gently. "If the moment were more serious, I'd suffocate. So let me say this, and I'll send you on your way. President Noland was right. Good already has come from my father's tragic life. My mother and I are free of his abuse. And maybe someday, I'll get to know this God who turns evil into good. Maybe someday I'll even forgive my father." He squeezed her hands and released them. He kissed her lightly on the cheek, then waved Cade over.

Standing a head taller, Cade gripped Max's shoulder. "I hope you'll come to Charleston soon."

"Not soon, but one day." Max nodded toward Liesl. "Take care of her." And he walked away.

The noon traffic through Washington was lighter than usual and the two sedans soon arrived at Liesl's small brick home in Georgetown. It stood among much larger homes, the kind occupied by Washington's old guard and new elite. Though the stately, tree-lined neighborhood seemed to welcome her home, she dreaded what she might find.

Agent Tucker remained outside while Liesl led Ava, Cade, and Ian to the door of her house. She held her breath as she turned the key. Ben's description of the break-in the week before was still fresh: *They really messed up the place.*

But when she opened the door and stepped inside, she was surprised to see everything in order, or close to it. And no black ski mask hanging from the chandelier in the dining room, as he'd reported. Someone had restored her home. *Thank you, Ben.*

But what they couldn't replace was all the music Kozlov and his thugs had taken. She opened the cabinets behind the piano and shuddered at the empty, yawning space. She felt the intruders' presence, their hands rummaging through her life. She was about to slam the door shut when Ian rounded the corner. He bent to peer inside one of the empty cabinets. When he straightened, he looked at her with clear understanding. "We'll get new music for you, honey." He put his arm around Liesl's shoulders. "The Lord will restore what the locusts have eaten."

Liesl didn't understand, and it showed.

"The book of Joel. You and I will read it together one day. For now, though, all you need to know is that God will right the wrongs, if you'll let him." He scratched his beard. "Now, I think I'll go clean out the penicillin growing in your refrigerator. Excuse me."

She thought she would burst with affection for him. What led these O'Brien men to wander into her life at the same time as an assassin? Good from evil, as the president said?

There wasn't time to ponder it anymore. She had to get moving. In her bedroom, she grabbed clothes from hangers and drawers and stuffed them into suitcases, then emptied jewelry and cash from a safe she kept under her bathroom sink. *Odd that it wasn't tampered with*, she thought. *Maybe there wasn't time.* She thought of the 911 call from the mystery jogger, who'd also made calls to Juilliard inquiring about her. Who was he? Had he surprised Kozlov and his men before they could take more than the music?

She looked quickly about the house for anything she couldn't afford to leave behind. What did she really need anyway? Again, there wasn't time to ponder. Ava was all but pushing her out the door. "Langley's waiting," the agent persisted.

When everyone started filing out of the house, carrying an assortment of suitcases and other containers, Agent Tucker moved from his post near the street to the cars in the driveway. Alone, Liesl made one more round through the house, knowing she'd probably never call it home again. She'd pay off the remainder of the lease, which was almost up for renewal, and close the door on an era.

She was passing by one of the living room windows when she noticed a small gray car drive slowly past the house, its windows tinted. She paused to study it, a reflex she would have to unlearn, she told herself. There would be many passing cars to come. *Shake this out of your head.*

She closed the lid over the keys of the piano and made sure the damper was still on. Until she could move it or sell it, she would keep damaging moisture from inside the instrument. She looked back at the empty cabinets. *Locusts?*

Turning the dead bolt in the front door, she hurried toward the first sedan, its engine running. Ava and Agent Tucker were standing near the rear of the car discussing something. Just before she climbed into the backseat, where Cade and Ian were already settled, she saw the same gray car approach again from the opposite direction. This time it stopped in front of the house.

Who are you? Something shifted inside Liesl. *What do you want?* She couldn't stop herself from moving toward the car. *I will not be afraid.* Cade called to her, but she kept walking. The car inched forward. But she didn't stop.

When Agent Tucker made a quick move toward her, the car pulled away and disappeared around the corner.

"Liesl! What are you doing?" Agent Tucker shouted, running toward her. She didn't answer.

He took her arm and led her back to the car. "What's the matter?"

She looked toward the street. "It was nothing. Someone stopping to look at a map, I guess. It was nothing." But she knew better.

Chapter 45

*J*ust because they can't find him doesn't mean he's here." President Noland paced as he talked to Ben and Ava, who had returned to the White House after delivering Liesl and the others to the ranch.

"No sir, but according to intelligence I received just this morning, it was definitely Evgeny Kozlov who chased Max through the airport in Tel Aviv," Ava confirmed. "Surveillance cameras picked him up and a positive ID has been made. When Vadim Fedorovsky and Pavel Andreyev were arrested, the rest of their mutinous brotherhood was rounded up as well. But not Kozlov."

"Evgeny would know better than to return to Russia now," Ben added.

"But why would he come back here?" Noland asked. "Certainly the Russian embassy can't afford to harbor him, even if the ambassador was part of the plot, which is only conjecture at this point."

"Evgeny Kozlov needs no harboring, sir," Ava stated confidently. "He's lived on the run most of his life. The world is his warren, if you'll allow me a metaphor. He can drop into a hole anywhere, anytime."

"But why here?" Noland pressed. "Why now?"

Ben looked steadily at the president. "One reason, sir. Liesl."

Noland stopped pacing. "But she has nothing else of value to him. Her role ended with the sonata code."

"So did Kozlov's career," Ava declared.

"You mean revenge."

"We've seen it before," Ava said.

"And there was an incident this morning, sir," Ben added.

"Where?"

"At Liesl's house. A car slowed up and stopped in front as she was closing it up, then sped away when she approached."

"Approached?" Noland's eyebrows spiked.

Ava sighed. "I'm not sure why she did it, sir, but she just walked right up to the car before we could stop her. And she's still planning to leave for Charleston tomorrow."

Pacing again, Noland said, "Liesl can't live in a vacuum anymore, or be spooked by every stopped car. It appears she understands this already. I say let her go, but provide reasonable security for a while. What did you have in mind, Ava?"

"She doesn't know it yet, but I'm going with her." She caught Ben's surprised look. "I'll see this assignment through to the end, sir." She hesitated. "It would be my, uh, pleasure to do so." She glanced between the two questioning faces before her, both clearly waiting for elaboration. "I've become rather attached to Liesl, though she might argue that, and I just want to make sure she's okay. That's all."

But that wasn't all. Ava had warmed to the whole trio from Charleston, and wasn't ready to sever her ties with them. There was something childlike and innocent about Liesl that drew Ava's protective instincts beyond her official CIA capacity. And something so soothing and reassuring about the O'Briens. She couldn't define it, only feel it at the core of her. She wished her son to know these people, especially Ian, who'd needled his way so far into Ava's subconscious that she often found herself thinking about him when he was nowhere near.

"I can always call on the locals for help if I need it," Ava added, as if justifying her Charleston-bound plans.

"Ava, you've done a remarkable job so far," Noland said. "I have no doubt that Liesl remains in good hands." He eyed her carefully. "I'm not usually this involved in such matters. But this young woman helped save us from catastrophe. She deserves whatever help we can give her."

Chapter 46

*T*he atmospheric thermals of November cavorted like kites over Charleston that morning, dipping and soaring in great swooshes of warmth. Liesl was nearly euphoric as she bounded down the worn stairs and into the living room. Like raising the heavy drape on a theatrical stage, she flung open the broad casement windows and summoned the rest of her life to begin. As if on cue, a gutsy wind rushed in from the harbor with a declaration on its breath. *Life that was lost is found again.* Liesl heard the words as clearly as if they'd been spoken. She closed her eyes and inhaled every syllable.

An autumn-red maple leaf fluttered inside the open window and landed on the white piano beside her. Liesl picked it up and twirled it in her fingers, which had been too long from the keyboard. Spontaneously, she sat down and lifted the lid over the ivory keys, some of them now cracked and needing replacement. Soon, she was flying through the runs and trills of *Autumn Leaves*, relishing every nuance of the childhood instrument that had spawned her illustrious career.

She wasn't mindful of the open window and the sounds carried through it until she heard wild applause and through-the-teeth whistles from below. A feeling like warm, soft honey seeped into her cheeks and spread them into a wide-open smile. She rose from the piano and leaned out the window, quickly reminding herself to have the house fitted with new screens.

In the front yard, Cade and Ian had dropped their rakes to the ground to free all four hands for clapping. "Don't stop!" Ian called, finally shoving his hands into faded overalls and rocking on his heels.

Cade stood nearby, grinning up at her, his dark hair shining in the bright sun. "Can you come out and play?" he teased.

She shook her head. "Later." She waved them off like two scoundrels attempting mischief, and headed for the kitchen. Ava was mixing pancake batter for a late breakfast.

"You don't have to do that," Liesl said, pulling a coffee mug from a white-painted cupboard. "You'll make us fat."

Ava chuckled, as she'd done more frequently in the last few days, Liesl had observed. She had wondered how the sensitive musician had ever morphed into the stern, no-nonsense CIA agent. But hadn't she, herself, undergone her own seismic transformations on the battlefields she'd just inhabited?

The kitchen smelled of fresh-roasted coffee beans, something Ava had introduced to the Tidewater Lane domestic equation. She'd purchased the roaster their second day back in Charleston and seemed to revel in serving the group each morning. What was happening to the woman Liesl had scorned for so long, yet whose company she now welcomed? As she sipped the hardy brew, she watched Ava's straight back, the strong arms stirring the batter, the pewter-streaked hair that lay too flat against her head, her drab clothes that rarely budged from neutral. She looked much older than her fifty-something years, Liesl thought, and decided to do something about it. "Ava, why don't we go shopping one day for new clothes."

"You have a closet full," Ava noted without turning around.

"Not for me. For you. And let's visit a salon."

Liesl feared she might have overstepped her bounds. The great thaw that had begun in their relationship was still a little crunchy. To her surprise, though, Ava turned toward her with an expression of thinly veiled delight. "Are you serious?" Ava asked.

"Perfectly. Let's make a day of it. King's Street boutiques, lunch at one of the old inns, and some serious coiffing. What do you say?"

Before Ava could answer, the back door banged open and Ian lumbered inside, a pair of hedge trimmers in his hand and a small twig lodged in his beard. He sniffed the air with relish. "It's about time the yard crew got some breakfast." With no hesitation, he walked up to Ava and peered over her shoulder. "One of those hotcakes needs turning there. See the bubbles on top?"

With one hand still on the skillet handle, Ava rounded on him, then her eyes dropped just below his chin. "Tell me you don't feel that tree limb dangling from your face."

Liesl burst into long-overdue peals of laughter. She was still laughing when Cade walked in. "I'm sorry I missed it," he said, glancing curiously from face to face. When he landed on his grandfather's, he understood. He stepped forward and yanked the twig from the gnarled gray beard, drawing a yelp from Ian. "Okay, that's done," Cade said. "Now can we eat?"

The next two days spun into a whirlwind of household chores. Though to Liesl, it was more like caressing the home she loved. Their first day back, she'd made a list of everything that needed cleaning, repairing, or replacing before she would bring her grandmother home. She was delighted to find the others so willing to help. No, she was shocked—especially by Ava. She and Liesl had polished furniture, scrubbed mildew from bathroom fixtures and walls, brushed away cobwebs, and hosed down the porches. Liesl had produced a color wheel and selected new paint colors for the interiors and a fresh new white for the outside. She'd already contracted a paint crew to begin the following week. Cade and Ian had volunteered to clean all the windows, once Ian had finished repairing them. Cade, of course, would take the high-ladder jobs.

After removing the faded and rotting curtains, Liesl had scheduled a seamstress to come measure for new window treatments. The oak floors would be reconditioned and the rugs steam-cleaned. In the yards, the men worked to "beat back Borneo," after Ian was warned again to leave the camellias alone. "If someone will tell me which ones they are," he'd grumbled.

The apartment, too, would be refurbished. Cade's home was Liesl's too. How that would evolve, she didn't know. For now, she was content to know he was near. While dusting her bedroom Thursday afternoon, she remembered what he'd told her that night at the ranch: that he'd fallen for her. What did that mean? Did he love her? Surely it was too soon for him to know.

But not too soon for her. She was certain she loved him, more fiercely each day. She just couldn't tell him. Why? What was wrong with her? Something drew her to the window. She leaned her forehead against the pane and looked down into the yard. The white steeple reflected the head-on rays of a kneeling sun, but the little porch sat in full, indigo shadow. In vivid detail, Liesl recalled the figure of a man on a moonlit night, sitting alone in a plastic chair, light glinting off glass as he raised the bottle to his mouth. How many times she'd told him "I love you." How many times, through the drowning bog of drink, had the words returned void? That's why she'd said them no more.

Friday afternoon, Liesl and Ava returned to the house carrying shopping bags filled with new clothes in Ava's size six. When the women got out of the car, Ian turned from polishing a downstairs window and gawked openmouthed at Ava. Her flat and faded hair had been replaced by a frisky new chestnut-brown cut that spiked here and curved there, partially lifting the time-worn lines on her face. The effect was more than even Liesl had hoped for, and Ava was unabashedly pleased.

"What have you done to that woman?" Ian hollered to Liesl. But his scraggy smile gave him away. He was impressed. And what was that on Ava's face? A blush? Liesl could hardly believe what she was seeing. But Ava was too fast. She hurried inside with her new self and left Liesl and Ian marveling in Ava's wake.

"I think she likes you, Ian." Liesl was only half teasing because the blush she'd seen was wholly genuine.

Oddly, Ian didn't pounce on that as Liesl expected him to. Instead, he just nodded in the direction of the now-closed front door and said, "She's a smart woman." Then he returned to his window cleaning, adding one more thing. "Cade took a break to check his e-mails. You know he's closing in on a job, don't you?"

An uneasy guilt crept over Liesl. She'd been far too focused on herself and the house to seriously consider the state of his career. It had been so long since she'd placed anyone else's needs above her own, she'd almost forgotten how to do that.

"Ian, how can I help him?"

The old man stopped his industrious scrubbing and turned to her. "Do you love him?" he asked bluntly.

His eyes searched hers. He was protecting Cade. She understood that. But she wondered if Ian knew his innocent question had pinned her down to a critical choice. Reinstate the barricade. Live insulated and alone. Or step into the open and yield to God's plan for her life. Could she be sure what that was? Was it enough to be sure of her own heart? Had God shown her that much already?

Her lips parted and the words flowed like a freshwater spring just tapped and rushing toward the surface. "Yes, I love him."

Ian laid a gentle hand on her arm. "Then tell him."

The basement door opened and Cade emerged. "I got the job!" he called.

Liesl looked uncertainly at Ian. "He'll tell you," he whispered.

"I may not have it next month," Cade said, waving a piece of paper in his hand as he approached, "but it's mine now."

"You'll have to fill her in on it, son."

Cade put his arm around Liesl. "Pop, do you mind if we take a walk?"

"Better check with the warden. And when you do, try not to stare."

Cade looked confused. "Ava got a makeover today," Liesl explained.

"That's a good thing, right?" Cade asked.

"Judge for yourself," Ian said. "But watch what you say. She's still got a gun in her pocket."

Liesl led Cade to a swing on the upstairs porch. "It's just easier to stay here," she told him. "Having that cop follow us store to store today, even though he wasn't in uniform, was awkward." She sighed. "This has got to end soon."

Cade held her hand and slowly rocked the swing.

She drew up her knees, then turned her full attention to him. "Now, tell me about this job."

For the next half hour, Cade spoke hopefully about a new magazine launching in Charleston and his role as managing editor. The magazine's new publisher and executive editor also had been laid off from the *Post & Courier* newsroom. It would be a city magazine covering the arts, history, people, and Charleston lifestyle. "But no stories about renegade Russian agents," he reassured her.

"And in this downturn economy, there's every opportunity for the magazine to fail," he added. But the light in his eyes didn't reflect that. They brimmed with optimism. She would not distract him with an ill-timed announcement of her feelings for him.

Chapter 47

*T*hat night after dinner, Liesl suggested they all spend a workday at the island.

"Suits me fine," Ian declared. "I've been wanting to take a whack at that noisy screen door, and there are some loose boards on the front steps."

"The sooner the better since I'll be back at work next week," Cade added.

They all turned to Ava, whose objections usually came quickly. She was sporting a new pair of designer jeans and loose-fitting cotton sweater in bright coral. Liesl was still amazed at the transformation. It was another new beginning to celebrate. The house had come to life again. Cade had landed a new job. For almost a week, there'd been peace and normalcy on Tidewater Lane. How could she not see even a coral sweater and perky hairdo on Ava as more proof that life had risen to a higher plain?

Ava looked guarded, and Liesl made her appeal. "Come on, Ava. We all need it."

In such a short time, Ava had become a matriarch of sorts, respected and deserving of the growing affection of this loosely tethered "family."

"Okay," Ava said, "but just for the day."

Liesl clasped her hands in anticipation. The island was her last frontier, the last place she would need to raise her flag of freedom—like her aunt

Bess had raised her backyard cross. Liesl resisted the nagging question of who had replanted the weathered crucifix and why. *Trespassers, that's all. Someone who thought they'd do the owner a favor in return for unauthorized lodging in the cottage, in return for the broken lock or window it took to gain entrance.* Hadn't Aunt Bess run them off before? In the future, Liesl might have to do the same. It was to be expected, not feared. *No more fear.*

Early the next morning, the *Exodus* churned east through a brisk chop in Charleston Harbor, the boat's high bow pointed toward the sunrise. On this clear, blustery day, the pilgrimage of fishing boats headed for the harvest further split the waters into troughs of rolling wakes. Cade had to hold the wheel tightly to maintain course alongside the flotilla—and to restrain his gag reflex. He'd found that handling the wheel and focusing on the horizon helped fend off his stomach's embarrassing tendencies.

He glanced at Liesl, seated quietly beside him, her long hair unfurled in the wind. He was glad for the serenity he saw in her. He looked behind him at Ian and Ava perched on the stern bench, each wrapped warmly against the morning chill and trying to talk over the growl of the twin outboards. Ian was telling her about his charter-fishing business, and Ava was doing a lot of nodding. A gust of wind blew open the front of her jacket, and Cade saw the handgun holstered firmly against her side.

Turning north into the Intracoastal, the waters calmed and Cade accelerated slightly. Sighting the entrance to the creek, he slowed and banked left into the now familiar channel, framed by a marsh turned golden with the season. Easing back on the throttle, he settled the boat into a slow drift toward the last turn before the cabin. When the little dwelling finally came into view, Liesl stood up and leaned against the windshield, watching intently. Cade couldn't read her eyes behind her dark glasses, but her mouth was tight, her jaw firm. She must have sensed his eyes on her. When she turned his way, the hard line of her mouth softened instantly into a smile. Cade wondered if it was real or camouflage.

With the rising sun behind it, the front of the house seemed to hunker in the shadows. "Glad to be back?" he asked as they approached the dock.

She nodded briskly and hurried toward the bowline, preparing to snag the forward cleat on the dock.

Cade checked the stern and saw Ian ready with the other line. In minutes they were tied up and the *Exodus* was bobbing peacefully against the current.

"Okay, this is how we're going to do this," Ava announced with full authority. "Liesl, you stay here with Ian while Cade and I scout the house and grounds. You don't come anywhere near until I call for you. Understood?"

"Come on, Ava," Liesl protested. "There's nobody here."

"Nope, that's the way it's going to be or we head right back to the house." Ava, every bit the CIA agent in charge, wasn't budging.

Liesl looked up at the sky and sighed. "Go ahead."

Leaving Liesl and Ian standing at the end of the dock, Ava and Cade walked the perimeter of the house first. When they reached the back door, Cade suddenly grabbed Ava's arm. The door was open. "I'm certain I locked it," he whispered. For the first time, Cade wished Agent Tucker were along. He knew now that they'd fallen too quickly into a lull, a dangerous complacency. And Liesl was at risk.

Ava drew her weapon and pushed ahead of him toward the door. With her fingers, she signaled 1 . . . 2 . . . 3 . . . and they burst into the house. No one was there, but there was a pot of hot coffee on the stove and one of the back-bedroom beds was still warm.

"Get Liesl out of here!" Ava ordered, withdrawing her cell phone. "I'm calling for help. Whoever it is can't be far. I'm staying."

"I'll stay with you. Pop can leave with Liesl."

"No! You go with her." Ava's face grew red and pinched. "I should *never* have let this happen." She unlocked the front door and rushed out. Cade followed her to the dock.

"Back in the boat!" she ordered. "And hurry!"

"What's wrong?" Liesl cried.

"Someone's been here! Just now! They left the back door open."

Liesl started for the house.

"No!" Ava shouted, reaching for Liesl's arm, but missing. "Get in the boat!"

Instead, Liesl broke into a run. Cade took off after her. "Liesl, stop!"

"It's just a squatter!" she called over her shoulder.

She shot up the steps and into the house, Cade right behind her. She quickly scanned the living room, where Cade and Ava had noted a dirty food plate resting on a sofa cushion. Liesl saw it too. Then she headed for the kitchen, where she touched the pot of coffee and quickly drew back her hand. She looked at Cade with pleading in her eyes. "It's just someone fishing the creek who decided to hole up for the night, Cade."

"Then where is his boat?" he asked bluntly, regretting his sharp tone.

"Maybe he came over from the old fish camp dock. They used to do that sometime. That's all it is, Cade. I'm not running away anymore!"

"Liesl, please. Ava's already calling in help. They'll find who it was. And if it's like you say, we can come back."

"No, Cade," she said, wandering toward the bedroom door. "I'm sure that—" She suddenly went still.

"Liesl?"

She didn't respond, didn't move, her eyes fixed on something inside the bedroom.

"What's wrong, Liesl?"

She turned slowly toward him, and what he saw on her face startled him. Her skin ashen, eyes glazed, she seemed to look right through him. Then, without a word, she swept past him and bolted through the open back door.

Cade ran to the front door and yelled once for Ava, then took off after Liesl. But she was well down the path through the deep hammock behind the house, the same path she'd warned Cade off of the night he'd chased someone into the trees. Was it the same someone?

He pulled the small automatic handgun, the one he still hid from Ava. Soon, her footsteps sounded behind him and he cared less about brandishing the gun than who it was Liesl might be closing in on.

Just ahead, he heard the thrashing of a runner through the heavy underbrush, her trail visible in the soft sand. He hoped Ava could follow his.

It wasn't wise to call out and alert whoever else was out there. He could only pray he'd reach Liesl first.

But that didn't happen. He lost her trail.

She could hardly feel the legs pumping beneath her, as if they were operating without her. But they knew where she had to go. Surely her mind would catch up.

The old fish camp was just ahead. It was the only other place on the island to hide. She stumbled once on the muddy path and scraped the back of her hand against a tree trunk strung with a thorny vine. Soon, she felt the sticky track of blood down her fingers, but didn't dare stop. She slowed only when the ground turned to patches of mud and the path took a ninety-degree turn along the creek. She'd reached the other side of the island. The camp dock would be just around the point.

When she rounded the turn, her legs suddenly stalled and a cry lodged in her throat. There was no breath to release it. The man on the dock dropped the line from his hand and stepped away from the small boat tied up beside him. He stared hard at her, then started toward her. Hesitant steps. Down the dock. Closer now. The sun catching him full in the face.

She went limp.

He stopped in front of her, his sorrowful eyes boring into hers. "Hey, Punkin."

Liesl staggered backward, arms reaching for support, something in real time, not a vision. Surely that's what this was. Without taking her eyes from the man, she touched her hand and felt the blood, still moist. Then the image of the cap flashed before her, the same faded red ball cap she'd just seen lying on the bed at the cabin, no longer enshrined inside the wooden box in her parents' wardrobe. It had signaled only one thing.

Dad!

No sound would come. No feeling in her body. Until he extended his hand toward her and she looked down at it, crackled-brown and scarred, the wide gold wedding band scraped and dull. "I'm so sorry," he whispered, and his sunken, red-rimmed eyes filled with tears. She watched them spill one by one into the sand.

Helpless to stop it, powered by something she didn't understand, all the patched-over wounds inside her burst open, their toxins fleeing her like exorcised demons. In their place rose the thing she'd battled for so long, a thing she'd never believed could be so quenching.

Forgiveness.

Without a sound, without looking in his eyes, she took his hand in hers and kissed it, her tears spilling against his calloused flesh and her own bleeding hand. In an instant, she remembered another time blood had trickled over her—in the bell tower, *fleeing from* this man. Now she had run with every wild hope that she would find him. Alive again! Wasn't life what blood was supposed to give? The image of a cross suddenly blazed in her mind and she gripped her dad's hand even tighter.

She felt a tremor in his hand; as his whole body began to convulse with grief, she wrapped her arms around the broken man and held on. *Lord, you did this! Only you could have brought him back from the dead.*

She squeezed her eyes shut and finally spoke. "Oh, Dad."

Wracked with sobs, he tried to speak but she wouldn't let him. "Shh," she said gently, clinging to him as if he might be snatched away.

Just then, Cade and Ava burst through the trees, guns drawn. "Get away from her!" Cade shouted.

Liesl released her dad and swung around. "It's okay," she called in a breaking voice. "My dad has come home."

Chapter 48

Cranking the outboard on his decrepit boat, Henry Bower motored his daughter, Cade, and Ava back to the cabin. Liesl couldn't tear her eyes from him. The long arms and legs were spidery. His thick golden hair had grayed, thinned, and retreated to the lower half of his head. His skin was like worn leather, almost crusted, and splotched as if it had been blistered many times over. He sat quietly behind the wheel, stealing soulful glances at Liesl and avoiding eye contact with the others.

The shock of finding her dad alive had almost suspended Liesl above reality. From inside another dimension, she'd heard Ava ask hard questions of Henry Bower in those first moments on the dock, felt Cade's reinforcing hand against her back as if she might topple without it. Still, she'd struggled to connect the man in front of her with the father she'd lost, to bring the two together in real time.

Now, as his small boat plied the creek waters, the words of the hymn she'd heard from the bell tower of St. Philip's rang in her head: "I once was lost but now I'm found." *Are you found, Dad? Or still dead?*

Approaching the cabin, they saw Ian standing on the dock, his head bobbing agitatedly. Cade waved to him and shouted, "Everything's okay, Pop!"

Now Ian's hand came up to shield his eyes from the morning glare off the water. "Who's that fella there?" Ian barked. "Where'd that boat come from? And why am I standing here all by myself?"

Cade murmured something apologetic to Henry Bower about the complexities of communicating with Ian O'Brien. But Henry Bower seemed indifferent to anything but his daughter. When they reached the dock, Cade tossed the lines to Ian, who handily tied down the boat, then whirled to face the stranger.

"Ian," Liesl said, a tremor in her voice, "this is . . . my dad."

"You're . . . well, my goodness, is that so?" Ian turned a what's-going-on-here eye on Cade.

"It's a story you're probably going to hear until you're sick of it," Henry said with mild amusement. He picked up his duffle bag and went straight to the *Exodus*, which had so often housed him, and climbed aboard. "I'll stay out here for now," he announced, his eyes locked hard on Liesl.

After encouraging the rest of them to return to the cabin, Liesl joined her dad. They sat opposite each other near the stern, where Liesl watched his eyes dart to the faded stain on the floor. She ached with the pain that pinched his face. She was about to break the long awkward silence between them when they heard the mounting percussion of wings above them. A great blue heron swooped over the marsh and landed across the creek, pecking into the pluff mud for whatever that primitive stew could offer.

Henry nodded toward the bird. "He does that a lot better than I could."

Liesl cocked her head at him.

"Living off the land," he explained, staring deep into her eyes. His bronzed face unleashed a hesitant smile and a key turned in a recessed lock inside her. His smile. In the better days, it had covered his face, open-mouthed and harboring an exquisite mischief. It occurred to her just then that she had never seen him flash that particular smile at anyone but her.

"I was there at Harvard," he announced without preamble. "And Washington. New York. And here. I've been watching you wherever I could find you."

Liesl leaned closer as if that would help her understand.

"You just couldn't see me." He laid a hand on his upper left arm and winced slightly.

"Are you all right?" Liesl watched him move that arm into a different position.

But he ignored the question. "You're waiting for the story, I know." He shifted on the seat and began. "When I left Charleston, I wound up in Mexico. I fell in with a band of transient beach bums. We traveled together, drank together, spent nights in jail together. But every chance I got, I visited a library and pulled up microfilm news of Liesl Bower. None of the guys would have believed I could've fathered a girl like you. It was just as hard for me to believe. So I never told them. No need to think I still had a family. Why not cut you all loose?"

Liesl lowered her eyes for a moment, fighting tears. When she looked back, he seemed not to have noticed her emotion, his eyes searching the horizon as if for strength to tell the rest of the story.

"One night, one of my wasted friends didn't see the jetty rocks beneath the pier and dove headfirst into them. When he surfaced dead and his face unrecognizable—his body size close to mine—I saw my chance. I planted my identification and your pumpkin necklace on him, and paid the others to swear to police that it was my body they had drug from the surf. I took his IDs."

Liesl remembered the phone call from Mexico that morning. She could still hear the woman's efficient report of the death. She remembered how bitterly her mother and grandmother had mourned, and anger surfaced unbidden. "That was hurtful," she allowed herself to say.

He shook his head vigorously. "No, it was my gift, or so I thought. I didn't know your mother was sick. That she would be gone so soon." He hung his head and cleared his throat.

Liesl wished to move on. "Keep going."

Henry looked back at the great bird still hunting along the shoreline. "I struck off on my own, working odd jobs around marinas, digging for food wherever I could find it, like that bird. I was just a mass of protoplasm taking up space. Cheap liquor in, cheap liquor out, and a mind gone to mush. Until the day I read about Devoe, the circumstances surrounding his murder, and the frightened young woman who'd witnessed it. That's the day I threw the bottle away and came back to life."

Liesl clung to every word.

"I had to get back to you. Not your life. I was already dead to you. But there was still a father in me somewhere, and he sensed his child was in trouble."

The tears sprang from Liesl's eyes. "You were near me?" she choked.

He nodded. "In a flophouse not far from your apartment in Boston. I got to be pretty good at trailing you."

Liesl was clearly uncomfortable.

"Creepy, isn't it? What a dead man can get away with. You wouldn't have recognized me if you'd passed me on the street, which you almost did a couple of times. I had a long ponytail and a full beard. I wore dark glasses day and night, and an assortment of hats."

"And Washington?"

"Yes, again. I'm the one who called the police when those guys broke into your house." He touched his arm again. "They wore masks, but I saw their weapons clearly."

Liesl looked at his arm. "They hurt you?"

He nodded. "It'll heal."

"Let me see."

"It's okay."

"Let me see it!"

Slowly he unbuttoned his shirt and exposed a four-inch gash held together with store-bought surgical tape. "See. I cleaned it and closed it myself."

Liesl shook her head. "No, that wound needs attention right away!"

He didn't respond as he rebuttoned the shirt.

"I'll take care of it," she declared.

She thought of something Ava had reported to her: the same man who called Washington police also called Juilliard about her. When she told Henry, he shook his head in surprise.

"They could match the calls?" He thought a minute. "But of course they can. They can do everything but keep people like me from getting close to you."

He told her about losing her in New York and finding her again in

Charleston. About watching her at the island, on the dock with Cade, at the boat landing on the Ashley just the week before. And about his shock when she came after his car outside her Georgetown house. "I never meant to frighten you. I just couldn't stay away."

Then he told her about visiting Lottie over the years, always in disguise.

"And along the way, I lost my taste for drink. Who would have thought that could ever happen?" His voice was shallow and dry.

He looked back at the cabin. "I didn't think I was ready for you to find me."

"But you were, weren't you? That's why you took the hat from the house. You knew I'd find it missing. One day."

He dropped his head again, and Liesl saw the eyes slide back to the stain on the boat's floor. She read the torment in his face.

"It was an accident, Dad. Aunt Bess said so."

His shoulders began to heave, and Liesl moved closer to him on the bench. She put her arm around him and he buried his head against her neck. They remained that way until they heard wings beating the air again. They looked up to see the bird rise from the wet, black muck and sail high over the marsh, its long, serpentine neck straining for altitude.

"You can do that too, Dad," she said, her eyes still on the heron. "God can make it happen."

"God?"

She studied the near-dead eyes that had once sparkled with light. "It's like lost and found, Dad. I wasn't homeless on a beach, but I was just as lost as you. All the fame and glory and riches the world can heap on you last just until you close the door, until you're alone with yourself. That's when the void inside begins to howl. And you can't make it stop because the only thing that can fill the void is God. I never believed this worldly sophisticate with the fine clothes and world-class career would ever say such a thing. But that truth has begun to burn in me, Dad. I think the *found* part is just beginning. For us both."

Henry sat up straight and composed himself. "I'm grateful for whatever makes you happy, Liesl." He looked down at his hard-worn hands and smirked. "But I'm used to the howl. It keeps me company."

Something suddenly occurred to Liesl. "What about the cross behind the cabin, Dad? It was you, wasn't it?"

He looked away. "It just didn't seem right for it to lie on the ground anymore. I raised it for Bess. And you."

Abruptly, he stood up. "And now, I need to go."

"What do you mean *go*?" Liesl panicked.

"Not far. But I can't stay here, not with you. I can't just suddenly move back into your life."

Liesl jumped up and clutched both his hands. "Do you know how tired I am of watching people I love disappear?" She didn't wait for a reply. "You're coming home with me to Tidewater Lane—where you belong. And we're going right now!"

Chapter 49

THREE MONTHS LATER

iesl pulled the emerald-green silk gown from her closet and checked its fastenings. Ever since a critical hook-and-eye on another gown tore loose during a performance, Liesl had been obsessively diligent about her wardrobe. She checked the hem of the flowing dress for any place the toe of her shoe might catch, then tested the pearl-button closures at the end of each long, sheer sleeve.

There was a slight tremor in her fingers as she ran them over the finely tailored gown. It wasn't like her to be this nervous, not this long before a concert. In a week, she would perform at Avery Fisher Hall in New York, sharing the billing with violinist Itzhak Perlman and the New York Philharmonic Orchestra. Both very familiar to her. Why should she be so nervous? But she knew why.

She hadn't returned to New York since it bared its teeth at her that night on a dark street where lamplight had suddenly filled with frightening faces. Willing the horrid memory to flee as quickly as she had that night, she slipped into the dress and went downstairs to show her grandmother. Liesl had converted a small study off the kitchen into a main-floor bedroom for Lottie.

The new caregiver Liesl had hired to tend her grandmother was helping the fragile woman get dressed. For the first month after Lottie had returned home, Liesl had stubbornly insisted on caring for her grandmother's every need—fed by guilt, she reluctantly admitted, at having left Lottie for too long in the hands of strangers. Liesl finally realized, though, that a different arrangement was in order. She not only had resumed her concert schedule but had joined the music faculty at the College of Charleston. Now, retired nurse Margo Blanchard had become a welcomed fixture in the home.

When Liesl appeared in the doorway, Margo gushed over the dress, then turned toward her patient. "Miss Lottie, look at this child of yours," trilled the ever-cheerful woman with the long, tight braid wrapped neatly around her head. "Oh my, if she's not a vision!"

Liesl was now sorry she'd paraded herself into the room. She had only wanted her grandmother to see the gown she'd given Liesl several Christmases ago, though she feared Lottie probably wouldn't remember it. She was wrong.

Lottie's good hand rose to the air and her eyes blinked wide with pleasant surprise. "Oh, Liesl. The Christmas dress! It's still so beautiful. Come here, dear."

The joy of seeing her grandmother so alert trumped her self-consciousness at Margo's effusive praise.

When Lottie grew tired, Liesl returned to her room to finish her packing and change into jeans and a black cable-knit sweater. Later, she headed back downstairs, her sneakers thudding softly against the old treads and her hand sliding down the familiar path to the carved-wood pineapple atop the newel post. *Like nothing ever changed*, she thought. How could such an old everyday routine deliver such pleasure? For weeks now, some down-deep spring kept bubbling up and filling her with joy over the simplest moments back in the old house. It was a peace she hadn't known since her family had gathered around to inaugurate the new playhouse with the steeple on top. *Lord, I don't know how long you'll let this last, but thank you for it.*

She paused at the foot of the stairs and looked across the broad entrance hall into the sunbathed living and dining rooms with their newly painted lemony walls, polished wood floors, and silky new drapes. Before settling in for a practice hour at the piano, she pulled a light jacket from the hall closet and walked out on the porch. Februarys in Charleston were unpredictable. This one was colder and wetter than most, too wet to ramble through the yards with her morning coffee, as she'd done those first few weeks after her dad returned. Most of those mornings, he had joined her. They had lingered around the playhouse, recalling only what they dared, and dismissing the other times as if they'd happened to someone else. When the weather was warm, they'd wheeled Lottie onto the porch with them. She had known Henry instantly, but couldn't recall how long he'd been gone or why, and there was no recollection of his "death." Some days, though, she didn't know him at all. He seemed not to mind.

Liesl was intent on resurrecting her father's good humor and considerable skills. She'd even encouraged him to drag out his long-dormant tools and make a few repairs around the house. She was still amazed at where that had led.

Henry and Ian had forged a partnership tasked with restoring the old house to its original luster, inside and out. But they didn't stop there. The two fraternal fishermen, who could talk ad nauseam about gutting fish, had merged into O'Brien Charters. The new sign at Ripley Light Marina said so. It hung on a post next to the spry old sport fisherman Ian had just bought with proceeds from the sale of his Keys boat and house. Both had sold quicker than expected. Proof, Cade had declared, that his pop belonged in Charleston with him, though Cade didn't belong in a fishing boat with Ian. Cade had christened his grandfather's new boat with a bottle of Pepto Bismol.

Liesl glanced at her watch, then hurried back inside to begin her work at the keyboard. Just before noon, she heard Cade's Blazer pull up in front of the house, and her stomach did its usual lurch at the sound. When she heard the front door open, she jumped from the piano bench and rushed to greet him. Today, he was dressed in a charcoal suit with his tie loosened. She wrapped her arms around his neck and nuzzled his cheek, inhaling the soapy scent of him. He drew her close and kissed her lightly the first time. The second time, he lingered, his lips full and sweet on hers.

There was no point in withholding what was in her heart any longer. Without knowing why she chose that particular moment, she finally released the words. "I love you," she said, emphasizing each word.

He searched her eyes. "Are you sure?"

"Oh yes, Mr. Editor Man. Very sure."

"Aren't you supposed to tell me something like that when I'm not in a rush to eat lunch and get back to the office?"

"Carpe diem," she said with a half smile.

"Seize the day, huh? Okay. Two can play this. So here goes." He picked her up and carried her to the piano where he set her down on the closed lid, eye level to him. "If you love me, marry me." He waited.

And waited.

Finally, she responded with one word.

"When?"

Chapter 50

Three hours before the concert, the sky over New York issued snow flurries so sheer they disappeared on contact with the limo's windshield. Liesl and Ava relaxed in the backseat, watching Manhattan's rush-hour throngs, heads down, navigate the crowded sidewalks.

"I don't miss it at all," Ava spoke into the frosty window.

Liesl slid sideways in her seat to see the woman more clearly. The two had become fast friends since Ava had permanently relocated to Charleston, a move that took everyone by surprise, even though Liesl had suggested it. "After all we've been through together, how can you just dump us and head back to New York?" she'd teased. "Your son is career military. Probably will never live in New York again. Just soften your vowels and head south."

So Ava Mullins retired from the CIA, returned to music, and signed on to teach at a Charleston high school. "That way, I can still use my law enforcement skills," she'd quipped.

Now, she turned to face Liesl. "You know, I can hear your piano from my place." She'd moved into a carriage-house apartment a block from Tidewater Lane.

"I hope I'm not breaking the noise ordinance. But probably so." Something else occurred to Liesl and she smiled mischievously. "Did you catch anything last night?" She raised one eyebrow.

Ava gave her a scolding glance. "Meaning?"

"Bait many hooks?"

Ava snickered. "You just have your fun, because I sure am, bait or no bait."

"What's it been now? Three nights in a row offshore with O'Brien Charters?"

Drawing a contented sigh, Ava clearly wasn't going to tangle with Liesl's broad insinuations. "Those are the two funniest men on the planet, you know that?"

"Yeah, and one of them thinks you hung the moon over that planet."

It tickled Liesl to see Ava try to suppress the smile and fail. Ava turned her face from Liesl and looked out the window. "Don't be silly. Ian's almost sixteen years older than I am."

"And acting like a schoolboy with a crush."

As they approached Lincoln Center, Ava changed the subject. "I've asked NYPD to offer added support tonight. Retired or not, I'm still your case manager."

"The case is closed, Ava. That wasn't necessary."

"Maybe not, but there'll be a guard, maybe two, outside your dressing room door."

The limo stopped next to Avery Fisher Hall and discharged its heavily bundled passengers. They hadn't forgotten what February in New York was like.

Once inside the building, Liesl went straight to her private dressing room where she shed the long, fleece-lined raincoat. Beneath it were jeans and a slouch sweater. She hung up the emerald-green gown, tucked the matching satin pumps under a chair, and laid out the necklace and earrings she would wear. No bracelets, no rings. Nothing to interfere with her hands' acrobatic dance over the keyboard.

While Ava went in search of the NYPD guards, Liesl headed to the stage. Though she'd been in rehearsals with the orchestra a couple of days now, these last-minute checks were critical. She walked across the stage toward the gleaming black Steinway concert grand, exchanging greetings with those in the orchestra who'd also arrived early. Seeing that the leather tufted piano bench was still properly adjusted to her height, she opened the lid over the keyboard and removed the soft cover over the keys. To determine if further tuning was necessary, she launched into a few finger-limbering scales and passages from the first piece she would perform. There would be two.

Then came a test of the sound system. A series of adjustments by those in the control booth made sure the piano wasn't drowned out by the orchestra, that the instrument's higher register wasn't too shrill, and that the great hall would, once again, live up to its reputation for celestial sound. There was no taking chances. A faulty sound system could make even a Steinway sound like a child's toy.

When Liesl finally returned to her dressing room, she was pleased to see no one about. She needed time to herself, to mentally prepare for the rigorous performance to come. And to pray. She still wasn't sure how that should be done. All she could do was talk to the Father in whatever words came naturally, as if he were seated beside her. That simple act had never failed to revive her.

She'd just kicked off her sneakers and settled into an overstuffed chair when someone knocked at the door. She groaned inwardly, but went to answer it. When she opened the door, a huge bouquet of flowers filled the doorway, a pair of hands around their vase.

"For you, Miss Bower."

Something about the voice.

Then the flowers moved through the doorway, carried by a delivery man in a rain jacket with the hood over his head. He didn't look at her as he closed the door, crossed the room, and placed the flowers on a table against the far wall. He paused for an instant before turning around, one hand slipping into a front pocket.

It happened all at once. The gun emerged. The hood came off. And the face—that face—appeared. "Don't scream," he warned her.

She raised both hands to her mouth and stopped breathing. *Oh, God, help me!*

Then, Evgeny Kozlov did a curious thing. He lowered the gun and placed it back in his pocket, his eyes steady on her. He motioned for her to sit down.

She stumbled toward the small bench at the dressing table, mind racing. If she screamed, he would shoot her and whoever came to help. Was there a knife in a drawer? Maybe scissors. Yes! She'd seen them yesterday. But which drawer? There was no time to search.

"You're terrified. I know this. But I didn't come to harm you—not this time. Not even in the alley that night in Moscow. You should have fled from Devoe then. I knew the Americans had reached him, that they would use him. I had been sent to warn him of what we would do to him and his wife. But not you. Not then."

Her voice came in a ragged whisper. "And . . . now?"

"My battle with you is over. It's all over. No one hunts you anymore."

"Wh-why are you here?"

"I was supposed to kill you. And young Max Morozov." He seemed oddly composed. "No more music."

Someone passed by the closed door, and Kozlov shot a hand into his gun pocket. After a moment, the hand reappeared and hung limply at his side. "But now, you are free. This is what I came to tell you. It is me they hunt."

As he backed toward the door, Liesl made no move, no sound. "You can tell your CIA friends that I was here," he said, "but they will not find me." Liesl watched as he, again, clutched the gun inside his pocket and turned to go. At the door, he looked back once more. "My comrades think I betrayed them. I didn't. I believed in them. But no more. They are not fit to rule over my Russia. They are reckless and arrogant." He paused. "But I tell you this, you Americans—you must never stop watching them." And he was gone.

Liesl couldn't move. The shock nailed her to the bench. The lunging in her chest wouldn't stop. She looked at the clock on the wall and watched its second hand sweep sluggishly through time. As she watched the incessant march around the orbit of meaningless numbers, struggling to regain her senses, his warning returned to her. In one hour, the orchestra would file in. The audience would take their seats. Who among them must be watched? *Who must we never stop watching?*

Another knock at the door. "Liesl, it's Ava. May I come in?"

Liesl couldn't answer.

"Liesl?" Still no answer. The door flew open and Ava rushed inside.

"Evgeny Kozlov just left." It was all Liesl could manage.

Ava's eyes flashed. "Are you hurt?" she demanded.

"No."

With that, Ava shot through the door, and Liesl could hear her shouting commands. A commotion ensued in the hallway, feet pounding the floor, and more shouts. But Liesl felt wholly removed from it, as if she'd had nothing to do with it. She walked calmly to the door and closed it, catching a glimpse of herself in the big mirror surrounded by lights. *Nothing happens to your children that hasn't first passed through your hands. That's what Aunt Bess always said. So if that's true, Lord, then tell me what I'm supposed to do with this.*

Chapter 51

When the house lights went down, Itzhak Perlman entered the stage to a rousing reception. After a short interval, the conductor raised his baton, and the orchestra plunged into the concerto. Soon, the famed violinist inserted himself into the music, dazzling the audience, who, at the completion of the piece, rose to a standing ovation.

Perlman took his bows and exited the stage. After a slight shuffling of music in the orchestra, the audience awaited the next performer. No introductions of solo artists were given this night. None were necessary. The wait for Liesl Bower, however, grew tedious. The conductor shifted his weight from one foot to the other, casting frequent and wary glances into the wings. In their complimentary box seats near the stage, Cade, Ian, and Henry also began to squirm. Next to them, Rev. Francis Scovall of West Park Christian Church watched expectantly for the young woman who'd fled blindly through his door one night not long ago. Cade caught the man's concerned eye. "I'm sure everything's okay," Cade said. But he wasn't.

"Where is she?" Ian whispered too loudly, tugging again at the stiff, white shirt collar. The three of them had flown in that morning for the concert. They were surprised to find their box was directly across from President Noland's. Though he wasn't in attendance that evening, his box was nearly full. The only person Cade recognized in it was Ben Hafner, who'd smiled and waved to them when he took his seat.

"Shh, Pop. She'll be here." But as soon as he said that, he noticed a man enter the president's box, approach Ben, and speak something into his ear. Immediately, Ben stood and made a move to leave, but the messenger evidently persuaded him to take his seat. Cade didn't like the expression he saw on Ben's face. There was no reason to believe it had anything to do with Liesl. But that's exactly what Cade believed. He was about to jump from his own seat when he saw her.

Her green gown shimmering in the stage lights, her golden hair swept over one shoulder and caught in a glittering clasp, Liesl walked slowly across the stage. She paused in front of the piano, bowing slightly to exuberant applause, a frequent and favorite artist on the New York stage.

But tonight, there was something different about the familiar face. A different set to the jaw, a flare in the eyes. Instead of taking her seat at the piano, she continued to stand, quietly studying the audience of foreign ambassadors and others whose fingers touched the power switches of the world. She looked out at Cade and saw the anxiety on his face. She nodded brightly toward him, hoping it signaled that all was well. Then her gaze swept quickly from Ian to her dad, who appeared about to burst with pride.

Certain of what she was about to do, she remained standing and waited for silence, catching the flicker of curiosity on faces closest to the stage. Then she began her message. "In a moment, I will play Chopin's *Scherzo No. 2 in B-Flat Minor*. It will take us into a storm of conflict, into escalating strife . . . then mercifully deliver us into the calm." She looked from one side of the great hall to the other, then high into the balconies.

"I see this as the conflict between *nations*," she proclaimed boldly, then paused, intensely studying her audience. "But hear this from the one who rules over *all* the nations: 'Blessed are the peacemakers.'"

She took her seat at the piano. And there was music.